The INNKEEPER *and the* FUGITIVE

PARADIGM
PRESS

MARTHA KEYES

1

Kildonnan, February 1763

Ava MacMorran stopped at the edge of the trees and curled her toes in her boots, checking for any remaining feeling. After trudging four miles over wintery Highland terrain, there *was* none. It must have been her blood, still running hot from the encounter with her father, that had warmed her enough to reach the inn, for the February air was unforgiving. It would only become more so as the light of day gave way to dark.

Her stomach rumbled, and she reached for the bannock in her pocket, unfolding the paper it was wrapped in and taking a bite. It was dry and bland—she certainly could have made a better one herself, but she hadn't baked a single thing since shortly after her mother's death.

Rewrapping it and setting it back in her pocket, she picked up the small bag that held the few things she had brought along with her and, with a quick glance around, stepped out from the protection of the trees and toward Glengour Inn. If she was fortunate, she might be able to sit by the fire and warm herself before departing with the traveling tinker. According to the maids at Glenlochan, Ava's home, the man and his wife made a practice of drinking a dram and sharing a bowl of porridge before continuing toward Fort William.

As Ava reached the side of the inn, her eyes shifted to the man emerging from the front door, and she tugged her hood down farther over her face. She had chosen Glengour Inn rather than The Maidenhead in Craiglinne not only for the tinker but because she knew her father would seek news of her at the latter first. It was much closer to Glenlochan, and whenever they left Glenlochan—not nearly frequently enough for Ava's taste—it was The Maidenhead which was graced with the MacMorrans' patronage.

But it was certainly not out of the realm of possibility that someone familiar with Ava's face might be here at this precise time—fate was sometimes unkind in that way.

She shivered involuntarily at the prospect, only to do so yet again as she thought on what her future held if she returned home rather than face the risks before her.

"You will marry him if I have to *force* you, Ava," her father had said. His anger came much more quickly these days. He never would have said such a thing when Ava's mother was still alive.

There was no sign of the tinker's cart yet, but it couldn't be much longer now or they would lose the last of the daylight before reaching Largnagour midway to Fort William. After a moment of debate and another tug on her hood, Ava hurried to the splintered and warped front door of the inn and pulled it open, causing a small bell hung over the top to tremble and ring. She stilled, not eager for anyone to be alerted to her presence, but the din inside was loud enough to cover the sound of the bell.

She had only seen Glengour once before—and even then only in passing—and apparently her memory had done the place an injustice. Its interior couldn't compare to the newly constructed Maidenhead, but it was cozy and inviting, with tartan tablecloths covering the two tables she could see in the coffee room from her position in the entry way. A striped, ginger cat jumped down from the nearest bench and curled itself around her legs, drawing a smile from her, only to continue out of the open door.

"Wait," she whispered urgently to the feline, but it skittered across the stones in front of the inn, ignoring her entirely.

She hurried to shut the door behind her, anxious to guard the welcoming warmth and hoping the cat was allowed such freedom. It was customary for the innkeeper to greet travelers, but none appeared, and she was grateful for it. She had thought an encounter with the innkeeper inevitable. In the event that her father sought word of her here, though, the less people aware of her presence, the better. Perhaps she would be able to slip away with only the tinker's knowledge.

A week ago, she had overheard two maids speaking of the tinker's impending arrival. It was a short snippet of a conversation largely focused on the new innkeeper at Glengour and his rumored attractiveness. It had been enough, though, to provide the spark of an idea in Ava—one that had grown with the kindling provided by her father's intractability regarding her marriage. Today, she had given him one more opportunity to change his mind, but far from doing so, he had threatened her with force when she had broached the subject and thrust at her all the reasons why the marriage was desirable.

As nonchalantly as she could manage, Ava had asked one of the maids for confirmation of the tinker's expected arrival, explaining that she was considering purchasing something from him. She had dressed as shabbily as she could, taking long forgotten items of clothing from the bottom of her trunk— the less she stood out from the other travelers, the better. She would already draw attention as a young woman on her own.

She curled her toes again in anticipation of the feeling they would soon regain—only to lose it again on the journey with the tinker. Perhaps he would have a blanket she could throw over her legs and, if she found a better option in Fort William to continue her journey to Glasgow, she would pray she had enough money to take advantage of it. All would be well once she reached Dermot McCurdy.

She tried to envision the comfort she had always felt in his presence, a result of their long and steady friendship—years of playing together as their fathers worked and discussed work. It seemed such a distant memory now.

She took a few hesitant steps forward and spotted the dancing flames of the fire she had been looking forward to. She gazed longingly at the table nearest the fire, but she would have to make do with admiring it from a distance; there were too many people in that part of the room. She comforted herself that, once she arrived at the McCurdys', there would be fires aplenty.

She fought back the nerves that came along with such a thought and the fear that this plan of hers might end as a colossal failure. But that fear couldn't persist for long. Dermot had assured her, time and again, that he would do anything for her, and his meaning had been clear, even if it had been some time since they had been able to see one another.

Ava took refuge on the side of the staircase opposite the coffee room, wiggling her toes as they slowly regained feeling. Her legs were aching for the chance to sit, but she had to content herself with leaning against the wall as the minutes passed. There was no telling how much time had passed, but she had begun to sweat under her hooded cloak when she began to wonder when the tinker would arrive. Several people had entered and left the inn since her own arrival. They must have been frequenters of the inn, for they hadn't waited to be greeted but had gone straight into the coffee room, including the two women carrying a wooden cask together.

The afternoon light was beginning to dull and would soon fade. Ava had only one option, and she did not relish it. She made her way to the coffee room and inspected each face she could see among the people seated at the tables and bar. She breathed a sigh of relief that none of the men were familiar to her.

The two women Ava had seen earlier—one with a kertch covering a head of graying hair, and the other with a folded, brown plait emerging from her snood—spoke to a man near the fire. He had his back turned to Ava and was a full head taller than either of the women, with a queue of hair that glinted golden in the light of the candles scattered throughout the room. When he shifted his weight to reveal a bit more of his profile, Ava immediately knew she was looking at the innkeeper. "*Braw, blond, and bonnie,*" one of the Glenlochan maids had said.

Ava entered the coffee room, keeping her eyes on the innkeeper, who was smiling politely at the two women, while the younger of them blushed rosily. A large cask stood beside him, holding what Ava assumed was whisky. She stopped ten feet away, not wanting to intrude on the conversation but impatient to ask about the tinker's whereabouts.

The innkeeper glanced down at the cask beside him, his brows furrowing slightly, though his expression was still a pleasant one. "'Twould be much easier for me ta send the large cart for whisky every two weeks or so. Then ye wouldna have ta come so often—or take time out of yer day at all."

The older woman—the mother of the younger one, Ava guessed—gave a tittering laugh at odds with her advancing age. "What? And take away the pleasure of seein' ye?" She swatted at Mr. Campbell's arm—a solid mass beneath his coat. "Nay, then, Mr. Campbell."

Ava raised her brows. The innkeeper smiled at the women's words, and Ava could see why he had gained a reputation for being attractive. Apparently, he was too busy flirting with his customers to greet newcomers.

A small draft of cold air whipped at Ava's cheeks, and footsteps approached from behind. Her heart stuttered, and she hurriedly turned her head to the side. It was too soon for her father to have done anything more than perhaps note her disappearance—he had left for Benleith after their altercation and was expected to dine there as well, presumably to discuss with Angus how to handle her discontent with the match—but she was still too nervous to look at whoever had just arrived.

Once the footsteps retreated, she glanced at the innkeeper, who now held a note in his hand, one that seemed to be distracting him from the women standing before him. They seemed oblivious to his preoccupation, though, and the mother continued to prattle on.

Ava sighed resignedly. At this rate, it would be midnight before the women let the innkeeper be so she could speak with him.

She looked at the nearest man sitting at the bar. His eyes had a glazed over look, as though he had been in that same position for hours. She stepped toward him and cleared her throat.

"Excuse me, sir," she said. "I dinna wish ta disturb ye, but I'm lookin' for the tinker. I was told he'd be here this afternoon. Do ye ken if he's been here yet?" She spoke naturally, adopting the speech she had been accustomed to use most of her life rather than the more stilted speech her father had ensured she was taught since his knighting. It felt good to shed the artificiality.

The man's head came around to look at her and seemed to bobble slightly as his eyes slowly focused on her. "Ye missed him." He gave a sort of hiccough and covered his mouth with a hand. "Left two hours ago. Perhaps three." He picked up his cup and tried to drain it, though only a few drops came out.

Ava stared at him, but he seemed to have forgotten her in his preoccupation with the emptiness of his cup.

The tinker had already come. He was gone.

Her eyelids flickered, roaming around the room at the various men laughing and chatting with a whisky in hand, seemingly without a care in the world, even as her own world seemed to crumble.

The maid at Glenlochan had been so certain of the tinker's habits—always in the afternoon, as he came from twenty miles north—and Ava had been so anxious for an escape from the looming prospect of marriage to Angus that she had pounced on the idea. Now what was she to do?

She took two steps backward, bumped into a chair, and hurried from the room as quickly and unobtrusively as she could manage. It was too late in the day to find a way to the next inn on the road to Fort William—unless she stole a horse, perhaps, but a solitary, miles-long ride in the dark with the bracing February wind blowing at her was lunacy. Besides, she didn't wish to steal anything.

And yet, she couldn't return home. She couldn't marry Angus MacKinnon. The match might provide Angus with the land he wished for and her father with the money for his next investment scheme, but a life with Angus would bring Ava nothing but misery, whether her father believed it or not. Angus had not been convicted of the crimes brought against him a few months since, but Ava—and most people with their wits about them—knew he was guilty. Even the sight of him sent a chill through her. How her father could even contemplate marrying her to a man accused of abduction and attempted murder was beyond her.

No, she would face almost any future before joining herself

to Angus, and marrying a man who loved her, even if she was not in love with *him*, was her best option.

She reached into her pocket and brought out the small, leather coin purse within. It was only half-full, and she fingered the hard, round pieces inside. She could afford a room for the night at Glengour, but it would deplete the resources she would need to find her way to Glasgow and then to Ardgour House—assuming she could find someone to take her there. If only she'd had time to write Dermot, she would have been spared the necessity of making this journey herself. But there had been no time. Her father wished for the wedding to take place within the week. Her letter would barely have arrived by then, to say nothing of the time required for Dermot's journey to Glenlochan to come get her.

The light was fading quickly, along with Ava's hope.

She took in a deep breath, and her lungs filled with the humid, whisky-scented air of the inn, which suddenly felt suffocating. She lifted the latch of the front door and stepped out into the gathering darkness. The bracing cold was a shock to her face, her lungs, and her mind, jolting her from her despair.

She clenched her jaw. She wouldn't accept defeat at the first sign of trouble. She needed time, that was all. Time to decide upon a new plan. The dark had a way of making problems seem insurmountable. A good night's rest and the light of day could do wonders for the mind and heart.

She glanced up at the windows of the inn. Could she slip into a vacant room unnoticed? The innkeeper was certainly distracted enough with...other matters.

As if on cue, the inn door opened, and the two women emerged. Ava hurried around the side of the inn, waiting for them to bid farewell to the innkeeper and start on their way.

"Och, ye're a kind soul, Mr. Campbell," said the older

woman. "As if ye didna have aught ta do besides seein' us ta the cart. I'm sure Henrietta is verra flattered."

Their footsteps drew nearer, and with light feet, Ava scurried behind the inn, where she could remain concealed. The three of them seemed to be headed for the stables.

"Mark has the afternoon off," Mr. Campbell said, "so I've been seein' the guests ta their horses." It seemed like a subtle refutation of the woman's insistence upon feeling flattered, but Ava doubted it would be taken as such, and she couldn't help a small smile, even amidst her own troubles.

"Ye'll never have a wink o' sleep, then," said the younger woman, and even in the dark, Ava could see how her mother nudged her closer to Mr. Campbell.

"Nay, Miss Shaw," he said. "'Tis no trouble. And besides, the rest o' the men walked."

"So, we're the last ones ta have this honor," the mother said.

Their voices grew muffled, and Ava could no longer hear the conversation. Not that she wanted to. She was embarrassed on behalf of the women.

She could see the stables from where she was, lit by a torch on either side of the opening, and her mind began to work. If there was no more work to be done in the stables and no one to supervise things there, perhaps she could find a place to sleep within, to rest her mind before applying herself to the problem at hand.

She waited in the dark for the women to emerge from the stables in their small cart, accompanied by Mr. Campbell, who stopped briefly to take both torches in hand. As he reached the front of the inn, he bid the women farewell, and Ava snuck forward and peeked her head around the wall, watching for him to reenter the inn. The younger woman turned to look over her shoulder at him, but he did not reciprocate the coy gesture, having already disappeared into the inn.

Gripping her bag with one hand and holding up her petticoats with the other, Ava hurried toward the stables, turning the corner and slipping behind the wall, her breath coming quickly. Her heart thudded against her chest, her every sense on the alert. The fear and danger made her feel more alive than she had in an eon. Her mother's death had overwhelmed her with grief for months, but for some time now, Ava had felt deadened to other emotions.

There was no sound to indicate she was in any danger of being discovered, and she relaxed her shoulders and breathing, looking at her surroundings. With the torches gone, it was dark in the stables, the only light coming from the lantern at the front of the inn. She blinked as her eyes adjusted. She was standing beside three haystacks—two large and one small. Beyond, there were a number of stalls, a few of which contained horses, whose breath created cloudy wisps as it entered the cold night air.

She set down her bag and, with a quick glance back toward the inn, made her way down the row of stalls toward a closed door. They had to keep the equipment somewhere—including the blankets. But the door was locked.

Yet another disappointment in a day already full of them. But, she reminded herself, still none of it compared to the alternative. Angus MacKinnon's face swam before her for a moment, and she shuddered, dismissing the unsettling image as she strode back toward the haystacks.

If she could manage to cover herself in enough hay, perhaps she would be able to stay warm enough. The only other option would be to sneak into the inn somehow, but she would rather not do that. It was bound to go wrong, and it would certainly draw unwanted attention.

A mew sounded, and Ava whirled around. She let out a breathy chuckle of relief at the view of the cat she had seen earlier, now perched on one of the stall doors, staring at her with its intent, glinting eyes.

She stepped toward it slowly. "Ye gave me a fright," she whispered.

The cat only stared at her, and she approached it with a hand out. It submitted to her touch hesitantly, but when she stroked it from its head, along its back, and down to its tail, it raised up onto its legs to allow for her ministrations. Its warmth permeated her gloves, and as she stroked it again, its rhythmic purring began.

"If only I had a coat like yers," she said then turned toward her bed for the night.

The shortest haystack seemed the most obvious option for her needs, and she tried to spread out the hay, distributing it more evenly and pushing the excess to the side. She untied her cloak and settled in, trying to ignore the way bits poked her side and legs and ankles. Taking her cloak, she draped it over herself then grabbed the extra hay and pushed it over her legs, feet, and stomach in as many layers as she could manage.

She couldn't help a laugh as her body disappeared from view. It was better to laugh than cry, after all, and she could feel tears hovering under the surface, ready to push through if she allowed them to.

The cat jumped down from its perch, mewing and walking toward her.

"What? Have I stolen yer bed?" Ava asked.

It lowered its head, as if in expectation of being petted, and Ava obliged, running her hand along its back again then trading hands so that both might feel its warmth. It nuzzled its head up against her chest, and after a few minutes, took its place on her lap.

Ava smiled and lay back, continuing to pet the creature, feeling its purring reverberate through the hay and letting it calm her until her eyes dropped closed.

2

Hamish Campbell reached for a rag to clean up the spill created by Mr. Milroy. He had finally managed to shake the presence of the Shaws an hour ago—they had stayed far longer than was necessary to bring one cask of whisky.

Glenna Douglas took the rag from him, giving him a significant look that told him to see to the increasingly incoherent Mr. Milroy. He was one of their regular patrons. Properly, Hamish was the innkeeper, but Glenna had been there far longer, and she worked every bit as hard as he did. Neither of them had had a moment to sit and breathe since the day had begun—an unusually busy day for February—and the letter in Hamish's pocket still sat unread, though he was ever-conscious of it.

The bustle of activity in the inn was finally calming, though, and Hamish guided the stumbling Mr. Milroy to the doors. The man had been seated at the bar for hours.

"Perhaps I should walk ye home, Mr. Milroy," Hamish said.

The mans' eyebrows snapped together, and he waved a dismissive hand. Hamish barely dodged the flailing gesture.

"I dinna need a chaperone," the man drawled.

Hamish knew better than to press the issue. Mr. Milroy was quick to anger when inebriated—which he often was.

He yanked his arm from Hamish's hand and tottered through the door and out into the night. Hamish sighed as he watched the man make his way toward the road, stumbling over one of the paving stones in front of the inn and saying, "I dinna need yer help," as though Hamish had offered it again.

Footsteps sounded behind him, and Glenna appeared. She looked as exhausted as Hamish felt. "So, ye managed ta escape the Shaws, then."

"Och," Hamish said, "only just."

She smiled broadly. "Henrietta wishes ye'd asked her ta marry ye yesterday, I reckon. What's takin' ye so long?"

He shot her an unamused look and closed the door. Hamish had no thought of Henrietta—or any woman. Not when he had nothing to offer them.

"We could make our own whisky," Glenna said after his silence continued. "I ken how ta do it."

He raised a brow. "And when would ye manage ta do that? With all the extra time ye have layin' about, ye reckon?"

Her lips pinched together in recognition of his point. "Once the cook arrives, I'll have more."

Hamish stopped and turned to face her. "I dinna think she *is* comin', Glenna. She was meant ta be here nearly a fortnight ago."

Glenna's head fell back and her eyes shut, as if in despair. "But we canna go on as we've been."

"Nay, ye're right. We'll have ta put out another advertisement—or perhaps one of the two women we didna hire is still at liberty ta take the position. But no' all days will be like today. 'Twas much harder with Mark gone, and he'll be back in the mornin'." Remembering the letter in his pocket, Hamish pulled it out, and his heart skipped at the thought of what it might contain. He had been waiting for a response from Sir Andrew

MacMorran for even longer than he'd been waiting for the new cook's arrival, and he had nearly given up on receiving one.

"What's that?" Glenna asked with a nod at the letter. Her eyes widened. "A letter for ye?"

He nodded. Neither of them were accustomed to receiving letters. Glenna's family was too near to necessitate it, and Hamish had no one to correspond with.

"Och! Go on, then." She gave him a little push toward the door to his lodgings, a small building attached to the office just inside the front door. "Read yer letter. I'll see ta cleanin' up. 'Tis only Mr. Buttar left, and ye ken he's no trouble."

Hamish hesitated, impatient to read the letter but reluctant to leave things to Glenna. She gave him another push, though, and he surrendered to curiosity.

He paused in the doorway, though, turning back to her. "Thank ye, Glenna."

She smiled and left to the coffee room.

Hamish didn't have any sisters, but he had spent the first years after his father's death with kin, and he had more familial affection for Glenna than he'd had for any of them. He had always felt like an outsider, an afterthought, an intruder with his kin. Not so at Glengour. He and Glenna were in a strange situation, working together so closely, though neither of them was married. But Glenna had assured him more than once that she was not worried by the gossip it might produce.

Each time he broached the subject, she would dismiss it out of hand. "People will say what they say, and there's nothin' ye can do ta prevent 'em. Besides, we have Mark to vouch for us, and no one would dare doubt my reputation."

Hamish stepped through the office and into his quarters, shutting the door behind him. He broke open the wafer and stepped before the light of the fire to read the letter's contents.

Mr. Campbell,

I beg you will forgive the delay in responding to your letter. I have been much occupied with arranging the details of my daughter's marriage and will continue to be for some time to come, as her departure to Benleith requires new arrangements be made for my other children. I would be happy to meet with you after these matters are taken care of, though I fear I cannot promise the response you are hoping for.

Regarding Dalmore House, assuming the Crown was inclined to look with favor upon your request—something which is by no means assured, given the actions of your father—you would be obliged to pay back the significant debts which encumbered the estate upon its attainder. I am not well enough acquainted with the number to state it with confidence, but I believe it is somewhere in the range of eight thousand pounds sterling.

In any case, I will inform you when I am at liberty to meet with you.

Your servant,

Sir Andrew MacMorran

Hamish read it again, his eyes focusing on the number near the bottom. Eight thousand pounds. He knew his father had been in debt, but it was more than he had thought. After living for so long on soldier's pay, the sum felt astronomical to him. Lachlan Kincaid, who employed Hamish, was paying him more than a fair wage to run things at Glengour, but Hamish would die before he had even earned the half of Dalmore's debts.

It looked as though he would require more than money, too. He needed connections—someone to vouch for him to those in power, as though the last nine years of service in His Majesty's Army proved nothing when weighed against his father's disloyalty to the Crown.

Sir Andrew's final words, too, felt more like a way of preventing Hamish from attempting to respond than a true statement of intent to meet with him.

He sighed.

Perhaps he simply wasn't meant to have a home—or any of the things that came along with it.

He set the letter on the crooked wooden mantel and scrubbed his bearded chin with a hand.

Would he be the innkeeper of Glengour his entire life? Lachlan had offered him the position as a way to provide him with an honest wage and a roof over his head. He had insisted Hamish was doing him a favor, sparing him the need to seek someone else for the position. Hamish had gladly accepted the offer, knowing it would put him in a position to seek the favor of Sir Andrew, the man in charge of Dalmore.

But the path to Dalmore had never seemed so impossible as it did now.

A clopping of hooves on stone sounded outside his window, and Hamish hurried over to peer into the dark. A horse with a man astride stepped into the light cast by the lantern on one side of the front door, and Hamish hurried out of his quarters to meet him outside.

Glenna was making her way there, as well, and she shot Hamish a harried look. They had both hoped they'd seen the last of the guests.

"Get some sleep, Glenna," Hamish said as he reached the door. "I'll see ta him." He was glad for the distraction, in truth.

She searched his face, and for a moment, he feared she might ask him about the letter. But there was no time for such a discussion, and she nodded, her shoulders dropping with relief.

"There are a few extra bannocks in the kitchen if he's hungry," she said. "I hope ye're able ta sleep soon, as well. Wake me if anyone else comes." Her gaze rested on him expectantly, and he offered a reassuring nod before opening the door.

Hamish greeted the man and, after tying his horse to the iron ring on the side wall of the inn, saw him to one of the vacant rooms upstairs. He had been traveling all day and was anxious for a place to lay his head, which suited Hamish very well. He did his best to be an agreeable host to the assortment of travelers who passed through, but tonight, he was feeling too weary and disappointed to offer conversation.

Once the man had been sufficiently instructed to know where to find the privy and what he could expect from his stay at Glengour, Hamish fetched one of the torches and returned to the horse, which, though undoubtedly as tired as his master, seemed eager to be fed, as he lipped at the bits of dead grass which stuck up between the paving stones after managing to survive the winter—and the efforts of countless other horses to consume them.

"Come on, then," Hamish said, untying him. "Ye'll get nothin' worth yer time there."

With heavy, shuffling steps, he led the way to the stables, praying there would be no other travelers to interrupt the sleep he hoped to achieve once the horse was settled, watered, and fed.

3

Ava woke to the feeling of cold and the clopping of approaching hooves. She blinked away the sleep in time to see the cat's tail disappear around the side of the tallest haystack, explaining the sudden chill its vacancy had left her with.

As the sleep shed enough for her to remember where she was and why it would be concerning to hear hoofbeats drawing near, she scrambled up, clutching her cloak and sending bits of hay floating in the air while she looked for a place to hide. But aside from the haystacks, there were only stalls and the locked door, and if a horse was about to be housed in one of the empty stalls, selecting one for a hiding place would be a risky endeavor.

She chose to keep her current position near the haystacks, slipping behind the tallest one with her heart thudding louder than the horse's hooves. The light from a torch increased, casting strange, moving shadows that brought an eerie feeling to Ava as they drew nearer

"We'll put ye next ta Bullet," came a man's voice, and the

creaking of a stall door sounded shortly after. "Come on, now. In ye go." The man gave a grunt, and a shuffling of hooves and footsteps followed.

Ava's eyes widened as she noted her leather bag nearby. The majority of it must have been covered in the process of blanketing herself in hay, but the handle and one side now protruded conspicuously. She could only hope the man was too focused on conversing with the animal to notice anything else.

If she reached out her foot, she might be able to nudge enough hay to conceal the rest of the bag. The stable door creaked and shut as she cautiously extended a boot, slipping it under the hay within its reach.

A sudden thud made her jump, and she retracted her foot hurriedly, sliding back behind the haystack, though the sliver of the man she saw before doing so told her it was Mr. Campbell, the innkeeper.

"Och," he said. "An impatient beast, aren't ye? No need ta kick." He sounded tired. What time *was* it? Ava had no idea when she had fallen asleep or for how long.

The muffled sound of footsteps on the dirt met her ears, and Ava instinctively held her breath. Was he coming for hay?

Should she seize her bag and run? She had no idea what sort of man Mr. Campbell was. If he was anything like Angus MacKinnon, she might be obliged to take drastic measures to protect herself. A pitchfork might do in a pinch.

But there was no time to think through the possible scenarios, and the rustling of hay, followed by a confused, "What's this?" told her that her bag had been found. It was only a matter of moments before Mr. Campbell began looking for the owner.

As if to ensure Ava had no opportunity to avoid discovery, the cat reappeared nearby, curling itself around Ava's legs and mewing. She cursed it silently.

If Ava had learned anything from being found after trying to escape lessons as a child, it was that confidence was crucial to credibility. She would simply have to ask for a room. The dent it would make in her meager purse made her cringe, but there was no helping that at this point—unless she managed to escape before paying the bill. Her conscience balked at that, but these were desperate times, and a conscience was beginning to feel like a luxury.

She stepped out from her hiding place, and Mr. Campbell startled, rearing back and blinking at her, pitchfork in one hand and her bag in the other. The cat followed Ava and continued to brush itself against her legs, oblivious to the delicate situation she was in.

She hurried and reached for the bag.

His eyes narrowed briefly as he surrendered it, and comprehension suddenly dawned on his face, making her stomach clench. Did he truly know who she was? How? She certainly would have remembered *him* if she had ever seen him.

"Ye must be Dorcas," he said, with the beginnings of a relieved smile. "Dorcas MacGurk?"

Ava's brain worked quickly. Whoever this Dorcas MacGurk was—unfortunate soul that she was with such a name—Ava knew two things about her. Firstly, that Mr. Campbell did not know her by sight, and secondly, that he looked somewhat pleased to see her.

"Aye, that's me," she said with an attempt at a smile.

"I didna hear ye arrive."

"I arrived on foot," she said truthfully, keeping her eyes on him for any clues about what he expected of this Dorcas. Had he thought she would come on horseback? In a carriage? Why was he relieved to see someone he obviously didn't know?

"We'd given up on ye," he said, and a flash of frustration crossed his face. "I was about ta put out another advertisement."

Oh. Dorcas MacGurk was being hired at Glengour. She was to be employed there.

Ava felt a bit of relief. Someone employed by the inn would certainly not be made to pay for a room. If she could maintain the ruse until morning, she could leave without her purse any lighter. Where she would go and how she would get there once she left Glengour, she was still unsure. She could only deal with so many problems at once, though.

"What're ye doin' in here instead of inside?" he asked.

It was a good question, and Ava scrambled for an answer that would make any sense at all. "I was nervous, and ye seemed busy when I took a gander inside, so I thought' I'd familiarize meself with the inn." On an impulse, she reached for some hay. "I meant ta let the horses ken me a wee bit—give 'em each a handful of hay."

His gaze took her in from head to toe. "Did ye fall in?" There was a hint of a smile on his lips, as though the thought amused him.

She looked down at her petticoats, still covered in hay, then looked back up at him. "Aye," she said flatly. "Aye, I did."

The hint of a smile morphed into a full one, and Ava better understood why the maids at Glenlochan had been fawning over Mr. Campbell. Between the smile, the twinkle in his eye, and his sturdy figure, he looked as though he might easily sweep a woman off her feet.

There was another loud thud nearby, and Mr. Campbell looked over his shoulder. "Ye can give that handful ta the crabbit one in the third stall. And then we should get ye some sleep. Ye'll need ta be up before the sun ta begin cookin'."

Ava nodded, hiding the strange mixture of chagrin and relief this information caused her as she set down her cloak. If Dorcas was expected to be up before the sun, Ava would be obliged to choose between leaving Glengour while it was still dark or waiting to do so until she had completed whatever was expected of her as—evidently—a cook. She had a fair amount of experience in the kitchen, so *that* was at least fortunate in the event that she was required to answer any questions. Though, she couldn't be certain her particular experience would serve her well at a place like Glengour Inn.

She obediently walked over to feed the kicking roan the fistful of hay she held, which was consumed so eagerly that her hand came away with an appreciable amount of slobber on it. She wiped it in hurried disgust on her petticoats and went to retrieve her cloak while Mr. Campbell tossed another pitchfork of hay into the stall.

His sleeves were rolled up to the elbows, and the muscles in his forearms oscillated as he used the pitchfork like a broom to sweep the hay back into a pile.

"Och, I've made a grand mess of things in here today," he said more to himself than to her. Ava looked away from his arms and pulled her lips between her teeth, keenly aware that she was the one who had made a mess of the hay.

She reached for her cloak and flung it over her shoulders, tying it at the neck. Mr. Campbell stuck his pitchfork in the hay and brushed off his hands, though they slowed as he looked at her. His eyes narrowed, focused on her cloak.

"'Twas you who asked about the tinker, was it no'?"

She swallowed. How had he overhead her question? He had been so distracted when she had asked the man at the bar.

"Ye've been out here since then?" he asked.

She tried for a smile. "I didna wish ta disturb ye—and the women ye were in conversation with didna seem ta wish for interruption." She couldn't stop the bit of amusement that crept to her lips at the memory, and Mr. Campbell pulled a face. Apparently his ability to sweep women off their feet was not one he welcomed.

"But I had the cat ta keep me company while I waited," she said.

Mr. Campbell looked down at the feline, who was seated beside Ava and licking a paw. "Aye," he said with a chuckle as he crouched down to pet her. "Mary prefers ta be the center of attention."

"Mary?" Ava asked, too curious to resist. As common a name as it was, it was not generally given to animals.

"Aye, Bloody Mary more properly. Named for her love of chasin'—and killin'—rodents." He looked up at Ava. "What did ye want with the tinker?"

"Ta buy somethin'." She paused. "A pot." It was the first thing that came to mind. "I'm particular about what I cook in." She knew a flash of pleasure at her quickness of mind.

Mr. Campbell looked somewhat surprised, but he stood and brushed off his breeches. "I'm afraid ye'll have ta make do with what we have until he and his wife return next month."

She feigned disappointment but gave a nod. If all went according to plan, she would be married by then, certainly not tracking down tinkers to buy pots. Not that anything had gone according to plan so far.

Mr. Campbell jerked his head toward the exit. "Come, let's get ye some sleep. Tomorrow will be a long day."

He took the torch in hand again and walked beside her toward the inn. He was quiet as they walked, and Ava remembered the sudden thought she'd had upon his entrance to the stables, comparing him to Angus. It seemed silly now. He bore little resemblance to Angus MacKinnon, from all she could tell.

She felt a constant current of fear and excitement running through her at the situation she was in, but none of that fear was for what Mr. Campbell might do to her. Some people's character could only be appraised with time, while a few short minutes with others was enough to either reassure or urge caution, and her intuition told her that Mr. Campbell was not a danger to her. She cringed to think what Angus would have done in the innkeeper's shoes, finding a woman alone in the stables at night.

"Can ye tell me what my duties will be?" she asked, hoping this was not something he and Dorcas had discussed in detail through correspondence.

"Primarily, ye'll be in the kitchen, cookin' and bakin'. We've been gettin' requests for more hearty dinner fare, but with all the things that need seein' ta, we've no' been able ta meet that demand yet. And then, if time permits, ye'll be helpin' with the washin'."

"But no' distillin' whisky," she said.

His head jerked around toward her, and she smiled teasingly. "I take it ye have that well taken care of," she said.

His face relaxed, and he chuckled. "Aye. Mrs. Shaw would never forgive me if I took that honor from her."

"From her daughter, ye mean," she said as they turned the corner of the inn, coming into the front yard. Surely, Mr. Campbell wasn't so obtuse as to be unaware of what Mrs. Shaw intended between him and her daughter—though he might be forgiven for assuming it was Mrs. Shaw herself who desired an attachment with him. Glenlochan had felt much like a prison to Ava since her family had arrived there, but she was grateful for that now, for it meant she was unacquainted with people like the Shaws.

Mr. Campbell narrowed his eyes as he looked at her, but there was amusement in them. "Ye're like ta give me trouble, Dorcas MacGurk, aren't ye?"

"Nay, sir." At least not for long, she hoped.

He left the torch in a holder just outside the front door, trading it for the lantern by the front door. It was a tin one with small holes all over and a door which swung open.

"The door latch is broken," he said as he led her inside.

She followed him up two sets of stairs to the top floor of the inn where the ceilings sloped up steeply, meeting in the middle. He opened the door to the first room on the right of the staircase, standing aside for Ava to enter.

It was a small room, made even smaller by the slanted ceiling. A wood-frame bed stood before a small dormer window, which looked out over the front yard of the inn lit by the torch Mr. Campbell had left there. An unlit candle sat atop a crooked chest of three drawers.

Mr. Campbell stepped inside and over to the piece of furniture, using his own flame to light the candle, after which he proceeded to light the fire in the grate.

"This peat has been waitin' for ye for some time now." He rose and looked about the room. "I hope ye'll be comfortable here, Miss MacGurk. It's no' much, and these rooms are on the long list of improvements yet ta see to, but . . . ."

Ava turned toward him with a smile. "'Tis perfectly fine." Certainly more comfortable than the haystack, but she was secretly glad she would only be spending one night in the bed. The bumpy shape of the blanket told her the thin mattress there was nearly as likely as the haystack to poke her. "Thank ye, Mr. Campbell."

"Hamish," he said. "Please call me Hamish. And it should be me thankin' *you*. We're in desperate need of help here. Ye'll see that for yerself. I'm glad ye're here."

She offered a wan smile, suppressing the twist of guilt and a desire to squirm. Whoever Dorcas MacGurk was, Ava was doing her reputation no favors.

Hamish opened the door to leave, and Ava hurried to say, "Mr. Campbell."

He turned toward her, brows raised.

"Hamish, I mean," she corrected herself. "Ye said ye'd given up on me. When did ye expect me?" It was a strange question, but Ava needed to know. Was Dorcas a day late? Five days late? It would be highly embarrassing—to say nothing of raising a host of questions—if the real Dorcas arrived during the short time Ava happened to be there.

Hamish stared at her. "February 12th. Almost a fortnight ago." He frowned. "'Twas you who chose the date."

"Aye," she said with a nod of acknowledgement, but she needed some explanation for her strange questions. "But I believe I wrote the *22nd*. Perhaps ye mistook the first two for a one."

"Perhaps." He sounded doubtful. "But today is the 24th."

She smiled through clenched teeth and shrugged her shoulders. "Promptness was never my strength. And ye ken how the roads are." Ava could only hope she never had occasion to meet the real Dorcas MacGurk, for the woman was bound to resent how Ava was playing fast and loose with her character.

"Promptness will have ta *become* a strength if ye mean ta remain here," he said with a hint of annoyance. "The travelers who pass through are often tired and hungry, and they will communicate their displeasure loudly if they're made ta wait too long for their food."

Ava gave a humble nod.

"Goodnight, Miss MacGurk."

The door closed, and Ava took in a long, deep breath, setting her bag on the floor as she took a seat on the bed. She removed her boots and lay back on the thin pillow, shifting in an attempt to get comfortable. As she had suspected, it was little better than the haystack.

She should sleep, but her mind was awake, attuned to the pressing problem of what to do next. Every minute she had passed in Hamish Campbell's company had made it more difficult to look on the prospect of serving him such an ill turn without a recoiling conscience.

But must conscience not submit to necessity? In this instance, at least, it certainly must. Her conscience could resume its full duties and strength once she reached Dermot. For now, though, she might need to stifle it a bit. It was that or submit to a life with Angus MacKinnon, and there was no question which was preferable.

She shut her eyes and allowed sleep to take over for the short time left for such a thing.

4

Hamish had fallen asleep almost as soon as he laid down, but when he woke before the rising of the sun, it was with bleary eyes and feeling hardly rested at all. He stifled a groan and threw aside the plaid he used as a blanket, inviting a chill to spread over his body. The fire had gone out sometime during the night, leaving his room not only dark but cold.

That was intentional, for the only way he could rouse himself at the required time was to make his room so cold that rising to light the fire was necessary. Once he rose to light the fire, he inevitably decided he might as well light the other fires and warm himself by going about his duties rather than getting back into bed.

Today was even colder than usual. It seemed the temperature had dipped significantly, for there was frost on the windows, and the draft of air coming from the fireplace was frigid, making his fingers tremble as they struck the flint.

A memory from last night flashed across his mind, and he hurried up once the fire in his quarters was lit, reaching for his breeks and pulling them on. Miss MacGurk hadn't appeared to him the lazy type, but her comment about promptness not being a strength had put him ill-at-ease. She needed to know that the pace of life at Glengour would not slow to accommodate her whims, and it was best to ensure she understood that right away.

He walked in the direction of Glenna's door, only to pause a dozen feet shy of it. It was the custom for him to knock when it was time to wake for the day, but he turned away instead. Another thirty minutes of sleep for Glenna would do her good. Neither of them had had such an opportunity for months now—Glenna even longer than that, for she had been at Glengour under the management of the prior innkeeper, Mr. Gibson, and it had been his custom to wake long after Glenna, leaving the preparations for the day largely to her.

He hurriedly lit the fire in the coffee room then scaled the two staircases leading to the uppermost level of the inn. The rooms there had been meant for servants, but there had been two nights in the last month when they'd had enough travelers passing through to require the use of the cramped rooms. If things continued as they were, they would be obliged to build another wing onto the inn. It was a good problem to have, being too busy, but it was also a fatiguing one.

Hamish reached the door where Miss MacGurk was sleeping and rapped three times. There was silence for a moment followed by a sudden and great shuffling within.

He frowned and leaned closer. "Time ta rise, Miss MacGurk."

The shuffling stopped for a moment, only to resume. He couldn't prevent a slight smile at the chaos his early visit had precipitated. What time had she expected to wake? Surely she understood that many of their guests preferred to be on their way betimes—and with porridge in their bellies.

His brows knit as he heard what could only be explained as the window opening. What the devil was she doing?

He knocked a second time, harder this time, and the door opened shortly.

Miss MacGurk stared out at him through the small gap, looking somewhat harried, though not, it appeared, as if she had just woken. Her eyes were too bright and her hair too orderly. Besides, she was already dressed.

"Ye're awake," Hamish said in mild surprise.

She smiled, though there was strain in it. "Aye, of course. 'Tis my first day. Wouldna wish ta be turned off afore I've even begun."

His gaze moved to the cloak tied about her neck, and she looked down to follow the object of his focus.

"I was just a wee bit cold," she said.

One eyebrow went up. "Aye, that's bound ta happen when ye open the window. In February."

She glanced quickly behind her. "I wished for a bit of fresh air. Helps energize me." She smiled at him then went over to shut the window. It stuck, though, and Hamish was obliged to go over and help.

"If frigid air is what ye require, ye can open the door in the kitchen. Ye'll no' be cold for long in there," he said significantly. "'Tis the warmest room in the house in the winter—and in the summer, ta say nothin' of the smoke that often fills it." He put out a hand to invite her to precede him. "Shall we?"

Another strained smile, and she slipped out of the room.

Hamish closed the door and followed, taking the opportunity to observe her from behind as they descended the narrow stairs. He had yet to see her in anything but dim light, but it was apparent despite that fact that she was a beautiful young woman—far younger than he had expected—with wavy auburn hair and a nose that turned up slightly at the end. There was a surprising degree of elegance to her movements, but her behavior so far was, to put it mildly, strange.

It was normal, of course, for a person to be nervous when

taking on a new position, and he hoped that was the case for Miss MacGurk. He also sincerely hoped that she was a capable cook despite her young age. He didn't think he could bear turning her away and being forced to survive more of the madness they had become accustomed to while they waited for the position to be filled.

Hamish dithered between giving her clear and precise instructions on what to do and leaving her to her own devices so that he could observe her. He settled for something in-between, showing her around the kitchen and larder then saying, "Porridge and coffee are always what's needed first, and for that ye'll need ta light the fire."

She stared at him for a moment then, seeming to understand this was her call to action, nodded and turned toward the hearth.

Using the tinder box on the mantle, she lit it deftly enough. Oddly, that small gesture reassured Hamish. He had begun to fear that there had been a terrible misunderstanding in their short communications and that perhaps Miss MacGurk was *not* fit to be a cook in such an establishment. He still had his doubts, in truth. She couldn't have been older than two and twenty—hardly the matronly figure one was accustomed to finding in such a role. Perhaps the *miss* in front of her name should have alerted him to something, but he had merely assumed her to be a spinster.

She rose and turned toward him, and, finding him still watching her, raised her brows.

"Right," he said, straightening. "Ye ken where ta find what ye need. Ye can ask me any questions, of course. I'll just be cleanin' up in this corner over here."

It didn't need cleaning. Glenna had arranged things nicely, but he needed an excuse to linger. All the Kincaids' hopes for the inn could be frustrated if the cook was a bad one. No one would choose to break their journey at Glengour rather than

The Maidenhead if they knew they would be subjected to abominable fare. They couldn't compete with the newly constructed facilities, so they needed to shine in other places.

He kept an eye on Miss MacGurk as she boiled the water and cooked the oats, but she seemed to keep every bit as much of an eye on him, for they caught eyes nearly a dozen times in the course of the next half hour, each time smiling awkwardly and hurriedly returning to their duties.

The fire provided light to an otherwise-dark room, and more than once, Hamish found his eye caught by the sheen of Miss MacGurk's hair. Perhaps it was only the firelight, but it glowed and gleamed red as she stirred the coffee. It was difficult to describe the color—not red like a summer apple, nor orange like leaves of the autumn trees. It was something in-between—its own unique color.

When she caught him watching her yet again, Hamish cleared his throat and set down the pot he had been rubbing down. It was past time to wake Glenna, and he could only imagine up so many things to do in the kitchen when there were plenty of tasks around the inn he truly *should* be seeing to.

He had let Glenna sleep longer than he had intended, and he could already hear movement upstairs—the first stirrings of guests waking. They would be down soon, making trips to the privy and wanting food and drink before continuing on their way. Mark was likely in the stables already, feeding the horses. He had spent the night at his family's home in Kildonnan, as he often did.

Hamish knocked on Glenna's door but, instead of turning away as he usually did, he called her name softly. She wasn't aware of Miss MacGurk's presence yet, and he wanted to prepare her.

She answered his call after a short time, looking out from the door with a wool shawl about her shoulders and eyes that still drooped heavy from sleep.

"I need ta speak with ye a moment," he said.

She nodded and stepped out of her room into the short corridor from which three doors branched off. The one behind her was to her bedroom, of course—a small, dingy room that Hamish had tried to persuade her to abandon more than once for one of the upstairs rooms—one to the cellar, and one to the laundry through which the kitchen could also be accessed.

"The cook arrived last night," he said.

Glenna's eyes widened. "She did?"

He nodded.

Glenna grimaced apologetically. "And I was already asleep. I should 'ave been there ta help ye. I'm sorry, Hamish. Ye might've woken me."

He shook his head. "Nay, 'twas better ye slept. Heaven kens ye needed it. I only showed her ta her room and went straight ta sleep meself. There was nothin' ye could have done."

Her mouth twisted to the side, betraying how guilty she felt despite his words. "How is she?"

He hesitated a moment. How could he describe her? "Young," he said. And pretty. The shimmering of her curls, tied back at the crown of her head, came into his mind. And then there had been her teasing comment about whisky and the Shaw women. That had taken him by surprise. "I'm no' certain she has the experience needed, but perhaps I'm wrong. She may just need a bit of guidance from us."

Glenna nodded. "I'll get dressed straightaway, then." She turned away from him only to stop. "Oh, Hamish."

He raised his brows.

"The letter ye had?"

He managed a smile. "'Twas nothin' worth discussin'."

She looked at him searchingly then nodded with a slight smile before closing the door slowly.

He sighed and turned away. After Sir Andrew's letter, his long-held hopes of finding a way to reclaim the Campbell estate seemed ridiculous, and he was glad he had not made his intentions known to anyone aside from the Kincaids.

He turned his mind away from his morose thoughts. He would be curious to see what Glenna thought of their new worker. It was her opinion that would decide things, for she had been the one managing things in the kitchen up to now. There had been so much else for her to do, though, that she had only been able to offer the most basic fare: bannocks and porridge, usually, sometimes supplemented by radishes or other things from the garden when it bore a decent harvest.

For his part, Hamish hoped Glenna would approve of Miss MacGurk. He was desperate to unload some of their burden, and the thought of waiting to find someone else made him wish for his bed.

Descending footsteps sounded on the staircase behind him, though, reminding him that he had guests to see to. He hoped Miss MacGurk had managed to make an edible pot of porridge. It would be wise for him to taste it before sending it out to whoever was coming down.

5

Ava glanced at the door Hamish had disappeared through then down at the porridge in the pot that hung over the fire in front of her. The familiar smell brought a lump into her throat. She had thought that the memories the smells of the kitchen brought about would abate with time, but that had not been the case so far. She could almost feel her mother's presence there, and she wanted to lean into it.

She turned away from the pot. This was not the time. She needed to use this time on her own to act. When Hamish had knocked on her door earlier, she had been on the verge of leaving the inn, with no idea of what the time was but any prospect of further sleep long gone.

His knock had precipitated a crisis, though, preventing her from leaving unseen, and she had opened the window, hoping she might be able to climb down the roof and jump to the ground. But, the gust of chilling wind that had come in from outside and the dark abyss below her had quickly removed that option. She would freeze to death before she could reach the next inn on the road, to say nothing of the broken leg she would likely have if she attempted the required jump.

Now, she was finally alone, but the leather bag with her belongings and money was upstairs in her room. She couldn't leave without it, but if she tried to retrieve it and leave the inn now, she would certainly encounter Hamish along the way. Such was her luck since leaving Glenlochan.

There were other options. She could simply apologize and tell him that she wouldn't be able to fill the position after all. She could sabotage her own work, forcing him to dismiss her—assuming the real Dorcas never arrived to throw off everything. But a woman two weeks past her promised arrival date was likely not coming at all.

Ava walked over to the window and looked out into the dark. The sky was just beginning to lighten behind the hill, and the world was covered in a blanket of frost. She gave an involuntary shudder. It was certainly tempting to stay in this kitchen, with warm toes and surrounded by familiar smells.

And perhaps she needn't give that up. Perhaps there was yet another option to consider.

What if she *didn't* leave? What if she became Dorcas MacGurk, Glengour's cook? At least until she could get a message to Dermot and he could come for her. She had no doubt that he would, and then she would be spared the necessity of finding a way to Glasgow.

To leave now would mean to face the unknown—and to do it alone. Ava couldn't pretend she had no fears at all about what might happen on the journey from here to Glasgow. She wasn't a fool. There were dangers of all sorts. They had seemed preferable when weighed against the prospect of being forced to marry Angus MacKinnon, but now, away from Glenlochan and with the anger toward her father no longer blazing bright enough to bury her fears in flame, the road before her was daunting indeed.

She hurried over to the fire and peered into the pot of oats, hurrying to take it from the fire. Her mother had always insisted on removing them when there was still a bit of liquid left. "The oats should be swimmin' in the shallows," she would say.

Voices coming from the coffee room grew louder, and Ava cocked an ear.

"...lookin' for a young woman who may have passed by this way yesterday." The voice made all her muscles tense. She recognized it easily. It was her father's servant, Gunn.

She looked around the kitchen wildly, and her eyes settled upon the door that led out to the back of the inn. If Hamish told them of her presence in the kitchen, her only choice would be to run, leaving behind her clothing, her money, and the bag of spices she had taken from the kitchen. Strangely, it was the thought of leaving behind that small spice pouch which made her eyes sting. It was the only connection to her mother she had been able to take with her in her hurry to leave.

There were a few bannocks sitting upon the large table in the middle of the kitchen, and Ava picked one up. She would need food, if nothing else.

"Nay," said the feminine voice, unfamiliar to Ava. "I canna say I remember anyone fittin' that description. Though, 'tis verra possible I've forgotten or didna notice. We had a great number of people passin' through yesterday. Was she alone?"

Ava strained to listen over the sound of her own heart beating in her ears. Thank heaven it wasn't Hamish answering Gunn's questions.

"We believe she may have left with the tinker," he said.

Ava's eyes widened. He must have discovered her intentions from the maids at Glenlochan. She had hoped it would take her father longer to deduce her plan.

"Och," said the young woman, "'tis possible, then, that I didna see her at all. He only stopped briefly yesterday—he was in a hurry."

The man grunted. "Do ye ken where he was goin'?"

"Aye, he goes through Fort William and down toward Glasgow by way of Dalnaspidal."

"With a day's advantage," said Gunn in a displeased voice. "Thank ye, miss." Footsteps soon retreated, followed by the closing of the front door.

Ava let out a shaky breath and looked at the bannock she held in her hand. Her fingers had clasped it so tightly, there was a scattering of crumbs on the floor beneath.

Gunn would follow the tinker under the assumption that he would find Ava with him. If she left Glengour now, she would do so on the heels of Gunn. But if she waited, would she be apprehended when he discovered she was not, in fact, with the tinker?

The shuffling sound of approaching footsteps caught Ava's ear, and a young woman appeared in the doorway to the kitchen. Her brown hair was plaited and wrapped around her head like a crown just behind her snood. She stopped in her tracks at the sight of Ava, who stared back at her.

Ava recognized the young woman before her. She was a Douglas, and Ava had seen her at the kirk any number of times, though she had never had occasion to speak to her. It was apparent that the recognition was mutual, for the Douglas girl blinked at her in surprise.

"Miss MacMorran," she said blankly.

Ava hurried over to her, looking for any sign that someone might have heard. But the only sound was muffled voices and scraping chairs in the coffee room—travelers waiting for their breakfast, undoubtedly.

The Douglas girl looked at her in confusion and glanced over her shoulder toward the coffee room. "Was it *you* that man was looking for? I didna ken ye were here, or—"

Ava took her by the arms, keeping her in place, for she seemed as though she might try to catch Gunn and correct her error.

"I dinna wish ta be found," Ava said in an urgent whisper. "Please dinna tell him."

The girl's wide eyes fixed on her, and she nodded slowly. "As ye wish, Miss MacMorran."

Ava shot another glance behind the girl, certain that Hamish would appear at any moment. "Ye mustna call me that."

Hamish appeared suddenly, and Ava dropped her hands from the Douglas girl's arms. Had he heard?

"We've two men waitin' for food and drink," he said, looking to Ava with a glint of a question in his eyes. "Is the porridge ready?"

She suppressed the desire to look at the Douglas girl to see what she thought of Hamish's question. "Aye. Only, I meant ta add a bit of butter."

He nodded. "Go ahead, then." He hesitated a moment. "I'll try some meself once ye've done so."

Ava felt a hint of annoyance at the implied distrust in her abilities as a cook. It was a silly thing to feel. She *wasn't* a cook, after all, but she knew her way around a kitchen and took pride in her capabilities there, just as her mother had.

"Would ye take the men their coffee, Glenna?" he asked, looking at the Douglas girl.

Glenna was still staring at Ava, clearly confused, but she blinked and nodded. "Aye. I'll take it." Her gaze lingered on Ava another moment as she walked toward the coffee pot and filled two mugs.

Ava ignored the staring, seeing to the task of serving two large spoonfuls of porridge into the bowls Hamish had retrieved and hoping Glenna would keep her confidences. He looked at it with a slight furrow to his brow, and the spoon he held in his hand, at the ready, wavered in the air.

"Perhaps it should cook a bit longer," he said.

Ava paused in the act of dropping butter into the bowl and looked at him. "Ye *did* hire me ta do the cookin', did ye no'?"

He shot her an unamused look, but there was a small twitch at the corner of his mouth. "Aye, I suppose I did."

She mixed the butter into the porridge, well aware how ridiculous her reaction to his doubt was. He had *not* hired her to do the cooking. She pushed the bowl toward him and stood with her arms folded across her chest, waiting. As he scooped a spoonful, she suddenly felt nervous.

She focused her gaze on his hair, which glinted in the light gathering in the kitchen through the dingy windows. The maids at Glenlochan had described him as blond, braw, and bonnie, but in both his brows and hair, there was nearly as much brown as blond, as though someone had haphazardly made brushstrokes of straw-colored paint over the rest of his dark hair. His beard was dark at the chin, growing lighter as it extended toward his ears.

His brows rose slightly, and he looked at her as he swallowed.

"Is it suitable for yer honored guests?" she asked, hoping his reaction was a positive one.

He took the bowl in hand, shaking his head, and her heart dropped.

"This one is only suitable for me." He scooped another spoonful into his mouth and chewed as he walked toward the door. "Prepare another ta be taken ta the men in the coffee room."

Ava shot him a look and reached for another bowl, a surge of victory filling her chest as she turned her back to him.

Glenna appeared again and glanced over her shoulder where Hamish had disappeared. "*Ye're* the cook we've been waitin' for?"

Ava shook her head swiftly. "Nay. But Hamish doesna ken that. He thinks I'm Dorcas MacGurk." She could hardly say the name without cringing. She would have to overcome that if she meant to take it as her own.

Glenna's brow wrinkled. "I dinna understand."

Ava lifted her shoulders. "I came here hopin' ta journey with the tinker, but when I arrived, he was already gone. Then Hamish mistook me for someone else when he found me sleepin' in the stables, and I was afeared he might throw me out or send me back home, so I didna correct him."

"But . . . but why would ye wish ta journey with the tinker? Why would ye no' wish ta return home?"

The clattering of mugs on one of the tables in the next room sounded, and Ava looked at the porridge, still sitting on the table.

"I can explain everythin'," she said, setting the bowls on a tray, "but would ye take these ta the men out there first? I dinna wish ta be seen if I can avoid it."

Glenna gave a bemused nod and took the tray from the kitchen.

Ava took in a deep breath and let it out slowly. There was no helping the fact that Glenna had recognized her. It should have occurred to Ava that Hamish would have workers who were not new to the area as he was. She was making silly mistakes, and she couldn't afford any more.

She looked around the kitchen—the chair in the corner by the warm fire, the abundance of food and drink, the familiar smell of oats and coffee. If she could stay here, safe and warm while Gunn followed a false scent, why would she not do so? A letter to Dermot could bring him here within the week.

But that was only an option if Ava could convince Glenna to guard her secret. It might require a bribe of some sort, but what could Ava possibly offer when she herself had so little? If Glenna refused to keep what she knew to herself, Ava would have no choice but to escape as soon as she could, preferably with one of the horses from the stables.

Ava tended to the fire, body alive with nervousness as she waited for Glenna's return. When she did arrive, she set the empty tray down on the table. "I'd like ta understand what brings ye here, Miss MacM—Dorcas, but there's work ta do, so I hope ye willna mind if I do it while ye speak."

"Of course," Ava said. "Only tell me what needs doin', and I'll help."

Glenna hesitated.

"I ken how ta bake and cook," Ava said.

Glenna's skepticism still showed through, and Ava couldn't blame her. Why would a young woman from Glenlochan know how to cook? "I promise ye, I ken what I'm about."

Glenna gave a little smile. "Verra well. We can start on the bannocks."

"Will Hamish be returnin'?" Ava asked.

"No' for a while now. He's gone ta the stables ta speak with Mark, and then he'll be seein' ta guests while I instruct ye."

They gathered the oats, flour, and water and set to work.

"So," Glenna said as she scooped handfuls of oats onto a long, wooden tray with ridges along the edge. "What made ye leave a place like Glenlochan ta find a tinker?"

Ava glanced at her. Could she trust Glenna? Her instinct told her she could. But she had thought she could trust her father, and that had proven to be a mistake.

But in such strange circumstances, an explanation was warranted, and Ava had nothing more believable than the truth.

"I'm escapin' marriage," she said, sprinkling flour over the oats.

Glenna's hands stopped, and she looked over at Ava, eyes intent. "Ta Angus MacKinnon?"

Ava clenched her jaw and nodded.

"I'd forgot 'twas you who was meant ta marry him," Glenna said, returning to pour water over the oats and flour. "Och, well,

I canna blame ye for choosin' ta chase a tinker over marryin' Angus. I take it ye've told yer father ye dinna wish ta marry him?"

Ava spread the oats more evenly. "I've told it ta him. I've yelled it at him. It doesna make a difference because it's no' about what I wish for—all that matters is what he wishes. Perhaps *he* should marry Angus."

Glenna gave a little chuckle, and both of them set to massaging the water into the oats and flour. "I dinna ken yer father, but I'd always thought him a reasonable man."

Ava frowned. "And ye'd have been right about that two years ago. But . . . he's changed since my mother's death. I hardly ken him meself anymore." Memories from the past two years flitted across her mind. "He's always had a temper under the surface, but 'twas only seen once in a rare while. Now he's quick ta anger. Unpredictable. Determined ta be obeyed." She shook her head and kneaded the dough with a fist. "I tried ta give him time, hopin' 'twas just his grief, but nothin' has changed. And when he told me he'd drag me ta the kirk if he had to . . . ." She sighed.

"Ye decided ye'd rather be a cook?" Glenna smiled at her.

Ava laughed softly and pulled some of the dough away from the mass to form a bannock. "Nay, 'twas my intent ta go with the tinker as far as he'd take me. Then on ta Glasgow."

Glenna looked at her with wide, surprised eyes. "And then what?"

Ava wavered a moment. The next part was difficult to explain to someone unfamiliar with her family's history. "I would go ta the home of a friend."

"A friend," Glenna said, and her tone urged Ava to explain.

"Aye."

"Ye're expected, then?"

"Nay," said Ava. "But I ken I can trust him."

Glenna didn't need to know any more about the relationship between them, and that was fortunate, for Ava would have struggled to explain it. Even when her father had moved them from Glasgow to Glenlochan three years ago, Ava had harbored little doubt in her mind that she and Dermot would marry one day. Their fathers had studied and worked together, keeping their families close until the health of Ava's mother had moved them away and their political loyalties had begun to shift.

Even then, after their distance had kept them apart, Dermot had traveled from Glasgow to pay his respects to Ava's mother at the funeral two years ago. He had left Ava in little doubt of the regard he held her in—or that she could rely on him if ever she needed help. Two years later now, she could still see the intentness in his eyes as he had swung onto his horse—one far finer than any they'd had as children—and said, "The next time I see ye, Ava, I hope 'twill be with money ta my name, yer hand in mine, and a minister afore us." She knew from his last letter that he had managed the first part of this—he was a respected businessman now. He wrote in proper English, too, rather than the Scots they had been raised with, and she had responded to his letters in kind, using them as a way to practice the speech her father had wished her to learn.

Glenna's brows rose. "Him?"

Heat crept into Ava's neck and cheeks, and she turned to set three bannocks in the nearby pan. "Aye. Our families are verra close." Or they *had* been before her father had moved them to the Highlands, and before Dermot's father had shifted his political views.

Ava walked over to the window and looked out at the view behind the inn. The sky was lightening behind the hill, but the world was still covered in a blanket of frost. She gave an involuntary shudder. She didn't wish to go out into that icy wilderness. She wished to stay in this kitchen.

She could feel Glenna's eyes on her and the questions that were coming.

"And ye still intend ta go?"

"I . . . I dinna ken what ta do now."

Glenna turned toward her, leaving the pan half-full of bannocks. "Ye canna make such a journey alone. 'Tis too dangerous. And certainly too cold. Ye'd freeze before ye'd made it halfway."

Ava looked to the window again. "I ken. But I canna go home."

"Stay here, then," Glenna said, as if it was the most obvious thing in the world.

Ava searched Glenna's face. There was a deep kindness there. "I've thought of that—of sendin' a letter ta Dermot and bidin' my time here 'til he comes."

Glenna nodded encouragingly at the suggestion.

"Would ye keep my secret?" Ava asked.

"Aye, of course."

"Even from Hamish?"

Glenna hesitated a moment. "Why would ye wish ta keep it from him?"

Ava didn't respond right away. She had no particular reason to think Hamish untrustworthy, but the more people who knew the truth, the more likely it was to travel, and the distance between Glengour and Glenlochan was but a few miles. Besides, she disliked the thought of asking people to lie—it was enough to ask it of the kind girl before her.

The thought of hiding in plain sight made Ava's heart thud again. "The fewer people who ken the truth, the less likely it is ta reach my father." She could see the reluctance in Glenna's face. "'Tis a great favor ta ask of ye. I ken that. But I'll repay ye."

Glenna was quick to shake her head. "Nay, I dinna want money."

Ava smiled ruefully. "'Tis fortunate, for I dinna have much of that—no' right now, at least. But I'm determined ta do somethin' for ye ta show my thanks."

45

"Yer help here in the kitchen is enough," Glenna said, looking around them. "I canna tell ye how greatly we've needed someone." She looked at Ava with a pitiful smile. "When we began ta realize that the cook wasna comin', I cried. Though Hamish doesna ken that, and I beg ye willna tell him. He tends ta worry." She turned to the bannocks again, setting two more in the large, black pan.

"Ye can trust me, Glenna," Ava said. "I'll do what I can in the kitchen, and I'll do it gladly, but I dinna think I can serve the guests without riskin' bein' recognized."

Glenna waved a dismissive hand. "That's nay bother. 'Tis the cookin' and cleanin' up here I've grown ta dislike so much. I canna get anythin' done when I'm havin' ta tend ta the fire and whatever's cookin' on it. Ye'll have plenty ta do stayin' out of sight back here."

Ava smiled gratefully at her. "I *will* find a way ta show ye my thanks. Surely there's somethin' I can do besides what I've been hired ta do."

Glenna glanced at her with a glint of hope in her eyes then immediately looked back to the bannocks, picking up the pan and walking toward the fire.

Ava stopped her, taking the bowed handle in hand. "Ye've thought of somethin', haven't ye?" She pulled the pan away with a smile, and Glenna ceded possession of it. "That's for me ta do. Now, tell me how I can repay ye. Anythin'. Well, anythin' but money."

Glenna's hands fiddled in front of her apron as Ava set the pan over the fire. "'Tis nothin'. Only, I've always wished ta learn ta write." She sent a nervous smile at Ava. "But I'd be a terrible student, I reckon, and 'tis too much ta ask of ye. I'll think of somethin' else—somethin' less of a burden."

Ava walked over to her, feeling a rush of affection for a girl she hardly knew, and set a hand on Glenna's shoulder. "Writin' it is. We can start as soon as ye wish."

Glenna's face broke into a smile that reached to her eyes, making them shine with anticipatory joy. Suddenly, she pulled Ava into an embrace, which Ava received gladly.

Glenna pulled away abruptly, eyes wide. "Forgive me. I should no' have done that."

"Why no'?" Ava asked.

"Because ye're. . .ye're"—she looked toward the door and leaned toward Ava—"ye're Miss MacMorran."

"I'm no'. I'm yer cook, Glenna. I answer ta *you* now. Ye'd better get used ta that." She scrunched up her nose. "And I'd better grow used ta bein' called Dorcas."

6

Hamish received the coins from the hand of the departing traveler, wished him a fine journey, and went to the office to scribble down an entry in the log book. It was something he had incorporated into his management of Glengour, as the past innkeeper, Mr. Gibson, had kept hardly any records at all. If the man hadn't been in the Colonies now, Hamish would have had a stern word or two to say to him.

He had spent a great deal of his time fixing problems left by Gibson. Anytime he asked Glenna a question about why something was in such a state, the response was inevitably, "Mr. Gibson preferred no' ta waste the money on that."

Hamish glanced up and, through the open door, noted Glenna emerging from the kitchen with a plate of bannocks to offer the two men seated at the table nearest the window. A frown settled on his brow, and he set the quill back in its stand, striding over to follow Glenna into the kitchen.

Dorcas was there, prodding at the logs with a poker. Tending to the fire was a necessity, but not enough to prevent her from serving the food to guests. Since she had begun her duties yesterday morning, he had yet to see her serve anyone.

"How are things comin' along here?" he asked.

Glenna and Dorcas shared a glance, responding in unison. "Verra well."

Hamish's brows went up as they smiled at the coincidence. The two of them seemed to have reached a good understanding in the short time they'd spent together. "Do ye feel ye ken what's expected of ye, then, Dorcas? And how ta go on in here? Or do ye still need Glenna?"

"Nay, she's well capable of runnin' things on her own by now," Glenna said. "She's a much better cook than I ever was."

Hamish looked at Dorcas, who seemed to be watching him carefully. "Aye, the guests have been pleased with the food," he said.

Dorcas tilted her head to the side, narrowing her eyes. "I take it ye dinna feel the same way as them."

"Nay, 'tis no' that," he said, remembering how much he had enjoyed the porridge she had made the last two days. It would be much easier to rise in the morning when he knew such food awaited him. "I thought ye might be overwhelmed, given that Glenna has been the one servin' the guests."

"Och," Glenna said, "Dorcas is a bit shy. I like talkin' with the guests, and they ken me already, so I dinna mind it. There's plenty ta keep her busy back here, ye ken."

Hamish looked to Dorcas, who was busy brushing at a spot on her skirt. Nothing about his interactions with her had led him to think of her as shy. On the contrary, she gave the impression of being quite confident. He had come to the kitchen a number of times throughout the day yesterday, though, and he had to admit she was a good worker—and certainly skilled enough in the kitchen to meet what was required of her.

The bell on the front door rang, preventing him from responding. He glanced at Dorcas once again. Everyone had secrets, but he had the impression that Dorcas MacGurk had more than her fair share.

Striding through the coffee room, he looked at the newcomers: two men dressed in rugged clothing and cocked hats. Hamish recognized them, though he didn't know them by name. They came to the inn from time to time, and when they did, he found that their gazes were frequently upon him. Glenna had once identified them as associates of Angus MacKinnon—and the men responsible for most of the goods smuggled into the area.

Hamish greeted them cordially and invited them to choose where they wished to sit. They selected a table rather than the bar, and when Hamish returned with their glasses of whisky, the taller of the two addressed him.

"Will ye no' sit down and have a drink with us, Mr. Campbell?" he asked.

Hamish had the feeling they had intended to ask him such a question since arriving, and his senses were immediately on alert, but he smiled and agreed to the suggestion, retrieving a glass for himself and joining them. He had a reputation for being a friendly innkeeper, and it was one he wanted to maintain.

The men maintained benign conversation for some time— long enough for the only other men in the room to finish their drinks, pay Glenna, and be on their way—but Hamish was aware as soon as the tide turned.

"Ye've done a great deal with the inn since takin' over," the man named Fowlis said, looking around the room. Between the two men, he was clearly the one in charge.

"Aye," Hamish replied, "and we've a great deal yet ta do."

"'Tis a location ta be envied," Fowlis said. "Along the coast —and situated close enough ta Ireland ta benefit from it." Though his tone was merely conversational, his eyes were fixed on Hamish.

"Aye, I suppose," Hamish said. "Though, 'tis much farther from Ireland than other places."

Fowlis shrugged. "Why leave everythin' ta those in the south? Sometimes the distance is worth the trouble, ye ken." He paused a moment. "Have ye no' tried tea from the Colonies? I imagine ye use enough of it ta curse the duty on it—and the duty on salt, too. How can ye serve yer weary travelers a fine meal after a hard day's travel in the harsh winter winds if ye dinna have salt ta preserve yer meat and fish?"

Hamish knew where the conversation was going, but he couldn't very well counter what Fowlis was saying. He was right. The cost of imported items had soared since the Act of Union, with the cost of some things now seven times what it had been before. It was a topic of frequent conversation and complaint, even after all these years, and people were eager to find a way around the duties whenever possible. It was to fight against exactly such interference that so many had sided with the Jacobites.

In any case, Glengour's salt supplies were dismally small at the moment.

Fowlis's gaze never left Hamish's face. "Perhaps ye wish ta provide yer guests with such things—and ta see that others in the area have access, as well." He raised his brows at Hamish. "The winter has been a milder one than usual, but 'twill no' always be so." He took a sip of his whisky.

Hamish had few qualms about involving himself in smuggling—he, too, believed the crippling taxes to be unfair, and the downtrodden in the Highlands were disproportionately affected by them, for they were already obliged to pay higher prices due to the cost of transporting goods from Glasgow, Edinburgh, London, and the like. It was so often the poor who were made to suffer for the whims of those in power.

But Hamish had more to consider than his own feelings about smuggling. Glengour Inn belonged to the Kincaids, and his position there was only thanks to their generosity. He doubted they would wish for him to become entangled with

Angus MacKinnon, even if they had nothing against smuggling in general.

It seemed unwise, too, to involve himself in such activity when he was seeking the favor of Sir Andrew MacMorran—at least until he could determine what the man's views were on smuggling. If he was fiercely loyal to Parliament and the Crown, he might have little patience for anything that undermined their revenue.

"'Tis a great risk," Hamish said. "I would be puttin' meself and the inn in jeopardy."

"Nay, then," said Fowlis, rearing back. "There's no' been a successful case against smugglin' in years. We've the approval of all, from the cottars ta the gaugers themselves."

Hamish said nothing. He was too new to the area and had been too long away from Scotland to know whether what Fowlis said was strictly true.

Still Fowlis watched him. "There would be more than just salt, tea, and tobacco, of course," Fowlis continued, supported by the nodding head of his companion, Warnock. "Ye'd be paid a fine sum for lendin' yer efforts and yer fine establishment ta the cause of justice."

Hamish wasn't such a fool that he didn't realize what Fowlis was trying to do, but he was interested, all the same, in pursuing what the man had just said. "A fine sum," he repeated. He wasn't at all certain how much Fowlis considered to be "fine."

"Three hundred pounds per shipment," Fowlis responded.

Hamish stilled, staring at the man, who looked at him with the hint of a smile, as though he knew he had captured Hamish's attention.

"With a shipment every few weeks, well"—he grinned —"I'll let ye do the calculations yerself. And 'twould be easy work with the setup ye have belowstairs." He looked at Hamish significantly.

Hamish knew what Fowlis was referring to. There was a tunnel connecting the cellar of Glengour to a place just shy of the nearest beach. It had certainly been used by Mr. Gibson during his tenure as innkeeper.

Fowlis's glance was drawn to something behind Hamish, and Hamish looked over his shoulder in time to see Dorcas's head disappear back into the kitchen.

"Hired someone new, have ye?" Fowlis asked, gaze still trained on the place she'd left.

"Aye," Hamish said. "That's our cook."

An eyebrow shot up. "She doesna look old enough ta be a cook."

Hamish chuckled. "I had the same thought. But she has skill enough."

"Can she guard her tongue? Ye understand, I reckon, the care we must take with new faces."

Hamish raised his brows. "I thought ye said ye had universal support."

"And that we do, but ye never do ken what an outsider will do."

The bell jingled, alerting Hamish to the presence of another traveler, and he stood. "Can I have some time ta think on yer offer?"

Fowlis gave a slight nod of the head. "There's no' much time afore the next shipment comes. We'll be passin' through again in three days. Ye can give us yer answer then."

Hamish agreed and left to see to the old man who had just arrived, though his mind was full of the conversation he had just had—and the number Fowlis had given him.

Three hundred pounds. Not just once, either, but every time he helped with a shipment. With such a sum coming in regularly, paying off Dalmore House's debts was a real possibility. How could he refuse it?

7

Ava's heart thudded against her chest for some time after her quick gander into the coffee room. It had been a heedless thing to do, but it had become so quiet there, she had assumed it was empty.

She hadn't poked her head out long enough to see if she recognized the men, and she could only hope that was mutual. It would be difficult to stay out of sight at Glengour. She would have to rely on Glenna's help, certainly, and finding explanations to satisfy Hamish about her reluctance to set foot in the coffee room would not be easy. He was likely to have little patience for her supposed shyness.

With an armful of rumpled bedsheets in her arms, Glenna came through the door. "Looks as though things are slowin' down for a bit. Last night's guests have gone, today's havna arrived yet." She set down her burden on the edge of the table and took in a satisfied breath. "The best part of the day."

"Would ye like some help?" Ava asked, nodding at the laundry. "Do ye wash those in here?"

Hamish entered, a troubled frown on his brow. Each time

she saw him, she had to admit—to herself—that he was every bit as handsome as the maids at Glenlochan had said he was, even wearing a frown. She was momentarily distracted from her own problems, wondering what sort of things bothered Glengour's innkeeper. It was easy to think she was the only one with difficulties and dilemmas.

"Nay," Glenna said. "The kitchen becomes cluttered enough as it is. We've a room for the laundry—just through the larder."

"I've no' shown ye around yet properly, have I?" Hamish said.

Ava shook her head. There was good reason for that—she was trying to stay in the kitchen. But if she was going to stay, she would have to know the inn—the more she knew it, the better—and she didn't wish to give Hamish any reason to complain of her now that she needed his support to remain at Glengour.

"I'll take her," Glenna said. "'Tis the perfect time for it, while there are no guests about and needin' attention."

Ava sent her a look of gratitude. Glenna would understand if a guest came during their rounds and Ava needed to step out of sight for a time. Hamish would not. Glenna's excuse about Ava's shyness had been well-meant but not terribly believable given the interactions she and Hamish had already had.

"'Tis kind of ye, Glenna," said Hamish, "but I'd like ta show her around meself."

Glenna's eyes flicked to Ava and back to Hamish, and she nodded. "Of course."

"Come, Dorcas," Hamish said, jerking his head toward the door to the coffee room. Earlier today, he had begun referring to her by her given name—or her *assumed* given name—rather than as Miss MacGurk. "We'll start on the main floor while there's no one ta disturb us."

Ava managed a smile and preceded him out of the room,

suppressing the impulse to send a final look at Glenna. She couldn't expect Glenna to naysay her master to save Ava from a tour of the inn.

Hamish showed her the coffee room, which was mercifully empty for the moment, the door to the office where he retreated to handle the growing pile of paperwork which came with running an inn, and the room Glenna inhabited beside the laundry. It was in a cramped corridor behind the stairwell. Very little natural light reached there from any of the windows, and Hamish's blond hair and white cravat drew Ava's eyes as the lightest objects in sight.

"Is there a reason Glenna sleeps down here and no' upstairs?" she asked.

He chuckled. "Aye, because she's stubborn. That's the reason. She'd rather sleep in this wee room she's accustomed to than move inta one of the rooms upstairs. Seems Mr. Gibson—he was the past innkeeper—had her doin' the better part of the work, so it made sense for her ta stay close, where she could answer the door when travelers came durin' the night. Apparently, she's grown too fond of the room ta change now."

He turned toward the door opposite Glenna's and opened it, revealing what appeared at first to be a dark void. A creature came hurtling out of the abyss, and Ava shrieked and jumped out of its path, grasping onto Hamish's arm.

The same cat that had slept on Ava's stomach two nights ago stopped, looking up at them with eyes that flashed in the dark.

"Och, 'tis just Mary." Hamish nudged the feline with a foot. "Always manages ta find her way down ta the cellar—lookin' for mice, no doubt—only ta become stranded when the door is shut. She can whine louder than a newborn babe when that happens."

Mary mewed, slipping around Hamish's legs and then Ava's,

whose heart was still galloping and might have been to Fort William and back by now if it hadn't been confined to her body.

"Ye frightened Dorcas," Hamish said to the cat in a chastising voice, and it walked leisurely away.

Realizing her hands were still wrapped around Hamish's arm and suddenly very much aware of the good choice she had made in clinging to such a solid, muscular form if her life *had* been in danger, she released her grip.

"So," Hamish said, "shy *and* easily afeared." His smile teased her without mercy. "Perhaps Glenna will have ta move upstairs after all, if only ta keep ye company, for Mary has been kend ta roam around at night, and I wouldna wish for ye ta throw yerself from the window if she happens ta find her way inta yer room."

Ava shot him an unamused look. "I dinna think it worthy of note if a person takes a fright when a mysterious animal lunges at them out of the dark. No doubt ye're used ta such things here at Glengour."

His smile never faltered. "I hope ye're no' as scared of mice as ye are of cats, for ye're like ta see a fair number of them in the kitchen. Wait there a moment."

He walked away toward the front door of the inn, and Ava looked after him with a glowering look. She found it difficult to identify what Hamish made her feel, but if she planned to stay at Glengour, she had every intention of giving as good as she got.

He returned with a candlestick in hand, smiling at her as though he knew she was still frustrated by his teasing. "Come, now. I'll make sure we dinna find any more surprises in the cellar."

"You first," she said with a smile full of false sincerity. "I insist."

He held her gaze for a moment, laughter in his eyes, then

preceded her down the stairs. She considered shutting the door behind him rather than following, but her reason curbed the impulse, and she gathered her petticoats in hand and went with him instead.

The cold drew in around them as they descended the uneven staircase, and Hamish ducked his head to avoid the low ceilings. His large form blocked much of the light from the single candle, so Ava followed closely behind to avoid tripping on the stairs and tumbling into him—though she had no doubt he would catch her easily if she did so.

She struck the thought from her mind, picturing Dermot to remind herself of her aims and realign her focus. He was of respectable stature with brown hair and a clean-shaven, attractive face. She would be relying on him, not Hamish, for her safety—for everything—soon enough. She would do well to remember that. Why, then, did the thought of tumbling into Dermot's arms do nothing to her heart?

They emerged into a room with low ceilings, and Hamish offered her his hand as she navigated the final, crooked stair.

Ava let her eyes rove around the room. A few bottles of spirits lay upon a long wooden rack, and four barrels like the one Ava had seen the Shaws bring the night she had arrived at Glengour sat against the wall beside the rack.

"This is where we keep the drink. As ye can see, a few things are in need of replenishin'."

She looked at the whisky barrels again. "Well, that's easy enough ta rectify. I'm certain the Shaws would be more than happy ta oblige ye there."

He glanced over at her, narrowing his eyes in mock enmity. "I was referrin' ta the wine."

She met his gaze, raising an eyebrow and trying to suppress a smile. The candle threw shadows across his face and lit his eyes, which glittered at her. Wiling away her time at Glengour might not be so bad after all if it was to include these types of exchanges with Hamish. She hoped a friendship between them would keep him from suspecting the truth.

"Movin' along," he said, his gaze holding hers until he stepped farther into the room. "There's a wee cupboard over here where we keep the salted fish and meat we mean ta use soon. Normally, we keep it in barrels, but there's no' much left, as we've run out of salt." He opened the cupboard and put the candle near it to display the contents.

A skittering sounded, and Hamish grabbed Ava's arm, pulling her back and away from the cupboard just as a rat emerged, scampering frantically down the wall. It scurried across the floor and over Hamish's boots, and after a small clattering, there was blackness. He had dropped the candle.

Hamish cursed breathlessly in Gaelic as the scampering sound drew farther away and then ceased. His hand still clasped Ava's arm, every bit as tightly as hers had done just minutes ago upstairs.

She had managed not to scream, but only because she couldn't even breathe. Nor could she see. The cellar was pitch black—as dark as if she had closed her eyes, which strained to see anything despite the futility of the attempt. A shiver slipped down her spine and bumps spread across her skin as she thought of the rat and where it might appear next.

Hamish's grip loosened, but his hand remained on her arm, a fact for which she was grateful, as it was the only thing preventing her from descending into a panic. It was a reminder that at least she was not alone with the rat.

"Are ye well?" he asked, and she could still hear the slight breathlessness in his voice.

"Aye," she said. "Though, I dinna particularly wish ta stay here—if the tour of the cellar is over, that is."

He chuckled. "Aye. 'Tis over. I'll guide us out. Hold onta me."

He let his hand slide down her arm and took her by the hand, pulling her slowly along in the opposite direction.

Ava's wide eyes continued to search for any point of light, and her heart pattered with nerves as Hamish's hand held hers firmly during their slow progress. Finally, a sliver of light appeared above their heads—the gap under the door at the top of the stairs. When they had stood in that corridor earlier, Ava hadn't thought there would have been enough light to seep through such a crack, but it was glorious to her eyes now, a bright guide.

Almost simultaneously, there was a thud and a grunt, and Hamish's hand dropped hers. Impulsively, she reached out into the dark, and her hand found purchase in something solid, which she realized with embarrassment was Hamish's abdomen.

He took her hand up again.

"Forgive me," he said, his voice half a groan. "I forgot the ceilin' was so low right here."

They made it to the top of the stairs without further complication, and Ava let out a great sigh of relief once her feet were planted on the even floor again—a floor where, if there was a rat, at least she would see it.

Hamish dropped her hand and met her gaze with an apologetic grimace.

"And ta think ye teased *me* about mice," she said. It wasn't entirely fair, for she had little doubt she would have dropped the candle as well if she had been the one holding it when the rat had appeared.

"Aye, *mice*," he replied. "That was a rat down there. Giant, connivin' beasties they are."

Mary was laying on the floor in the corridor, staring up at them with lazy, tired eyes.

"What good are ye, anyway, Bloody Mary? What do ye do down there if ye're no' catchin' rats?"

The cat only blinked slowly at him.

He shook his head at her. "Lazy Mary, that's what I'll call ye now."

"Dinna pay him any mind," Ava said as she crouched down to pet the cat. "He's only embarrassed."

He scoffed.

They went outside next, and Hamish showed her the stables, the plot of farming land attached to the inn, the privy, and finally, the well.

"Ye'll be usin' this a fair amount," he said as he rotated the crank to raise the bucket.

Ava's eyes went to the red spot on his forehead, where he had hit the low ceiling in the cellar.

"It might give ye a bit of trouble at first—the crank can be ticklish at times—but ye'll grow used ta it soon enough. I reckon ye've used such a thing plenty of times afore. They all have their tricks."

"Aye," Ava said with a forced smile. Operating a well was not something she had done, but she would learn—and Glenna would help her. Anything she could do that put her out of the view of the local and traveling guests was a duty to be sought out and mastered.

He stepped back and nodded in an invitation for her to operate the crank herself. "We may as well bring in a bucket while we're here."

"Are most of the people ye serve travelers passin' through?" she asked as she turned the crank with as much strength as she could muster.

He tilted his head from side to side. "When I first arrived, 'twas so, but now, we have more and more of the tounfolk comin'—that's mostly at night, though, when they've finished their work and are eager ta relax or eat somethin' they dinna have ta make at home."

"Or ta bring a cask of whisky and flirt with the braw innkeeper," Ava said with a provoking smile.

He let out a chuckle and shook his head. "Ye're worse than Glenna, goin' on about that. And I dinna *flirt.*"

"Much ta the young lass's chagrin."

He nudged her with an elbow, and the gesture struck Ava—first, with the beginnings of a blush, and second, for how it would have affected Miss Shaw if he had done as much to her. The crank jolted suddenly, and Hamish grabbed at the chain, which had managed to slip from its proper place.

He looped it around the pulley again. "That's what I meant about it bein' ticklish. The bucket's almost up, though. Just a few more rounds." He kept one hand on the chain he had just readjusted and put the other atop hers on the crank. "Slow but firm for the final bit, or else the water sloshes out, and all yer work is for naught."

Ava swallowed, keenly aware of his hand on hers as the bucket emerged and Hamish reached for and unhooked it.

There had been nothing flirtatious about the gesture; it was purely practical—a way to ensure no water was lost, as he had said. But, still, it made her heart beat harder than was needful for the task she was performing. She pictured Dermot in her mind again.

"What do ye have against Miss Shaw, anyway?" she asked. "She's bonnie, she kens how ta make whisky, and she looks kind enough." It was more of a reminder to herself than anything, but Ava *was* curious.

"I've nothin' ta say against Henrietta."

Henrietta. They were close enough to call one another by their Christian names.

"Ye could do worse than her, and she could do much worse than becomin' an innkeeper's wife." Ava looked back at the inn behind them. "'Tis a good home."

He set down the bucket and turned toward Glengour. He shook his head. "It's no' a home. No' a proper one, anyway."

"What do ye mean?"

He shrugged. "'Tis where people come when they're *away* from home, when they're escapin' home."

Ava tensed, but he wasn't looking at her. He turned away from the inn, setting his hands on his waist. "When ye've been without a home as long as I have, ye begin ta appreciate what it means ta have a true one."

Ava thought of her own home and how she'd wanted nothing more than to escape it.

"And just what do ye consider a *true home*?"

His eyes narrowed a bit as he looked off behind her at nothing in particular. "Somethin' sturdy, established. Old and full of memories."

"Ye've plenty of memories here, I reckon."

"Aye, memories of rousin' Mr. Milroy from his drunken slumbers."

She pointed a finger at him. "And yet, ye're smilin' at the thought. 'Tis the people who make a home what it is, no' the buildin' itself."

His gaze held hers, thoughtful. "Henrietta is a fine lass, I'm sure, but I dinna wish ta take her ta wife." He rubbed a hand absently on the injury on his forehead then picked up the bucket of water, looking at Ava through curious eyes as they began their walk toward the inn. "I confess, I'm still surprised ta find ye as young as ye are. I had expected . . . ."

"An old maid?" Ava said, taking the bucket from his hands. There was no reason for Hamish to be carrying it for her. Gallantry had no place in their relationship as innkeeper and cook.

His gaze moved to the bucket in her hand, and for a moment, she thought he might insist on carrying it, but he didn't. Instead, he smiled guiltily. "Aye, I suppose. Certainly someone older than ye look ta be. How *do* ye come ta take on such a position at yer age—or ta have the experience for it?"

She should have anticipated such a question—twenty-year-old cooks were certainly not the norm—and her mind moved quickly, seeking how to respond. It would be safest to keep as close to the truth as possible. Too many intricate lies and she was bound to betray herself.

"I helped my mother in the kitchen from a young age."

He nodded his understanding. "Did ye no' wish ta stay close ta her, then? Ye came a long way."

Ava looked away from him. "She died. I decided ta make my own path—take the future inta my own hands." That was all true.

She could feel him looking at her, eyes searching and sincere, and they stopped before the back door that led to the kitchen. "I'm sorry ta hear about yer mother. Is that what ye meant when ye said what ye did about the people bein' the most important part of a home?"

She managed a smile and nodded. "Aye. A home without the people ye love is nothin' but a pile of stones—or worse yet, a pile of stones remindin' ye of everythin' ye once had." She could see the sympathy and concern in his eyes, and, fearing she was letting the conversation turn too personal and potentially dangerous, she guided it elsewhere. "For the people passin' through here, 'tis you and Glenna who make Glengour a place they want ta be. 'Tis no small thing, that."

"Aye, Glenna, Mark, meself, and now you, as well."

She thought on her plans to leave as soon as Dermot could come, thought of the position she would be leaving Hamish and Glenna in when that happened, of the fact that Dermot would never come if she was never able to send him word. If she didn't manage to get a letter to him, she *would* be here indefinitely, and that had never been the plan.

"I'd better get back ta my duties, then," she said, pulling open the door. "I reckon 'tis time ta be startin' on dinner."

Glenna was in the kitchen, fiddling with the fire, and once Hamish had left and they had discussed what to prepare for the evening's guests, Ava lost no time in asking the foremost question on her mind.

"I need ta send a letter ta Dermot, Glenna. Please tell me there's a way ta do that—some traveler who would be willin' ta take it—for payment, of course." Now that she had no intention of traveling to Glasgow on her own, she could spare a bit of the little money she had.

Glenna nodded. "I'm sure we can find someone willin' ta take it for ye—there's plenty of men happy ta carry a message if it means more money ta feed their families."

For the next three hours, Ava and Glenna worked without ceasing to prepare food for the remainder of the day: bread, pickled radish, and salted salmon. The last of these required them to make a trip to the cellar, and Ava followed behind Glenna, eyes searching all around the cold, shadowed room for signs of the rat she and Hamish had met earlier. She ignored the thoughts of Hamish's hand holding hers or the moment she had reached out for him in the dark, her hand finding purchase in his ribs—or perhaps they had been muscles. Her cheeks warmed at the embarrassing memory.

By the time the last of the travelers had turned in for the night, Ava was exhausted. It was a satisfying exhaustion, though, and the relief she felt at the prospect of a good night's sleep was palpable in Glenna and Hamish, too, as they cleared away the last few dishes and wiped down the tables in the coffee room.

"A busy evenin'," Glenna said.

"Aye." Hamish set the poker beside the fire and turned to look over the room. "I canna think how we would have managed without ye, Dorcas."

Ava was still becoming accustomed to answering to the name.

"'Tis true," Glenna said. "We're that glad ye're here."

She glanced at Hamish, who smiled and nodded at her in confirmation of Glenna's words. "And now, we blink and do it all again tomorrow," he said.

As Ava walked up both sets of stairs to her room, she found she didn't mind the prospect terribly.

8

Hamish lay awake for some time after climbing into bed. His conversation with Dorcas wouldn't leave him be. Even before he had known he would be leaving the army, he'd had the same goal: to make a home for himself—a home he could be proud of, one that would convey to the family of the wife he hoped to someday be worthy of that he was a desirable match.

Dorcas didn't know what it was like to live half of one's life homeless, like a ship with no destination, floating purposelessly on the waters. For all she had tried to hide it, he had seen the tenderness in her eyes as she had spoken of her mother, and he envied her that attachment. She had willingly left her home; he had never had such a choice, had never had a home to leave after Dalmore had been taken from his family.

It wasn't just his conversation with her, though. It was their interactions over the course of the day. For years, the only associations Hamish had with women were limited to those with women following the drum—most of them either wives of the men in his company or women who made Henrietta Shaw's flirtatious advances look like child's play. Such associations had

never particularly appealed to Hamish, available as they had
been.

He had always envisioned himself reclaiming Dalmore
House and seeking a wife fit to take on the management of it.
The estate wasn't particularly grand, but it had housed generation after generation of respected Campbells, and Hamish
wanted nothing more than to resurrect that tradition.

Never would he have imagined the first woman to capture
the veriest flicker of his interest would be a cook in an obscure
Highland inn.

She had asked him why he didn't take Henrietta to wife. It
was not as though it had never occurred to him—it could
hardly fail to, given the encouragement he received from her
and, even more so, from her mother. It had never appealed to
him, though, and he had assumed that was because Henrietta
was not of the upbringing he wanted.

And yet, today with Dorcas, Hamish had felt the undeni-
able inklings of attraction, far stronger than he would have
anticipated in someone he knew so little. What was he to do
with such information, though?

Hamish paused as he scratched another entry into the
registry in his small office at Glengour, squinting as he
glanced out of the window. Someone was approaching the inn
on horseback, and Hamish rose from his chair to go meet the
newcomer.

Once Hamish was outdoors and the man nearer, Hamish
recognized him, for he had passed through the inn a few times
in the past, only stopping for some sustenance before continuing on his way astride one of Glengour's fresh horses. He
always passed through weeks later on his return journey.

He swung down from his mount, which Mark took and led toward the stables as Hamish welcomed the traveler inside.

"I hope ye're hungry," Hamish said as he clapped him on the back.

"Aye," said the man, adopting a purposeful pace toward the inn. "Hungry as an ox, but with less time than one. Have ta be in Glasgow three days from now."

"Och." Hamish matched the man's pace and guided him into the coffee room. "Then we'd better get some food and drink in ye without delay."

He hurried into the kitchen. Dorcas was there, pulling a pan from the fire.

"Perfect," he said when he saw that it was full of bannocks. "We've a hungry traveler who needs ta be ta Glasgow without delay. I imagine he'll want a bannock ta eat here and two or three for the road."

Dorcas slowed her walk to the table. "Ta Glasgow?"

Hamish retrieved a clean plate and mug, setting them on the table. "Aye." He looked up when she came no closer, raising his brows.

"Would he ever take a letter for me?"

Hamish searched her face. She was looking at him so intently. "Do ye have it now? Ye can certainly ask."

She clenched her teeth. "Do ye have paper and a quill? It willna take long, but I've been waitin' for the chance ta send one."

"Aye, 'tis all in the office."

She hurried to set the pan down, picking up three bannocks and setting them on the plate as though they weren't steaming hot. She reached for the jug of ale and poured it into the mug. Everything was quickly set on a wooden platter, after which she looked up at Hamish expectantly.

He raised his brows. "Feelin' less shy, are ye?"

"I suppose so," she said with a smile, but it seemed slightly forced, and there was an air of urgency about her.

He led the way into the coffee room, watching as Dorcas paused in the doorway, taking in the people present there. She seemed satisfied, for she followed after Hamish, setting the platter down on the round table at which the traveler sat.

Hamish nodded at him. "A bit of food and drink for ye—fuel for yer journey. I thought ye might wish ta take a bannock or two with ye."

The man nodded and gulped down some ale.

Hamish glanced at Dorcas. The man was in such a hurry, Dorcas would have hardly any time to write the letter she had mentioned if the man did agree to take it.

"I understand ye're goin' ta Glasgow, sir," she said.

He took a bite of one bannock, nodding, though he didn't even bother looking at her.

"I wondered if ye wouldna mind takin' a letter for me."

The man's brow furrowed.

"I'll pay ye, of course."

"How much?" He took a bite of oat cake.

Hamish and Dorcas met eyes, and he saw the uncertainty there.

"Half a shillin'?" Dorcas said. It was a question, not an answer, though. "The letter is goin' ta Blantyre."

"Blantyre?" The man stopped chewing and looked at her. He shook his head. "That's out of my way."

"Ye can wait ta deliver it 'til after ye've seen ta yer own task."

The man had already turned back to his food, and Hamish watched Dorcas, seeing the way her eyes fretted. Whatever this letter was, she evidently set great store by it.

"Make it a shillin'," Hamish said. "Half now, half when ye return."

Dorcas's head whipped around to look at him, dismay in her eyes. She began to shake her head. "I—"

"Done," said the man, stuffing the remainder of the bannock into his mouth. "I leave in five minutes, with or without yer letter."

The alarm in Dorcas's eyes made them even wider, and her mouth sat open, as though she needed to speak but couldn't find the words.

Hamish reached into his pocket and pulled out the coins there. He counted out sixpence and handed it to the man, who slipped it into a pocket.

Dorcas pulled Hamish aside by the arm. "I thank ye, Hamish, but I dinna wish for yer charity." Her jaw tightened, and she glanced over at the traveler. "I canna afford ta pay the man a shillin'."

"Ye arrived at a bad time, Dorcas," Hamish said, and the embarrassment in her face made him glad he had offered the man a full shilling. "Candlemas just passed, which means ye willna be paid 'til Whitsunday—nearly three months from now. Consider this an advance on yer wages." He jerked his head toward the office. "Now, go write yer letter while ye've time ta do it."

Her lips were drawn into a thin line, and she held his gaze for a moment in obvious debate. Finally, her expression softened, and she grasped his hand between hers. "Thank ye, Hamish. I swear I'll repay ye before then."

He smiled at the gratitude in her eyes. He didn't even mind if she didn't repay him, in truth. "Ye'd better get on with it. There are wafers in the drawer on the left."

She nodded and hurried toward the office, disappearing through the door.

Hamish stared after her. For whatever reason, seeing that this letter was delivered was of great importance to Dorcas, and for an even less understandable reason, that made it important to him.

Hamish kept the messenger engaged in civil conversation

for as long as he could, but he was anxious to be off, and Hamish was obliged to insist the man take a bag for the two remaining bannocks in order to delay his departure. But when he had fetched the bag and taken his time arranging the oatcakes inside it, Dorcas had still not returned with the letter.

Just as the man was rising, she emerged from the office, letter in hand.

"Here it is," she said, running over with a face slightly flushed.

Hamish looked at the paper, clearly folded in a hurry, as she extended it toward the man.

"Och," Hamish said, reaching for it. "Ye've no' sealed it properly." The wafer was hanging on one side. He licked it and pressed it with his fingers, turning over the letter once he had finished. "There," he said. His eyes went to the name on the front. Dermot McCurdy.

The man took it from Hamish's hand, thanked him, and left.

Dorcas let out a grand sigh of relief. "Thank ye, Hamish. Truly."

He nodded. "I hope yer brother will ken now that ye're taken care of here at Glengour." It was a silly thing to say. He was fairly certain the name on the letter hadn't been that of her brother—they didn't even share a surname, after all—but he had been too curious about the identity of the person to say nothing. What was so urgent about writing to this Dermot McCurdy?

Dorcas looked at him, brows knit. "My brother?"

"I. . .I saw the name on the front and. . . well, I thought perhaps Dermot was a brother ye wished ta inform of yer safe arrival. Forgive me. I . . . ."

"He is," she said a mite too quickly.

"Oh," Hamish said. There was no pursuing the conversation any further if she intended to lie. Or was she lying? Perhaps it *was* her brother. Somehow. She was certainly acting strangely again, though, and it had occurred to Hamish—far more quickly than he cared to admit—that it might be a clandestine letter. A twinge of jealousy pricked him at the thought. Ridiculous.

He had no reason to be jealous. He had been conscious of the fact that she was harboring secrets ever since her arrival, and this was further evidence of how little he knew of her and her life before coming to Glengour.

He would do well to curtail the attraction developing within him.

9

Monday drew to a close, and with the end of the day came the time for Hamish to make a decision. Fowlis would be returning tomorrow for his answer.

Normally, he would have taken the opportunity put before him by the smugglers to go to Lachlan and ask for his opinion. But Lachlan and his wife were still wrapped up in the blissful cocoon of welcoming a baby into their lives, and Hamish had no intention of disturbing them.

It was Glenna, in the end, whose advice he sought out. She had lived in Kildonnan longer than anyone else of Hamish's close acquaintance. She would be able to tell him whether it would be wise or unwise to accept the proposal.

It was late, and the day had been long. Dark had fallen hours ago, and most of the guests had retreated to their bedchambers earlier than usual, perhaps eager for their beds to escape the cold and rain that crept into the inn through every crevice.

Having had no success in his search for Glenna in the kitchen, larder, or laundry, Hamish went to her room. The door was ajar, and muffled voices came from within. He peered inside the small, candlelit room and saw Glenna and Dorcas there, the former seated in a chair in front of the bedside table, leaning over what must have been a paper, for she held a quill in her right hand. Dorcas's gaze was fixed on the same spot as she leaned toward Glenna from her place on the bed.

"Aye," Dorcas said with enthusiasm. "Ye've done it perfectly. I never saw a better 'g,' I reckon."

Glenna sat back slightly and tipped her head to the side, as though evaluating what she had just written. "Ye canna mean that. I'm fair certain 'tisna meant ta have that great glob of ink at the top."

Dorcas brushed the comment aside. "Dinna mind that. 'Tis a matter of practice and confidence, and that only comes with time. What matters is that ye ken how ta form the letter, and ye certainly do. Ye'll be writin' in no time at all."

Hamish had been keeping a greater distance from Dorcas for the past two days, but it was difficult to do, given the relatively small quarters they worked in and how often he was obliged to relay information from arriving guests to her. He let his gaze take in the supportive hand she had on Glenna's back and the encouraging smile she wore. It was genuine, as though she truly took pleasure in Glenna's accomplishment.

That she should be teaching Glenna to write intrigued him. How had Dorcas gained such a skill herself? He would have to remember to ask her.

Much as he was tempted to stay and watch the lesson he had stumbled upon, he moved to leave. The floorboard he had been standing on whined loudly, betraying him.

Shuffling footsteps sounded in the room, and the door opened quickly, revealing Dorcas. The candle on the table threw its light from behind, creating an amber halo around her head, which was free of the cap she had taken to wearing while she worked.

"I didna mean ta interrupt," he said.

"Nay, ye're no' interruptin'," Glenna said from behind, rising from her seat. "Dorcas was only teachin' me a few letters before bed—kind of her, is it no'?"

"Aye, it is," he responded. Why hadn't it ever occurred to *him* to do as much? Perhaps because he, Glenna, and Mark had been far too busy for months now to devote time to anything but the tasks required to keep the inn functioning.

"What is it?" Glenna asked. "Has someone arrived? I thought I'd certainly hear if they did, but perhaps I've been too distracted."

Hamish shook his head. "Nay. Everyone's gone ta bed. I just . . . I had a question for ye." He glanced at Dorcas. He hadn't considered what it would mean to discuss this topic in her presence. What would she make of his predicament?

Dorcas's brows rose, and her mouth opened, as if she suddenly understood her presence to be a barrier. "Och, of course. I'll leave ye." She smiled politely and made to pass by Hamish in the doorway.

He stopped her with a hand. "Ye dinna have ta leave, Dorcas."

"Dinna fash," she said with a reassuring smile. "I'd better be gettin' ta bed. With all the guests sleepin' so early, they're like ta wake early too, ready for warm food." She glanced at Glenna. "Keep practicin' those letters—even if only ta write a few of them when ye've a minute ta spare. We can work on some of the other letters in yer name tomorrow."

She squeezed by, and Hamish watched for a moment as her figure disappeared into the dark corridor that led to the stairs. A haze of questions hung around Dorcas MacGurk, and he didn't know whether he had any right to the answers.

Hamish quickly acquainted Glenna with the visit he'd had from Fowlis and Warnock and the offer they had made in exchange for his services. She listened carefully, as she always did, not betraying any of her emotions in her expression.

"I suppose I wanted yer opinion," he said. "Ye mentioned once that Fowlis works with Angus, and I canna like that."

Glenna grimaced. "Aye. Angus will have his hands in anythin' that might give him a bit more power. But ye're no' likely ta deal with him yersel—'twould be Fowlis doin' that, I reckon. Angus prefers ta let others do the dirty work."

Hamish rubbed the short, coarse hairs of his beard. "And ye dinna think there's a danger in it? I wouldna wish ta do anythin' that might hurt Lachlan or Christina."

Glenna shook her head. "Dinna fash yerself over that. Mr. Gibson was used ta work with Fowlis. Did so for years without any problem."

Hamish raised a brow. "That isna particularly encouragin', given the end Gibson met."

"But it wasna the smugglin' that brought that about," she pointed out. "Ye couldna find anyone within thirty miles of here who'd turn against ye for the free trade. They're more likely ta fall down at yer feet and thank ye. These are things they *need*, ye ken. Just think what we might do here at Glengour with more salt. And tea! A fair number of travelers comin' through have asked for it—many have begun ta prefer it ta coffee or ale in the mornin'."

"Takin' on English airs," Hamish said with a chuckle. He let out a breath of relief. "Verra well, then." He envisioned Dalmore House—or what remained of it in his memory after so many years—and hope flickered in him. He might have a home sooner than he had thought possible. Perhaps Sir Andrew would be more willing to consider Hamish's request once he knew he would have the means of paying off the estate's debts, even if it took time.

The next day, Hamish was more than usually aware anytime the hoofbeats sounded outside the inn. Three times he went to the window in the office, only to discover that travelers were merely passing by Glengour.

The fourth time, he was rewarded with the sight of a cart turning into the short lane that led from the main road. But it was the Shaws with a cask of whisky in their cart.

He stayed at the window for a moment, watching as Mark took the bridle of the old, stooped horse pulling the cart. Dorcas's words from a few days before came to him again—her compliments for Henrietta and encouragement of him.

Was he being too particular? Blind to the merits of someone who would take him as a poor innkeeper, who had no expectation of being lady of a house like Dalmore? There was something to be said for that, certainly.

He went out to meet the Shaws, retrieving the cask in the back of the rickety cart. It always gave Mrs. Shaw a great deal of pleasure to watch him do so, and she would never accept his suggestion to go on ahead into the inn while he did it.

"Only see how easy he makes it look, Henrietta," said Mrs. Shaw. "Wouldn't it be fine indeed ta have such a braw lad by yer side?"

Henrietta looked up at him through her lashes, and Hamish tried for a smile. She was a kind girl, and Hamish had nothing to say against her except that she was too easily led by her mother.

"If ye'll follow me inside," he said, "I'll pay ye and give ye the empty casks ta take with ye. Ye're welcome ta a bannock while ye wait, of course."

Mrs. Shaw gave a little squeal of delight. "Ye're too good ta us, Mr. Campbell, treatin' us with such special consideration, which I'm sure we dinna deserve!"

Mrs. Shaw gave her daughter a nudge so that she and

Hamish were walking abreast, and Hamish allowed Henrietta to precede him into the inn before excusing himself to go to the kitchen.

Dorcas turned at his entrance, and he set the heavy cask down. "Do we have two bannocks ta spare?"

She nodded, glancing at a plate on the table, stacked with oatcakes. "Aye, I made plenty yesterday." Her eyes went to the cask, and her brows lifted as an amused quirk settled onto the corner of her lip. "Special visitors, I take it?"

He shot her an unamused look. "We've three empty casks ta send with them, so I told them they could enjoy a bannock while I see ta takin' this one downstairs and bringin' up the others. Where's Glenna?"

"Seein' ta one of the rooms upstairs—it seems that man with the squinty eye thought ta take his whisky ta bed with him. Spilled it all over." She set two bannocks on another plate. "Go ahead. I'll do the honors of takin' these ta the Shaws."

Hamish looked at her suspiciously. "What happened ta the shyness?"

She lifted a shoulder and picked up the plate, making her way toward the door to the coffee room. "My curiosity has got the better of it for the moment."

Hamish let out a soft chuckle as he hoisted the cask back into his arms and made his way to the cellar. He had to suppress a smile at the sight of Mrs. Shaw's chagrin that it was Dorcas rather than Hamish bringing her the bannocks.

Only when he reached the cellar door did Hamish realize his errand required a candle—something he could not carry while he held the cask. He would have to light a candle, take it down to the cellar, then return for the cask. With a sigh, he began to lower the cask to the ground just as Dorcas appeared with a candle in hand.

"Thought ye might need a bit of light—and someone who's no' afraid of rats," she said with the twinkle in her eye that never failed to charm Hamish. "Besides, I dinna think Mrs. Shaw is terribly fond of me." She opened the door and stepped down toward the cellar. "I'll help ye bring up the empty casks."

Hamish followed behind Dorcas into the freezing cellar and set the full cask next to those lined up against the wall.

"Which ones are empty?" she asked as she set the candle in the holder on the wall.

"Those last three." He nodded at the ones farthest from him. "But ye dinna need ta carry them, Dorcas. I can take two and come back for the last one."

She picked up the one on the end, tucking it under her arm so that it rested on her hip then reaching for the candle. "If ye dinna hurry, ye'll have no light again. And I reckon Miss Shaw would be sad ta see *another* injury added ta yer bonnie face."

He opened his mouth to retort, but she was already walking toward the stairs with the only source of light in her hand, so he hurried to awkwardly scoop up the other two casks and follow her up the stairs.

From there, Dorcas blew out the candle and led the way out of the inn. Hamish glanced over in time to see Mrs. Shaw turned in her chair to watch them, a somewhat leery expression on her face.

"I reckon ye're right about Mrs. Shaw," Hamish said as he set his two casks down in the small cart.

"Of course I am," Dorcas said as he took the cask from her arms. "I ken what jealousy looks like, and that woman has it written on her face plainer than that sign." She indicated the wooden sign above the entrance with *Glengour Inn* painted upon it. They walked back inside, and Mrs. Shaw was their first view, craning her neck to see them.

Dorcas looked at Hamish with a laugh on her lips. "I'm no' certain whether she wants ye for her daughter or herself."

Hamish elbowed her in the ribs. "Wheesht, lass," he said in a whisper. "She'll hear ye."

"Henrietta could've helped with that, Mr. Campbell," said Mrs. Shaw as they walked into the coffee room.

"Nay, then, Mrs. Shaw," Hamish said. "Ye've done all the work of makin' the whisky. Time for us ta take over."

Her eyes went to Dorcas, and she smiled at her in a way that left no room for doubting her feelings. "I've no' seen ye before here," she said. "Are ye the kitchen maid?"

"The new cook, ma'am," Dorcas said, smiling genuinely.

"Ah, still learnin', then," said the woman. "No wonder the bannocks were so dry."

Hamish raised his brows. Dorcas made some of the best bannocks he had ever tasted. They certainly weren't dry.

"Were they?" Dorcas asked. "My apologies. I'm glad, though, ta see that they werena so dry that ye didna enjoy them." She picked up both plates, which held nothing but the smallest of crumbs. "Would ye like a cup of ale ta wet yer throat?"

The clopping of hoofbeats sailed through the front door, and Hamish glanced in that direction, suddenly feeling anxious as he remembered that he hadn't yet seen Fowlis today.

"Here," Hamish said, pulling coins from his pocket and counting out the correct amount. "I'm sorry I canna stay and chat longer, but I must welcome the guests."

"I'll see that they have a drink before they go on their way," Dorcas said with a smile at the women.

Hamish hesitated. Mrs. Shaw seemed to have taken Dorcas in aversion, and a tongue as sugary sweet as hers could also strike like a whip at need. But he had little doubt Dorcas was capable of dealing with it. She, too, had a quick wit. Whether that should reassure or worry him, he didn't know.

She nodded at him, as if to offer assurance that she would keep a civil tongue in her head, and he hurried to the door. Sure enough, Fowlis and Warnock were dismounting, and Hamish greeted them with relief. Now that he had made a decision, he'd begun to fear they might never return, that perhaps he had missed his opportunity.

They handed off their horses to Mark and turned to Hamish.

"Well, then," said Fowlis. "What do ye say, Campbell?"

10

Ava brought Mrs. Shaw and her daughter two cups of ale, which only Henrietta thanked her for. Ava was fairly certain Mrs. Shaw would drink hers at a leisurely pace in hopes of having the opportunity to speak with Hamish again.

For her part, Ava didn't mind. She found it amusing to see the way Mrs. Shaw regarded Hamish like a fox might regard its prey. Besides, viewing Hamish as though he was intended for Henrietta Shaw was a good reminder. She was welcome to him, for Ava had plans and hopes of her own, even if she lacked a scheming mother to help her achieve them

Ava generally preferred to think of Mrs. Shaw rather than Henrietta, for Henrietta was young, pretty, and seemed to have the kind heart her mother lacked. To feel at all jealous at the thought of Henrietta and Hamish running Glengour together as husband and wife was nonsense, and Ava had no time for nonsense. Her day was occupied from sun-up to sun-down, leaving her little enough time to puzzle out her own problems and future—a future she hoped to face with Dermot.

"Would ye fetch my cloak?"

It took a moment for Ava to realize Mrs. Shaw was speaking to her.

"Aye, of course, Mrs. Shaw."

Biting her lip to keep from smiling at the woman's clear desire to set her and her daughter above Ava by utilizing her as a servant to the fullest extent possible, Ava walked toward the front door. Two brown woolen cloaks hung there, and Ava reached for both of them.

The door opened, and she glanced over to see Hamish on the threshold, the first of three men removing their hats and speaking amongst themselves.

Ava's heart stopped, and she whirled around, putting her back to them. She recognized one of them. He had been departing Benleith when she and her father had visited a few weeks ago. That visit, more than anything, had determined Ava against a match with Angus.

She pulled her cap down farther onto her forehead and hurried out of the entryway, pushing open the office door and stepping in with her heart thumping wildly.

She listened to the muffled sounds of the voices, recognizing Hamish's without difficulty, despite the fact that he seemed to be speaking in an undervoice. Rather than passing and continuing into the coffee room, the voices lingered in front of the office door.

Ava's eyes widened, and she looked around the room frantically. She had only been in the office once before, and her thoughts then had been consumed by the need to write her letter to Dermot as quickly as possible. There was another door on the other side of the room, and she ran toward it, pushing it open, and slipping inside just as the voices increased in volume, only to be shut out as she hurriedly pushed the door closed behind her.

She waited—waited for any sign that her escape had been

noted. But the low timbre of the men's voices continued in the office, their words unintelligible.

Heartbeat slowing, she looked at her surroundings. The fireplace on the wall to her right was equipped for cooking, though it was currently unlit. There was a small couch and two chairs in the room, though one chair sat in the corner. Upon its woven seat were various items—a folded plaid, a sporran, and a book.

Ava turned around fully to face the wall opposite the door she had come in. A bed sat in the corner there. Separating the sleeping and cooking areas was a small wooden table. The bed was made, though somewhat haphazardly, as though the occupant had woken late but was so accustomed to making the bed they hadn't been able to leave the covers thrown aside.

She must be in Hamish's lodgings. She had wondered where he slept, for his sleeping arrangements had not been identified or discussed during the tour he had given her of Glengour, and amongst the bedchambers on the same floor as hers, only one seemed to be in use—Mark slept there on nights when he was too tired to return to his family's lodgings in Kildonnan.

Seeing Hamish's quarters, Ava felt a bit of sadness. The room gave no more indication of who lived in it than any of the other inn rooms housing passing travelers for one night at a time, often with nothing more than the clothes on their back and a small pack.

All the same, it felt wrong to be there—particularly without his knowledge—but there was no door except the one she had come through. She would have to wait until she heard the men leave.

The thought of them unsettled her. What business had Hamish with Angus's associates? She had not expected him to consort with such people. Of course, he was obliged to serve them if they came asking for a drink, but to invite them into his office? What could they possibly be speaking of? And what would happen if word of Ava's presence at Glengour were to make its way to Angus?

Shivers erupted all over her skin. She was in hiding, and in many ways, that restricted her more than ever before. But she was also experiencing a new type of freedom, away from the prison Glenlochan had come to be, away from her father's demands and unexpected outbursts. But what if Hamish came to know of her true identity and betrayed her?

There was so much she didn't know, so many ways things could go awry. Surely, Gunn must have apprehended the tinker by now, and if so, he would have learned that Ava had not been in his company.

Her eyes widened. Perhaps they had enlisted Angus's men in their search for her.

A sliver of mistrust lodged itself inside her. Nothing good could come of a connection to Angus MacKinnon—she was certain of that, at least. She had seen her father become more selfish, more volatile as his acquaintance with Angus had developed. Why would Hamish be immune to Angus's pernicious influence?

Or perhaps she was letting her fears take over, creating unmerited suspicion. She didn't know what to think. All she knew was that the prospect of being forced into a marriage with Angus terrified her.

By the time the muffled speaking in the office ended, Ava felt thoroughly confused about Hamish and what to make of him. She found it too easy to enjoy his company despite her efforts to nip such feelings in the bud. The important thing was that Dermot would soon receive her letter, and he would come take her far away from Glengour.

She approached the door she had come through, setting her ear against it just in time to hear the sound of the office door closing.

She hurried over to the window and pulled aside the thin curtain, watching as Mark brought the horses and the men climbed into the saddles. They spoke a few final words to Hamish then urged their horses forward and out of the inn yard.

Ava let out a sigh of relief. They were gone. She could return to the kitchen where she was safe.

Just as she reached the door, it opened, and she froze.

Hamish, too, stilled in the doorway, gaze full of confusion. "Dorcas? What're ye doin'?" His brow frowned heavily.

She swallowed, and the fears she had talked herself into during her time in his lodgings swelled. She had come into his private lodgings uninvited. Plenty of servants had been dismissed—or worse—for less.

She shut her eyes for a moment, and the image of Angus's face just before her own hovered in her mind: the look of desire in his eyes, the way he had set a hand on her waist, as though he was in no doubt she would welcome his advances. She had pushed him away, and while she had feared what he might then do in his anger, he had merely looked at her with the edge of his lip curled up in . . . amusement? Intrigue? She couldn't say exactly what it had been, only that it had troubled her deeply.

"Dorcas?"

Ava's eyes flew open as she yanked her arm away from the hesitant hand Hamish had put on it. She held her arm where he had touched it as he blinked in surprise.

"Forgive me," he said. "I didna mean ta . . . ." He grimaced but left the sentence unfinished. The expression on his face, though—a mixture of concern, bewilderment, and embarrassment—was opposite of Angus's. The realization calmed her enough to think. An explanation was certainly warranted. He had found her in his lodgings, but she was acting as though he had attacked her.

"I'm sorry," she said. "I ken I shouldna be here. Only, I—I—I was helpin' the Shaws, fetchin' their cloaks when ye entered the front door with the men." She lifted her shoulders. "I panicked and hurried inta the office, only—"

"Only I brought them inta the office, and ye were obliged ta come in here."

She nodded, trying for a laugh to show she realized how silly her behavior must sound, but it came out weaker than she had hoped.

His eyes narrowed as he looked at her. "I canna understand ye, lass. One moment, ye insist on helpin' see ta Mrs. Shaw and Henrietta, and the next moment ye're runnin' ta hide."

He was right. It made no sense, but she couldn't explain it to him—not without putting her plans in danger.

"'Tis men I fear," she said. It was partially true, but he could be forgiven for doubting it. She had shown no fear of the messenger who had taken her letter to Dermot, after all.

His gaze flicked to the arm she still held, and he nodded. His jaw worked for a moment as he looked at her. "I mean ye no harm, Dorcas." The side of his mouth came up in the beginnings of a half-smile. "I canna speak for Mrs. Shaw, of course, but"—he held her gaze—"ye're safe here."

A lump rose in her throat, and she swallowed it down. Looking into Hamish's eyes now, her fears of him melted away. She tried to brush away the heaviness with a smile. "Ye'll protect me from Mrs. Shaw, then?"

He relaxed more at her attempt at lightness, stepping farther into the room. "Well, ye abandoned them ta fetch their cloaks on their own, so I canna promise anythin'. Mrs. Shaw was leavin' just as I sent the men on their way, and she didna hesitate ta tell me her opinion of ye."

Ava covered her laugh with a hand.

Hamish smiled, but his gaze became more serious. "We canna have ye runnin' away every time a guest arrives, Dorcas."

"It willna happen again, sir," she said, lowering her head slightly in humility.

His nose scrunched up at the epithet. "Just Hamish, if ye please. And dinna pretend ye're shy, Dorcas. I've kent shy people, and ye're no' one of them." He put a hand up as she began to respond. "'Tis none of my business why ye're pretendin' such a thing. What I care about is that ye're takin' on some of the load here, which ye are, and which I'm grateful for."

It was Glenna who had first said Ava was shy, but Ava didn't bother reminding Hamish of that fact, for she still had no explanation to offer him of why the lie had been necessary. She was merely glad he was not demanding she do so. He was a better man than she had allowed herself to think him just minutes ago.

"I'm sorry for intrudin' inta yer personal quarters." She glanced around at the sparse furnishings. "Though, in my defense, it wasna at all apparent ta me that it *was* yer space when I first entered."

He raised his brows. "And?"

She shrugged. "Well, 'tis little wonder ye dinna regard Glengour as yer home. There's naught in here ta give an idea of whose room it is except for its bein' attached ta the office."

He chuckled and took a half-seat on the arm of the couch, letting his leg hang and resting an arm atop his knee. "And what exactly do ye expect me ta do? Hang a paintin' of meself on the wall?" He gestured up at the ceiling. "Carve my name inta one of the beams?"

"If that appeals ta ye, aye. Anythin' ta put yer mark upon it and make it less"—she wrinkled her nose—"bare."

He looked around the room. "I dinna ken that I understand what ye have in mind, but I'll take yer suggestions inta consideration."

She waved a dismissive hand. "Do what ye wish. 'Tis no' my

affair. But how will ye fill the home ye've imagined if ye canna even fill a room like this?"

He looked at her through narrowed eyes, though his lips quirked up at one edge. "Ye seem ta have grand ideas of the sort of money an innkeeper has at hand for buyin' wee knickknacks and tapestries and the like."

"Fair enough. Perhaps I forgot. Ye dinna seem much like an innkeeper."

His brows went up. "Why's that?"

"Ye're too young. And no' fat enough." Her gaze traveled over his body—the broad shoulders, the strong forearm she'd held onto, the wall of a stomach she'd reached for in the dark. She hurried her eyes back to his face.

He let out a laugh. "Whereas *you* are the typical cook?"

She laughed, for there was no other response to his well-made point. He didn't know she had never set out to be a cook, of course. By now, she had expected to be with Dermot, preparing for a wedding.

But here she was, not four miles from home, pretending to be Dorcas MacGurk, hiding from associates of the man her father intended her to marry, and befriending an innkeeper.

"Who *were* those men?"

His smile dissipated somewhat, and he let out a large breath, tapping a thoughtful finger on his knee as his foot continued to swing slightly from the couch. "Free traders. I didna wish ta involve ye in any of it, but I dinna see how ta avoid it. I've agreed ta help them—ta allow them ta use the inn when the shipment arrives."

Smuggling. Of course Angus would keep such men among his close acquaintances. Freetrading was a necessity for most in the Highlands, and Angus was quick to capitalize on any opportunity to make an easy profit where he could. In any case, the inn was well-situated for concealing newly arrived goods.

"Ye dinna need ta help," Hamish said, misinterpreting her

silence. "I only tell ye so ye ken what ta expect whenever the shipment arrives."

Ava nodded. If Angus's men were involved, playing any part would put her open to discovery, assuming she was still here when the shipment came.

"When do ye expect it?" she asked.

"Hard ta say," he said. "A week or so. Two at most, Fowlis says."

She would have to hope it would be two. By then, Dermot would have had plenty of time to arrive, and they would be on their way to Ardgour House.

Glenna's voice sounded from the office. "Hamish?"

He stepped down from his seat on the arm of the couch and walked toward the door as Glenna's head appeared in the doorway from the office. Her eyes registered surprise at seeing the two of them there, and Ava felt her cheeks warm with embarrassment. Glenna could certainly be forgiven for coming to incorrect conclusions about the scene before her.

"Oh," Glenna said, staying behind the door, as though she was hesitant to step into Hamish's living quarters. "I didna ken where either of ye went. A man's just arrived, Hamish, and he wishes for a room."

"Aye, of course," Hamish said, and he hurried out with a quick glance at Ava.

Glenna's eyes settled on Ava, and she smiled politely.

Ava walked to the door. "I saw that man arrivin'—Fowlis?— and I recognized him from my last visit ta Benleith, so I hid."

Glenna would understand that. But Ava had no explanation for why she had remained here once Hamish had found her, or how both of them had come to forget that there was an inn waiting to be run and food needing to be cooked.

Glenna nodded her understanding, but whether she truly found the explanation sufficient, Ava couldn't tell.

"Dermot should be here within the next week or so." Ava

could hear how pathetic she sounded trying to reassure Glenna —or perhaps herself—that there was nothing to wonder at in finding her alone with Hamish in his quarters. She grasped at any other topic of conversation as they made their way to the kitchen by way of the laundry. "Have ye been practicin' yer letters?"

"Aye," Glenna said, and her voice was infused with enthusiasm, "but I couldna remember how ta write the two *n*'s beside one another. They keep comin' out wrong."

Ava smiled, relieved to have steered things away from uncomfortable topics. "Dinna fash yerself. We can work on that tonight."

The sooner Dermot arrived, the better.

11

Hamish sat in his office, going over the inn's finances before the influx of guests arrived for the evening. They could certainly use a bit more money, and Hamish had made the decision to take some of what he earned from working with Fowlis for the inn's exclusive use. It was only fair.

Outside, the light was beginning to fade as day shifted to night, forcing him to use a candle as he summed the income from February's guests and visitors and compared it against the inn's expenditures. He'd left the door ajar to better hear if he was suddenly needed, and it creaked as it opened a bit more.

He stretched his neck to peer over the desk and was rewarded with the swishing of Mary's striped tail as she disappeared under his desk and sidled up against his legs with a soulful mew.

Hamish set the quill in the stand and reached down to stroke her back. It was warm, a welcome sensation for cold fingers, as the office had no fireplace. Mary walked behind him and mewed again, and Hamish turned to see her sitting before the door to his quarters, staring longingly with her back to him.

"Nay, Mary," he said. "There's no mice for ye in there."

There was nothing of interest in there, in fact. Dorcas had made that clear.

Hamish rose from his seat and opened the door to allow the cat inside. "See for yerself if ye dinna believe me."

She crept inside, head lowered and alert to any sign of danger or excitement, and Hamish smiled slightly. What must it be like to be Bloody Mary? Living at an inn like Glengour was an adventure she never seemed to tire of, and she walked its corridors and rooms with a confidence befitting the monarch she had been named for. Glengour was her home.

Hamish looked around the room, and his smile turned to a small sigh. Dorcas was right. These lodgings might have been anyone's, and though Hamish was surrounded by people all day, when he retreated here at night, there was a loneliness that permeated its walls. The feeling had been his constant companion for years now, ever since his father's imprisonment and subsequent death in gaol, for his father had been his only family.

He had come to accept the loneliness as an inevitability—a fact of life for someone who had lost his family at a young age, as Hamish had. His years in the army had held it at bay somewhat, surrounding him with good men like Lachlan Kincaid and Alistair Innes, but even then, he had been aware of the uniqueness of his situation. Innes had had brothers and sisters to return to, as had Lachlan. Hamish had no one—no one to send him letters, no one to worry over his safety.

His quarters here at Glengour were the place he laid his head, but that was all. He distracted himself with his duties around the inn from before the sun rose to the time it had been set for many hours. Only when he had come in to find Dorcas in this room had he realized what a lonely place it was.

There had been a contentment in her company, in the teasing, even, and he found that it left this room feeling more bare and dull than ever—a stark contrast from what it had been for a few minutes while they had been there together.

He furrowed his brow, remembering the unsatisfactory explanation she'd given him for her presence there. He had no suspicion that she was doing anything untoward in his quarters, and he hadn't pressed her to confide in him what had driven her here upon Fowlis's arrival—the thought of her lying to him had kept him from pressing the issue. He wished she would confide in him, of her own volition, whatever it was that made her act so strangely at times. She seemed to have done so with Glenna, at least.

"Come, Mary," he said.

She stopped her inspection of the fireplace to look at him, but she made no move to obey his command.

"Och," He walked over and scooped her up into his arms, carrying her through his office and setting her down outside it, where he shut the door behind them. She sat on her haunches and blinked at him lazily.

"Go on and find a rat," he said, gesturing toward the cellar. "Make yerself useful. Earn yer keep."

She blinked again. He swiped an impatient hand in her direction and glanced up to find Glenna descending the stairs with an armful of bed linens in her arms, piled so high she was obliged to lean her head to the side to ensure she could see her path.

"Here," Hamish said, taking them from her.

She smiled and thanked him, and he led the way behind the stairs toward the laundry, setting down his load on the table inside the small room, which was cramped with racks for drying laundry and large basins with scrubbing boards.

"'Tis kind of ye, Hamish," she said. "I should have made two trips, but I was feelin' a wee bit lazy, so I tried ta take the linens from two rooms at once."

"Nay bother," he said. "Are ye findin' it easier now? Ta see ta yer duties with Dorcas here?"

Glenna began taking fresh linens from the pile of folded ones and setting them on the table beside the heap they had just brought in. "Aye, certainly. I've never been verra good with cookin' and bakin'—as ye well ken—so 'tis a relief no' ta be obliged ta spend so much time in the kitchen, worryin' whether I've spoilt the bannocks by forgettin' 'em over the fire again."

Hamish smiled, but Glenna wasn't looking at him. It was true that she had burned her fair share of food over the past few months, but most of that was due to the fact that she had been obliged to see to so many duties at a time. It was also true, though, that the bannocks Dorcas made simply tasted better—even burnt, Hamish imagined. The porridge, too, was better. And the fish. They all had a distinctive taste to them, and he thought he might be able to identify something Dorcas made by taste alone.

"So, ye're satisfied with the work Dorcas is doin'?" He took a pair of sheets and handed them to Glenna. "And ye like her well enough?"

She glanced at him quickly before adding them to the pile. "Aye. I had my doubts when I first met her, but those were quickly set ta rest. I've heard the comments of the guests when they eat the food, too, and they all rave about it."

"And it doesna bother ye that she doesna *serve* the food?"

Glenna gave a little laugh. "Nay, she's no' much help with servin' or chattin' with the guests, but I dinna mind doin' that. Everyone has their strengths."

Hamish nodded, keeping his eyes on her. What did she know about Dorcas that Hamish didn't? And why would she keep the secret of someone she had only just met when she and Hamish had known each other so well for months now? He tried not to let it bother him, the feeling of being the only one unaware of the truth. He wouldn't be surprised to find that Mark knew more about Dorcas than him.

"What about you?" Glenna asked. "How do ye like her? Ye seem ta get on with her verra well." She shot a glance at him, and Hamish's mind was taken to the moment she had found Dorcas and him in his quarters together. Had she assumed more than was merited? Hamish wasn't even certain what *was* merited. He couldn't tell if what he felt for Dorcas was mere friendship or something more, but he had an uncomfortable and growing suspicion that it was the latter.

"Aye," he said with as much nonchalance as he could manage. "I've nothin' too important ta complain of."

"Nothin' too important," Glenna repeated. She smoothed the folded pillowcase at the top of the pile and looked at him with a question on her brow.

Hamish folded his arms across his chest and shrugged. "'Tis none of my business, of course, but I *have* wondered a few things. The way she acts sometimes makes me think she's hidin' somethin'."

"What sort of thing?" A wariness entered Glenna's eyes, and Hamish hesitated, unable to brush aside another stab of loneliness at evidence that he had for some reason been left out of the circle of trust Glenna and Dorcas had made.

"I thought perhaps she might be. . .well, that she might be hidin' from her family and"—he touched the pillowcase Glenna had just smoothed—"waitin' for a lover." It sounded silly now that he said it, but he hadn't forgotten the way she had looked at him when he'd mentioned the letter she had sent with the messenger. Hamish hadn't forgotten the name on the letter either: Dermot McCurdy. A simple name shouldn't be such a matter of curiosity, surely.

Glenna didn't respond immediately, though her gaze was fixed on Hamish. "I reckon ye're no' far off there." She said it softly, almost reluctantly.

Hamish's brows rose. He was right? His chest tightened, a flash of jealousy and disappointment lodging there. Dorcas had a lover. He swallowed and nodded. "I suspected it when I saw the letter."

Her lips pulled into a grimace. "'Tis no' my place ta tell, and the truth is, I dinna ken much meself, but 'tis what I believe the truth of it is. She expects him soon."

Hamish forced a smile. "Well, I willna ask ye ta betray her confidences. I only wanted ta make certain ye're happy with her here and that we can go on trustin' her." He looked at the heap of sheets before her. "I'll leave ye ta yer work. I reckon we'll have a fair number of people here within the next half hour or so."

Glenna nodded, but the way she looked at him was more searching than he would have liked.

He left the room, and his smile faded once he was sure Glenna could no longer see him. So, Dermot was *not* Dorcas's brother. Of course he wasn't. It had been clear Hamish's mention of the letter had agitated her, and that would be nonsensical if she had only been sending a letter to her own brother.

What, then? Did she expect them to welcome Dermot McCurdy at the inn when he arrived? Or did she intend to leave with him? Either way, she should have told Hamish her plans, as they would affect him nearly.

He tried to push away the feeling of ill-usage at the thought. It had been silly of him to read anything into her behavior—it was far too easy to see what one hoped to see, and that was precisely what he had done. She had been friendly toward him, and he had assumed more. That was no one's fault but his own.

He kept his distance from Dorcas as much as was possible for the remainder of the day, busying himself with seeing to the arriving guests and relaying information at need to her by way of Glenna.

It had become the custom for Hamish to step into the kitchen in the mornings for his own bowl of porridge, but he forewent that tradition the next morning, deciding to use the meager ingredients he kept in his lodgings to make his own food once the departing guests had all been seen to and offered bannocks to take on their journey.

Hamish peered into the pot over his fire with a scrunched nose and, with a soft curse, pulled it away and onto the stone floor. He waved a hand over it, trying to disperse the emerging smoke. He must have burned the bottom.

He fetched the bowl and wooden spoon on the table and hurried over to the pot, skimming off the top of the porridge and dumping it into his bowl. There wasn't much left after leaving the burned bits, and he hadn't managed to avoid the charred oats entirely, but it would at least give him some energy for the tasks ahead.

Blowing on the steamy glob in his bowl, he scooped some onto his spoon and took a bite. His lips pulled up in a wry expression. It tasted of smoke and burning, which perhaps was a good thing, for otherwise it might not have had any flavor at all. The texture, too, was chewy rather than the perfect balance between soupy and doughy that Dorcas managed every day.

He pushed the bowl aside.

There was a knock on the door, and Hamish stilled, looking up. The only times Glenna had ever come to his door were when there was an urgent issue—generally in the middle of the night—and when she had been searching for him the other day. He didn't generally spend time in his quarters apart from sleep.

He hurried over to the door and opened it, finding himself face to face with Dorcas, who had a bowl in her hands and a smile on her face.

"Ye've been so busy, ye forgot ta come for yer porridge, so I brought it to ye." Her brows contracted, and she sniffed. "Is somethin' burnin'?" Her eyes took on a hint of alarm, and she looked behind her, as though she worried the smell was coming from the kitchen. She extended the bowl toward him hurriedly. "I'd better go—"

"Nay," Hamish said, stopping her with a hand on her shoulder. He immediately regretted the decision and pulled it away. "It's comin' from here." He jerked his head toward the fireplace beside him.

Her brows shot up. "Ye burned somethin'?"

He didn't want to answer her question, but there was no avoiding it. "Aye."

She went up on her tiptoes to peer over his shoulder, and the gesture brought her closer to him. She smelled of warm butter and spices—everything that had been missing from his porridge.

"What were ye makin'?" she asked.

He clenched his teeth, feeling the embarrassment run warm in his veins. "Porridge."

Her gaze flicked to him. "Porridge," she repeated, and her eyes went to the bowl she had given him.

He tried for a smile. "Thought I'd put my own skill ta the test. Ye make it look so easy."

"Oh, then—" she tried to take the bowl back, but he stopped her, holding the bowl rigidly. In all his life, he had never wanted to eat something more than the steaming porridge he held.

Her mouth broke into an amused smile, and she dropped her hands from the bowl, allowing him to keep it. "I take it things didna go as ye'd hoped?"

He smiled ruefully. "I reckon the horses will be glad for my attempt, at least. They're the only ones who'll be able ta stomach it."

"It canna be so bad as that, surely."

He raised his brows then turned away from her, hurrying to the table to set down the porridge she had brought and retrieve the one he had made. She looked at it with a slightly wary gaze when he returned with it.

Her nose scrunched up. "Quite lumpy, isn't it?"

He donned an expression of mock offense. "I prefer ta call it *hearty*."

She laughed and took the bowl, scooping a tiny helping onto the spoon.

"Och." He put a hand over hers and shoved the spoon deeper into the mess. "Ye canna truly get a sense for it with such a small servin'."

She shot him a look but put the heaping spoon in her mouth while he watched her with a hand over his mouth to keep it from betraying his amusement.

She chewed twice, and her face contorted a bit, as though she was trying to control it. The sides of her lips turned down, and her forehead wrinkled as she swallowed with effort. She managed something between a smile and a grimace. "No' so bad." The effort the words cost her was evident in her face.

"Perhaps ye wish for a wee bit of the burnt portion?"

Lips still smacking, she pointed it at the bowl. "Is that no' what I just had?"

He shook his head.

"I reckon I'll use my imagination. I've a fair idea what it would taste like." She handed him the bowl with a large exhale. "Well, there's a reason I'm the cook and ye're the innkeeper. Oh! I nearly forgot. I brought ye somethin' else."

She turned and stepped away from the door toward the desk in the office, whirling back around in a flash of bright yellow. In her hands, she held an old tankard, overflowing with gorse.

"A wee gift for yer home," she said. "I went out ta the well earlier and saw these. I thought they might bring a spot of cheer ta yer quarters."

Hamish blinked as he accepted the tankard, bereft of speech. He had been expecting more food—or perhaps a cup of coffee.

Dorcas tilted her head to the side. "No' the most elegant container for it, I admit, but—" She shrugged her shoulders.

"I...I...thank ye, Dorcas," Hamish stuttered out.

She smiled at him. "I'd better be goin' now, and *you'd* better eat that porridge I brought afore it grows cold." She turned and left the office, shutting the door behind her. She would take the back way to the kitchens, of course—past the door to the cellar and through the laundry and larder, as she always did.

Hamish glanced down at the flower-filled tankard in one hand and the burnt porridge in the other, mindlessly closing the door to his quarters then walking to the kitchen table, where he set them.

The bowl of Dorcas's porridge was sending up its last wisps of steam, and he picked it up, still staring at the flowers. Gorse was everywhere in the area surrounding Glengour. It was so ubiquitous, he hardly noticed it. But he had never seen it inside until now. It brought a cheeriness and warmth that surprised him for something so common.

The sound of wheels and hooves reached him through the window, and he hurried to the door, bowl in hand.

Whether it was because of the contrast to his own attempt at breakfast, the porridge Dorcas had brought him tasted particularly delicious today. He wished he had time to savor it, but he was obliged to eat it in a hurry to meet whoever had just arrived.

Hamish recognized the man speaking with Mark as a

Dunverlockie servant, and he wiped his mouth before walking out to meet him, hoping his rushed meal hadn't left any evidence on his face.

In the man's cart was a canvas-covered heap, and Hamish helped the servant unload it.

"Had a few sheep take ill," the man said. "The master said ta send two of 'em here for ye ta use."

"'Tis verra kind of him," Hamish said. "Convey my gratitude, will ye?"

The man nodded, and both of them carried a sheep, making their way toward the back of the inn.

"What news from Dunverlockie?" Hamish asked. "How does wee Sorcha do? And Christina?"

"Verra well, as I understand, though the wee bairn has a cry ta fill the entire castle."

Hamish chuckled, readjusting his burden. "And what other news do ye have for us?"

The man shook his head. "Dunverlockie is quiet—except for the bairn, of course. And ye'll have heard, no doubt, about Angus's weddin'."

"Nay," Hamish replied. "I kend there was ta be one, but I didna ken when."

The man gave him a significant look. "Never, perhaps. 'Twas meant ta be this week, but it didna take place."

Hamish's brows shot up. "Why no'?"

He shrugged. "Dinna ken."

Hamish carried on a conversation with the man as they laid their burdens down on the kitchen table, but his thoughts were elsewhere. Would Sir Andrew be upset by the turn of events? Would it make him less likely to agree to Hamish's request? Either way, it would seem the Glenlochan laird was now free to meet with Hamish. Whether he would remember his stated intention—or care about it—was another matter.

Dorcas and Glenna were in the kitchen, tending to the fire,

but they cleared a way for the gifts from Dunverlockie. Glenna offered the servant a dram, which he gladly accepted, and she escorted him into the coffee room to find him a place to sit before he made his way back to the castle.

"What's this, then?" Dorcas asked of the canvas heaps on her table.

"Mutton," Hamish said. "From Dunverlockie."

"Oh," she said with curiosity, lifting the end of the canvas to see. "And what do ye wish me ta do with it?"

He shrugged. "Whatever ye *can* do, I suppose. I leave that up ta you."

"Verra trustin' of ye." A mischievous light grew in her eyes as she glanced at him. "Ye certain ye dinna wish ta try somethin' yerself after the success of yer porridge attempt?"

He shot her a look. A light pattering of paws sounded, and both of them turned toward it.

"Och!" Hamish said, wrinkling his nose. In her mouth, Mary carried a dead rat. She stopped just in front of him and dropped it onto the floor like an offering. He stepped back quickly.

Dorcas clucked her tongue. "Ye've frightened Hamish, Mary," she said, echoing his words from their venture into the cellar a few days ago. "Ye ken how he feels about rats."

"No' frightened," he said. "Disgusted. I told her ta go make herself useful this mornin', but I didna expect she'd feel the need ta prove she'd listened."

Mary pawed at the rat twice then, apparently disappointed with its lifelessness, she mewed, looking up at Hamish and Dorcas as though they had deprived her of a toy.

"Take it outside, Mary," Hamish said sternly.

Dorcas looked at him with a quirk to her lips. "She's a cat, Hamish. No' a servant."

"Well, we canna have a dead rat in the kitchens." He looked at it with distaste.

"Nay, ye're right." Dorcas folded her arms and jerked her head toward the door. "Ye can take it out that way. Time ta face yer fears, I reckon." She stared at him expectantly.

Mary moved toward the table, raising up on her hind legs and reaching her front paws to the tabletop where the mutton sat.

Hamish hurried over and pushed the cat away. "Oh, no ye don't! Take yer filthy paws outside. I dinna want ye touchin' my dinner. Go play with all the mice and rats ye wish, but spare me the aftermath."

Mary shot him a resentful look under lazy lids. He gave a little kick in her direction, and she scampered a few feet then stalked out the back door.

"Ye've offended her," Dorcas said.

"Well, it's no' the first time she's done that. 'Tis as if she thinks I'll be proud of her. But dead animals are no' my gift of choice—except the ones on the table here. These, I can use."

Dorcas turned toward him, brows raised. "Can ye now?"

He tipped his head from side to side. "Well, no. But *you* can." He looked down at the rat on the ground, and let out a noise of disgust.

"Dinna fash yerself," Dorcas said. "I'll see ta it. Wouldna wish for ye ta faint, after all."

Hamish reached for the nearest rag and scooped up the rat with it. For some reason, the thought that Dorcas might think him too afraid to see to such a task was unpalatable.

Trying to conceal his revulsion, he walked with purposeful steps toward the door, well aware from her chuckling that Dorcas was enjoying the spectacle.

12

Ava sat on her bed and rubbed her thumb along the soft leather of the pouch in her hand. It was tied shut, but she could still smell the spices in the mixture faintly—particularly the nutmeg. She tugged on one of the strings, and the bow loosened and came undone. Uncinching the satchel, she brought it up to her nose and inhaled slowly and deeply, eyes shut.

The small, low-ceilinged kitchen of their last home—the last place Ava truly thought of as home—swam before her closed lids. Her mother's apron strings dangled from her waist as she mixed the dough in front of her, humming a traditional work song, accompanied by the crackling of the fire in the fireplace.

Emotion rose in Ava's throat, and she hurried to open her eyes. She had no time for such reminiscences. There was mutton waiting to be made into something suitable for dinner, and only one thing had come to Ava's mind. How many times had she made mutton pies with her mother? Of all her mother's recipes, it was the one Ava knew best. And it wouldn't be complete without these spices.

She pulled the strings on the pouch to close it and stood, leaving her room and making her way down the staircases. When she reached the bottom, she didn't allow herself so much as a glance into the coffee room but turned left, taking the back way toward the kitchens.

Glenna was there, standing by the mutton they had cut up, and as Ava came in, she clenched her teeth.

"I hope ye ken better than I what ta do with all this. My abilities in the kitchen have never been verra good, and I've little experience with mutton."

Ava set the pouch of spices on the table. "Aye. I'll be makin' mutton pie."

Glenna raised her brows. "A wee bit ambitious, is it no'?"

"No' if we get ta cookin' as soon as we can. I could make these in my sleep."

It wasn't entirely true. It had been almost two years since the last time Ava had made mutton pie. Once her mother had begun to fall ill, her father had prohibited them from continuing their time in the kitchen, fearing it would weaken her even more. Not long after, they had moved to Glenlochan. Her father had hoped the fresh Highland air would help. It hadn't.

Ava and Glenna labored together for the next three hours, painstakingly making the pastry dough, cooking the mutton and making the gravy, assembling the pies, and placing them on the stove.

Hamish came in at one point and stole a bit of pastry from the batch they had just rolled in the larder and transferred with care to the larger kitchen table. Ava whacked his hand with her own, and he gave her a look full of warning.

"Take care," he said, "or ye'll find yerself out of work for abusin' yer master."

She reached behind her and tugged the string of her apron, which untied easily. She pulled it off and handed it toward him.

MARTHA KEYES

"I wish ye good fortune feedin' all the men who'll be here in an hour or so."

He put up both hands in a gesture of surrender, eyes wide with mock dismay. "Nay. I beg yer forgiveness, Mistress Dorcas."

She lifted her chin, feigning superiority, and looked at him.

He took a knee and bowed his head. "Ye're queen of the kitchen, and I but a lowly serf."

She pursed her lips and shot a long-suffering look at Glenna, trying not to laugh at his dramatics. "Rise, then, oh serf. And get thee on thy way."

He stood and left the kitchen with a glance over his shoulder and a smile on his lips that made Ava's heart sputter like the bubbling mutton and gravy on the stove.

"Ye ken what ye're doin' in the kitchen," Glenna said as they added decorative pastry petals to the top of the second batch of pies. "I'd have thought ye had a cook of yer own at Glenlochan."

"Aye, we do," Ava said, glancing up to ensure no one was near enough to hear. "Afore my father was knighted—afore we came ta Glenlochan—my mother did most of the work in the kitchen. 'Twas somethin' we did together." She reached for the salt, grateful for the opportunity it gave her to conceal her face. Something about speaking of her mother while doing just the sort of thing they had so often done together made her eyes water. Her emotions seemed to be perilously close to the surface today. She would do well to take care.

"Tender memories?" Glenna asked, seeing through Ava's attempts to conceal her emotion.

"Aye, a bit," she responded.

Hamish entered some time later, just as Ava was pouring the gravy into the pies, which were perfectly golden brown and steaming. Glenna was seeing to the guests who were arriving

108

inside from the chilly March day and wishing for a plate of warm dinner.

"Come foragin' for food, peasant?" Ava said to Hamish as she poured the gravy into a second pie.

"Nay, then," Hamish replied, the picture of offense. "But I *have* come ta tell ye we have a number of people who've smelled the heavenly scent emergin' from here and are determined ta have a bit of it for themselves." He came up beside her and looked at the pies, raising his brows. "If those taste as good as they look, we'll have a verra satisfied group of guests."

Ava inspected her work with a discerning eye. "And I hope they do."

Hamish stepped away for a moment and returned with a knife and a fork. "Hopin' is too passive for me. 'Tis my somber duty as the keeper of this grand inn ta ensure the quality of what we're feedin' the guests."

She raised a brow. "Is that so?"

"Och, lass, of course it is." He cut into the pastry slowly but firmly, releasing a great waft of savory steam and a rivulet of gravy. He inhaled deeply and shut his eyes.

"Ye'd do well ta wait," Ava said, trying to conceal the pleasure she felt seeing his eagerness to try the pies—and the nerves that came along with it. She had made the pies a hundred times, but what if she had made a mistake this time? "Those are fresh from the oven. Ye'll burn yerself."

He used the fork to cut off the edge of the piece he had sliced. "Only takes a few blows ta prevent that." He tried to remove the filling from the pastry, and she put a hand on his to stop him, shaking her head.

"Nay," she said. "The pastry's the best part." Ava had spent many a day in the kitchen, watching as her mother made adjustments to the pastry recipe in order to make it more than just a container for the mutton—something to be discarded and given to the servants. She had certainly found success.

Hamish shot Ava a suspicious, sidelong glance through narrowed eyes, and she laughed. "I mean it."

He kept his eyes on her as his lips rounded. He blew on the piece three times then slipped the entire thing into his mouth.

She watched him chew, trying not to betray how anxious she felt. Was it because she wished for his approval? Or because his reaction represented the way the guests waiting in the coffee room would react to the pies?

He opened his mouth and breathed out, releasing a whisp of steam and blinking watering eyes.

"Told ye ye'd do better ta wait," she said, turning to cut more pieces as a way to distract herself. "The gravy hasna even set yet." She reached for the stack of plates sitting beside her, clean and ready for servings of the pie.

"Dorcas," Hamish finally said.

She glanced at him, and he was staring at her fixedly. She looked a question at him.

"Ye've no' been truthful with me," he said.

Ava's heart stuttered, and her breath came quickly. "What do ye mean?"

"I meant ta hire a cook, no' a sorceress, but there's no other way ta explain *that*." He pointed to the piece of pie he had cut for himself.

Ava gave a relieved laugh and turned away. "'Tis no sorcery." He hadn't just *liked* the pie; he had loved it.

"No one will believe ye." He cut another piece, blew on it more thoroughly this time, then set it in his mouth, shutting his eyes in enjoyment as she served up four plates. Once he had swallowed, he stared at her through narrowed eyes, nodding slowly. "A sorceress."

She shot him an unamused glance. "If people hear ye say that, it willna matter how good these pies are—we'll lose every last guest. Ye ken how superstitious the people are." She handed two plates to him. "Dinna make them wait any longer for their food."

Ava had made five full pies, and by the end of the night, not a solitary piece remained. Guests had asked for second and then third helpings—of which there were none.

When Hamish came into the kitchen at the end of the busy evening, he wore a tired but contented smile and shook his head at her in disbelief.

"I'm no' the canniest of men," he said as he helped her clean up, "but I ken one thing: we need ta find more mutton."

"There will be plenty for three or four days if we have nights like tonight again. And I can always make the pies with somethin' else if needed—salmon, perhaps."

He looked at her significantly. "If we dinna have fully half of the tounspeople here tomorrow night, I'll eat a rat from the cellar."

Hamish was not forced to follow through with his promise, for it was only midday when the first person came through—a man from Kildonnan—asking for a piece of Glengour's mutton pie. By six o'clock, the coffee room was full, and Ava was scrambling to make more than the six pies she had planned for.

"We need more pie." Glenna came hurrying in as Ava took two pies from the oven. "And ale. The men are eatin' *and* drinkin' more, and we're runnin' low on whisky."

"No' ta worry," Ava said as she cut into a pie. "The Shaws will be here soon, I reckon."

The bell on front door jingled, announcing the arrival of yet more guests, and Ava and Glenna looked at each other with wide eyes and incredulous smiles. Ava had only been at Glengour just over a week, but it was obvious that Glenna, too, saw the busyness as unusual.

Feeling overwhelmed with heat, Ava walked toward the door that opened to the back of the inn. They had left it open to let in cool air and let out some of the smoke, and she stretched her back and shoulders as she let the chilly March air kiss her warm cheeks.

"Let me get the ale," she said. She had been hunched over the table and fire for so much of the day, her body was screaming for a respite.

Glenna looked at her warily. "But . . . there's so many people."

"I'll go through the laundry ta get there and bring it right back here for ye ta take out ta the coffee room. If ye'll cut more pieces, we can be ready for whoever just arrived."

"Of course," Glenna said with a smile. "Ye need a wee break. I understand that. There's a candle by the stairs ta the cellar already lit."

Ava brushed her hands together to dust them off then slid them down the front of her apron as she walked through the larder and the laundry, breathing deeply. There was deep satisfaction in the work she had been doing, but she was exhausted. She had heard Glenna and Hamish pass along the praises of those who had tasted the mutton pie, but she had yet to see anyone actually eat it.

She paused at the cellar door. The chatter of the guests in the coffee room was a constant buzzing, interspersed with laughter. She peeked her head around the wall, looking toward the small window beside the front door. It was twilight, and she could barely see the outlines of trees from such a distance, but there were no guests outside.

With soft feet, she tiptoed down the narrow corridor and peaked around the staircase. She had only a small view of the coffee room—one full table and half of two others—but she watched for a moment, straining her ears to catch a glimpse of the conversation being had over the plates Glenna set down in front of two of the men.

"Och," said one of them as Glenna went back to the kitchen. "That's yer third, Durward. Would ye like ta take a fourth ta keep ye warm in bed tonight?"

The others at the table crowed with laughter, and the man named Durward looked at them, his expression impassive. "Aye. I *would* like that." He reached for the plate before the man beside him, pulling it toward him, but it was snatched back just in time.

"Ye'll no' take mine," the man said, and he hurried to take up his fork and eat it.

Ava smiled at the interaction and let her eyes wander the small view available to her. At the half-table behind the one Durward and his friends occupied, a man with his back to Ava turned in his chair.

She sucked in a breath and retreated behind the wall, heart kicking to full speed.

Angus MacKinnon. Here at Glengour. Had he seen her?

She laid her head back against the cold wall and shut her eyes. *Why* had she thought it wise to allow any bit of her face in view of the coffee room?

"One moment." Angus's voice met her ears as footsteps approached, and Ava's eyes widened. She hurried toward the closest door—the one to the office—well-aware that Angus had a full view of her back as she slipped inside and slammed the door closed. Once inside, she reached for the latch only to remember it was broken.

Her chest heaved with fear, eyes fixed steadily on the door.

She whirled around and rushed past the desk to the door to Hamish's quarters, pushing it open and slamming it behind her just as the office door opened and Angus's face appeared.

She slid the latch into place with trembling hands and stepped back to watch and wait. The slim piece of metal would be no real deterrent to someone intent on entering the room, and Ava didn't even need to turn and look around the room to know that there were no doors or sash windows for her to escape through. She was trapped.

The door rattled and the latch clanked, jolting Ava's heart.

Angus was trying to get in.

13

"I'm afeared we've run out of pie for the night, sir." Hamish delivered the disappointing news to the man asking him for a second helping.

The man set his plate back down with a discouraged, inaudible response. It wasn't the first time Hamish had been obliged to disappoint the guests, and it wouldn't be the last. But none of them seemed put out for too long, or else they were simply drowning their sorrows with the last of the spirits at Glengour.

"If ye wish for more, there'll be plenty tomorrow." Hamish was working on ensuring they had more regular access to mutton. The expense would be covered by what guests were willing to pay for the pies Dorcas was making. It had increased their revenue by quite a bit as guests consumed more ale and whisky as they ate.

Hamish stepped away from the table and glanced up at a movement that caught his eye.

He stilled, brows knitting at the view of a man opening the office door and entering. Hamish weaved his way through the tables, begging the pardon of a guest who called to him. "I'll be with ye in a wee moment, sir."

The office door shut behind the man, and Hamish picked up his pace, pushing the door open when he reached it.

The man's back was to him, and he seemed to be trying to force his way into Hamish's living quarters.

"Excuse me," Hamish said in a voice that was anything but polite. "Can I help ye, sir?" He put a hand on the man's shoulder, pulling him around.

Hamish stilled.

"Angus," he said in blinking surprise. Angus had arrived only a few short minutes ago, accompanied by Gregory and Ivor, asking for a taste of the infamous mutton pie. Glenna had been the one to seat them, though.

Angus turned fully toward him, smiling in the way so particular to him—far from the positive expression it was meant to be. There was something unsettling about it. Hamish had only interacted with Angus on a few occasions, but he had no liking for the man.

"I was looking for the privy," Angus said.

Hamish didn't believe him for a second, but just what he was looking for in Hamish's living quarters remained a mystery. "Ye'll no' find it that way. It can only be accessed through the front door and around the back, past the well."

"Ah," Angus said. "I see."

Hamish stepped aside to allow him free passage through the office door, keeping his tone and expression amiable while his eyes stayed fixed on the intruder. "Ye'd do well ta hurry. If ye dinna eat the pie on yer plate, and then ye return ta find it has been stolen, there'll be naught I can do for ye. The three of ye have the last pieces, and there are a half dozen men wantin' more."

"Of course." Angus gave a curt bow of the head and left the room.

Hamish stared after him, his smile disappearing as he did so.

Angus hesitated once outside the room and glanced behind him, as if to see if Hamish was still watching. He gave a quick, civil smile and turned toward the front door, from which he soon disappeared into the darkening outdoors.

Hamish quickly turned toward his quarters, slipping past the desk and pushing on the door. It didn't budge. He tried again, but it must have been latched on the inside.

"Is someone there?" he whispered through the crack. "I swear I'll break down this door if ye dinna let me in."

There was a pause, and Hamish set his shoulder against the door, ready to heave into it just as the latched lifted. He stepped back and prepared his fists as the door opened.

Dorcas was inside, and Hamish drew back in surprise, dropping his fists. "Dorcas," he said. He gave a small, uneven chuckle, trying to calm the pulsing energy he had been ready to use in a fight. "Hidin' again, are ye? If ye dinna like yer own room—"

He stopped. Dorcas held her fists up against her chest, as if trying to contain herself tightly. Her body was convulsing, her breath coming in ragged gusts, and her eyes held a hunted look, reminding Hamish whom he had found attempting to force his way into the room.

Without another word, he reached out his arms, wrapping them around her and bringing her toward him. She resisted for the briefest of moments then surrendered. He held her steady, as though by doing so, he might stop the shaking of her body against his. "Ye're safe, lass. I willna let ye come ta harm." His mouth rested against the cap on her head, which smelled of smoke and spices.

Had Angus known Dorcas was inside this door? Or was it mere happenstance? Who knew what he might have done if he had managed to find a way into this room. Hamish had heard enough stories, enough rumors of Angus's exploits that the thought made him sick, and he held Dorcas more tightly. In the short time she had been at Glengour, Hamish had come to care for her deeply—more than was reasonable for such short acquaintance.

Her body soon calmed, and she pulled back, blinking and looking away, as though embarrassed.

He fixed his gaze on her, hesitant to speak of what had just happened. But he needed to know. If Angus thought he could behave in such a way at Glengour Inn, he was about to understand how very wrong he was.

"Was he threatenin' ye? The man in the office?"

Dorcas shut her eyes, not immediately responding. She took a deep, trembling breath. "I dinna ken. I went ta fetch some ale, and I thought ta take a wee peek inta the coffee room." She lifted her shoulders. "I wanted ta see people eatin' the pies. 'Twas silly of me. But I saw him look at me from the coffee room, and"—her lips drew into a thin line—"I kend he meant ta come after me, so I hid in the office, but the latch is broken, so . . . ."

Hamish nodded, but his jaw was tighter than newly strung bow.

She looked up at him, and the smile she attempted tugged at Hamish's heartstrings. "I'm just glad ye came."

"I'm glad too." He reached for her hand, wanting to reassure her. "Shall I walk ye ta the kitchen?"

She shook her head. "I havna fetched the ale. I told Glenna I'd do so."

"Dinna fash yerself. I'll see ta that." He kept her hand in his, and together they walked into the office. As they reached the door, though, Dorcas hand resisted moving forward, and he looked back at her.

"I dinna wish ta see him," she said, and he could see the words cost her.

He nodded, remembering when he had first found her in his quarters. She had told him then that her shyness was really a fear of men. She had evidently not been lying. "I'll walk beside ye ta shield ye from view, and we'll go the back way."

They emerged from the office, and Hamish used his body as a sort of bulwark—she was small enough to make it fairly easy —as they navigated the short area which put them in view of the coffee room. Hamish glanced inside and noticed Angus taking his seat there, looking over his shoulder in Hamish's direction.

Hamish felt another flash of anger, but he focused his attention on the hand in his, keeping a firm and comforting hold on it as they entered the laundry and then the larder. It was dark there, but the light from the kitchen fire illuminated the space enough to show evidence of the pastry making that had happened there earlier—a tabletop covered in flour and bits of dough.

Dorcas stopped before they reached the kitchen door, pulling her hand from his. She smiled up at him gratefully, but there was a hint of shyness in her eyes. "I can manage the rest of the way."

He nodded, brushing his hand along his breeches to rid it of the empty feeling there now.

She hesitated a moment longer. "Forgive me for bein' so missish. I'm no' so weak normally."

"Dinna apologize." He smiled. "And dinna use such a word ta describe yerself. Ye're no' weak."

She sighed and with a sort of final, grimacing glance at him, disappeared through the door.

Hamish waited a moment, listening as Glenna greeted Dorcas and asked where the ale was.

"Hamish insisted on bringin' it," Dorcas said.

"We'll need a great deal more—and a visit or two from the Shaws if we're ta keep up with this, ta say nothin' of the mutton.

They canna get enough of it. 'Tis for the best ye're hidden away back here. I think if they kend who'd made the pie, ye'd have a half-dozen offers of marriage afore the night was over."

Hamish moved away and back toward the laundry, aware of the little flash of jealousy he felt at Glenna's playful words. He had promised himself not to entertain any ideas of women or marriage until he had exhausted every avenue to reclaim Dalmore House. His heart seemed to be resisting such a plan, though.

Possibly for good reason. Perhaps it was a fool's errand he was on and it would be better to accept a future at Glengour— and one with Dorcas. There was certainly an appeal to such a thought. It was becoming less and less likely he would hear from Sir Andrew.

He hurried down into the cellar, bringing the ale up with him, which he took to the bar. He would stay there all night if he needed to—until Angus left. He didn't intend to let the man out of his sight.

H amish found his eyes and mind traveling to Dorcas often over the next two days. Unless he had reason to go to the kitchen, he had little occasion to see her during the course of the day. But the bright tankard of gorse on his kitchen table kept her in his thoughts in the morning and night, and during the day, there were plenty of things to remind him of her, from the men inquiring about mutton pie to the antics of Mary to the haystacks in the stables where he had first found her.

The busyness continued, which meant that all three of them inside and Mark in the stables were occupied from well before sunrise until well after sunset with their tasks. In the evenings after the work was finally done, Dorcas and Glenna spent some time together in Glenna's room, practicing Glenna's letters, and Hamish tried—and failed—not to envy Glenna the company.

Dorcas had made no further mention of the incident with Angus, and Hamish had made no attempt to revisit the subject, either. He doubted she was aware of the identity of her pursuer, and Hamish thought that for the best. To know his power would only unsettle her more, and he had no desire to do that.

Hamish was obliged to make the journey to Craiglinne on market day, where he bought more mutton. It was a significant expense, but he had checked the numbers early that morning, and, with a slight increase to the price of the mutton pie, they would be well able to sustain the recurring costs.

Dorcas had tried her hand with great success at some sweet pies, and they hoped that the combination of offerings from the Glengour kitchen would help stabilize both the expenses of the inn and the consumption by the guests to a more sustainable level that required less of a frenetic pace than they had been obliged to take. She had been waking early to make extra pies that could be stored until they were eaten. Her skill and dedication amazed Hamish. And to think he had doubted her so much upon her arrival.

It was nearly eight o'clock in the evening when a donkey cart appeared in the inn yard, with a woman and man seated at the front. Hamish went out to meet them, shivering slightly with the chilly evening air.

He greeted the travelers, listening to the driver expressing the need for a room as he helped the woman down from the cart. She was a hefty woman, and she wore a traveling cloak, a kertch, and an expression of longsuffering. The lantern beside the front door made a few silver hairs peeking through the kertch gleam.

Mark came to take over the donkey and cart, and Hamish guided the two people toward the inn, listening as the man continued to talk about the state of the roads they had faced on their way from Fort William. His words came like the rush of a stream after rainfall, and Hamish suddenly understood the woman's exasperated expression. He had assumed her to be the man's wife at first glance, but she was quite a bit older than him, and she held her tongue too well for a woman who had been obliged to listen to such incessant yapping for years of her life.

It wasn't until Hamish had found the man a table and a mug of ale that he stopped talking long enough for Hamish to see to the woman. She stood at the base of the stairs with a small, well-worn leather portmanteau clasped in her hands.

"My sincere apologies, ma'am, for makin' ye wait so long."

Her eyes creased at the corners as she laughed. "Apologies for what? Givin' me a break from the jabberin'? 'Tis my thanks ye deserve!"

An irrepressible chuckle escaped Hamish's lips. "How can I serve ye, ma'am?"

"Well," she said, "the shoe is on the other foot, in fact."

He raised his brows. "And how is that?"

She let go of the portmanteau with one hand and held her hands out to each side. "I'm yer new cook."

Hamish stared.

She seemed to take note of his underwhelming reaction, for her hands dropped. "Ye *did* receive my letter, did ye no'?"

Hamish's head shook slowly from side to side.

Her lips pinched together and she shook her head. "I should have kent no' ta trust that man! I'm terribly sorry ta be so late arrivin', but my brother died unexpectedly, and there was no helpin' the delay, ye ken."

Hamish blinked rapidly, trying to overcome his confusion. "Ye must be mistaken, ma'am. The position has been filled."

Her brows snapped together, her good humor disappearing in a flash. "And ye didna think ta tell me as much? I apologize for the delay, but I didna think ye'd go on and hire someone else when we had it all arranged between us. Ye *are* Hamish Campbell, I assume? And this *is* Glengour Inn?"

He looked at her through narrowed eyes. "Aye. On both counts." He opened his mouth and shut it again, thoroughly confused. "Ye say we've corresponded?"

She gave an incredulous laugh. "Of course we have."

His confusion multiplied. Perhaps he hadn't been clear enough in his response to the two women who had responded to his advertisement but not been offered the position. "What's yer name, ma'am?"

"MacGurk," she said in exasperation. "Dorcas MacGurk."

He stared. It was all he was capable of doing. His mind was a blank, a bed of confusion.

Either the woman before him was an imposter, or the woman in the kitchen was.

14

Ava opened the door to the back of the inn wider, hoping to dispel more of the smoke that filled the kitchen. They had used wood rather than peat today, and apparently it had been wet from the rain two days ago. She had been fighting billowing smoke all day long.

One mutton pie was left of the six she had brought out from the larder for the day. For all the experience she had gained making them with her mother, she had acquired a great deal more concentrated practice in the past week, and she was getting much quicker—enough that she had made two never-before-attempted sweet pies yesterday, which had been rapidly consumed by the guests.

She breathed in the fresh evening air, reveling in the crispness and clearness of it after so much smoke-filled air throughout the day. Since her near run-in with Angus, she hadn't ventured from the kitchen, laundry, and larder except to slip inside Glenna's room or go up to bed once there were no guests left in the coffee room.

Neither had she spoken of the occurrence since. It had unsettled her deeply, and she hardly knew what to say of it. She didn't want to give voice to her fears. At the very least, Angus had seen enough to urge him to follow after her. But surely, if he had been certain of her identity, he would have said as much to Hamish when he had been discovered in the office—an explanation for his strange presence there.

Ava's gaze was suddenly drawn to the kitchen doorway. Hamish stood there, looking at her with an inscrutable expression on his face. Their interactions since the encounter with Angus had been charged with something she found difficult to explain. But something was different now. That much, she could see and feel. Whether it was a good or a bad thing was yet to be discovered.

Hamish stepped into the room, and Ava made her way to the fire, which had begun to emit more billowing gusts of smoke.

"How do ye go on in here?" Hamish asked.

She glanced at him as she picked up the poker and tried to rearrange the wood into a more suitable position. The fact that he was asking such an inane, civil question made her more anxious than if he had simply come out with whatever was on his mind.

"Aside from drownin' in smoke," she said, "fairly well, I reckon. We've one full pie left, which I hope will be enough for the last two or three people who may trickle in."

Hamish folded his arms and reclined with his shoulder against the wall, watching her as she worked. "Dorcas," he said, "do ye remember where ye saw the advertisement I put out?"

Ava's hand slowed, and she took in a slow, steady breath. This was dangerous ground to tread. Somehow, up until now, she had managed to avoid most of the questions that might give her away. She should have known it would not last, but what had inspired the questions now?

"For the cook position, I mean," Hamish added, as though she was unaware to what he referred.

She cleared her throat and tried to keep her tone light. "I canna recall now." She could feel his eyes boring into her, at odds with his relaxed position. She gave another nudge to one of the logs on the fire, releasing a surge of black air.

"Can ye recall the date ye saw it?"

She swallowed. He knew. It was the only explanation for such questions. But *how*? How did he know? Had Angus returned and conveyed his suspicions?

She set the poker in its place and turned to the table, trying to keep herself busy so she wouldn't have to look Hamish in the eye. She didn't know if she could manage to lie to him now. But if he already knew, lying would not save her from his anger—it would only heighten it.

She turned to him, forcing herself to meet his gaze.

His expression had a hard, unyielding quality to it. "Ye're no' Dorcas MacGurk, are ye?"

She held his gaze for a moment then, clenching her teeth determinedly, gave a brief shake of the head.

His jaw tightened, and his nostrils flared.

"How did ye discover it?" She hated asking the question. It seemed so callous, so self-condemnatory. But if Hamish meant to betray her to Angus, she needed to know now. She would snatch the last mutton pie and escape through the open kitchen door, heading for the trees on the side of the inn near the stables. And then she would run for her life.

"Dorcas MacGurk arrived a few minutes ago," he said, and his voice was hard. It cut her. She hated to know that Hamish was thinking ill of her. But she deserved it. She *had* lied to him. "The *real* Dorcas MacGurk."

"I'm sorry, Hamish," she said, and the words spilled out. "When I first came, I only meant ta go with the tinker, but when I arrived and discovered he'd already come and gone, I didna ken what ta do. And then ye mistook me for someone, and. . ." She lifted her shoulders. "I did what I had ta do ta survive."

Her explanation did little to soften his expression. "Who are ye, then?"

Ava pulled her lips between her teeth as the fear inside her blossomed. The only way to be certain he would not betray her was to lie again. But she couldn't. She was tired of lying, and she couldn't bear to disappoint him more. There were so few people in this world she felt connected to now, and Hamish Campbell was foremost among them.

"Ava MacMorran."

15

MacMorran. MacMorran. The word echoed in Hamish's mind as he stared blankly at the woman before him. She had a hand on the edge of the table, clenched tightly, but she looked ready to run at the least provocation.

"MacMorran?" he finally managed to say. He was no longer leaning against the wall or folding his arms, though he didn't remember ever moving from that position.

She nodded, and her eyes watched him intently.

"Do ye mean ye're Sir Andrew MacMorran's daughter?"

More than ever, she looked poised to make an escape from the kitchen. She might be able to get through the door fairly easily, but she couldn't outrun him. He had a much longer stride than her. But he wasn't even certain he would make the attempt to go after her if she *did* run. What was the point?

"Aye," she said. "Ye ken him?"

She *was* Sir Andrew's daughter. Hamish wasn't even certain what the implications of that information were, but he knew there were plenty to be reckoned with once he had time to consider them. How was this possible?

He scrubbed a hand over his jaw. "By name, aye. But I've

never met him." His eyebrows came together as he thought on the given name she had mentioned. Ava. "Were ye the daughter meant ta marry Angus?"

Her mouth turned up in a subtle show of disgust as she nodded.

Suddenly, it made sense, Angus's presence in the office. "And ye're here escapin' him?"

"Him and my father. My father wouldna listen ta me— threatened ta force me."

Hamish was hardly listening to her justification. All he could think of was the fact that Sir Andrew's daughter was hiding herself in *his* inn.

"How old are ye?" he asked. If she was no longer a minor, she had a right to make her own decisions—at least legally, she did. Whether people respected the law was another matter.

She hesitated. "I'm twenty."

He shut his eyes in consternation. He was harboring a fugitive at Glengour, and that fugitive happened to be the daughter of the man whose goodwill he most needed in the whole world.

"And of all the inns in Scotland, ye had ta choose *my* inn ta hide at?" He could hardly believe his ill-fortune. It was like something from a bad dream.

She looked at him, and for the first time, he saw a flash of anger instead of the defensiveness she had been showing thus far. "I never meant ta settle here. I only came ta find the tinker, as I told ye. I never meant ta be a burden on ye."

He didn't respond. She *hadn't* been a burden. She had been a godsend. Dorcas MacGurk had been a godsend, at least. Ava MacMorran, on the other hand . . . . How could a name change so much about her presence at Glengour?

"Ye're no' a burden." He said the words, but he knew he hadn't managed to do so in a convincing way.

"I ken ye're angry," she said. "And I deserve that ye should be. I'll leave now if ye prefer it, but I *beg* ye, Hamish." She walked toward him and put her palms together in a plea. "Dinna tell my father. I canna marry Angus MacKinnon. I'd rather starve or drown in the nearest loch."

He studied her for a moment—the fear in her eyes and on her brow, the wariness in her gaze. It hadn't occurred to him to tell her father of her presence here at the inn until she said it. Would it be enough to sway Sir Andrew in his favor?

It didn't matter. Hamish would never consign the woman before him—or any woman—to a life with Angus MacKinnon.

"I dinna ken him," Hamish said, and he couldn't keep the annoyance from his voice. "I told ye."

She grabbed his hand, and his impulse told him to draw it back. It was that which told him there was more to his anger than the revelation of her true identity. He understood why she had lied to him, but it still bothered him. It still hurt him. She had trusted Glenna, hadn't she? Then why not him?

"I'll gather my things and go," she said.

The suggestion irritated him even more. He didn't *want* her to go. Even after discovering she had lied to him this whole time, he didn't wish for her to leave. What did that say about him?

"Go where? Home?"

She shook her head quickly. "Nay. I canna go home. I willna. My father's been a tyrant since we came ta Glenlochan."

"Then what'll ye do?" Hamish had no intention of forcing her to leave, but he didn't care to say as much yet. Perhaps he wanted to punish her for using him as she had. Or perhaps he simply wanted to understand her better.

She lifted her shoulders. "Find my way ta Fort William, I suppose, and hope ta cross paths with Dermot on his way here." She looked at him squarely. "I'll manage. In any case, 'tis none of yer concern."

Hamish shook his head. "Ye'll no' go anywhere."

The muscles in her jaw tightened. "I *will*."

"Ye'll no'."

Their gazes held, a battle of wills, her eyes burned bright, sending him a warning look. "I didna leave home ta trade one tyrant for another."

Her words jolted him. Did she think him a tyrant? He forced his shoulders to relax. "I'm no tyrant. But I canna let ye go out inta the wilderness by yerself. Ye can stay here till yer . . . yer . . . till Dermot arrives."

She shook her head.

"Dinna be stubborn, lass. Even if ye find a way ta Fort William, how do ye expect ta find him? What if he passes ye on the road? What if he only makes a brief stop there and ye miss him just as ye did the tinker?"

Her eyes betrayed how his words were shaking her confidence, but her chin lifted higher despite it. "Then, I'll find a family in need of a cook there."

"And ye think they'll take on a lass of yer age? Unmarried?"

"*You* did."

"Aye," he said. "Because we were desperate for help, and I feared 'twas my mistake for assumin' ye'd been an old maid or a widow."

She kept her eyes on him, biting her lip. His point seemed to have been taken.

"So, we're agreed, then? Ye'll remain here until Dermot arrives."

There was a pause again as they stared at one another. Her brown eyes surveyed him carefully, and he tried to ignore the way they drew him to her.

She gave a curt nod. "Thank ye."

He smiled wryly at the reluctant way she said it.

"I'll continue ta help here," she said.

Hamish began to speak, but she talked over him. "I dinna have the money ta pay for a room, so ye'll have my work instead, and that's that. If ye willna let me work, I'll gather my things and go now. "

It went against Hamish's sense of propriety to allow the daughter of Sir Andrew to labor in his inn, but if the choice was between that and her leaving Glengour for Fort William on her own—which he had no doubt she would do, given her stubbornness—the former was unarguably preferable.

"Fine," he said. "Ye can teach Dorcas"—he shifted, feeling the strangeness of saying the name he associated with Miss MacMorran—"how ta make yer pies and help with the washin'."

She gave a nod.

"One more thing." Hamish sighed, crossing his arms again. "This Dermot . . . is he a respectable man?" He couldn't help himself. He felt protective of Miss MacMorran, and he knew nothing of the man she was waiting for. What if she was as mistaken in him as she had been in her knowledge of the tinker?

Her mouth twitched at the sides. "Aye. He's respectable. I've kent him since we were wee."

A long-standing attachment, then. How had Hamish let himself see anything more than friendship in her manner toward him? "And he has the means ta take care of ye as ye deserve?"

"He has a small estate near his father's, close ta Glasgow."

Hamish attempted to loosen his jaw, which clenched of its own accord. He couldn't help comparing Dermot McCurdy to himself and his lack of estate. "And ye trust he *will* come?"

She nodded.

The thought of her riding back toward Glasgow in the company of another man lit a fire inside Hamish—a jealousy he had no right to feel. She had known Dermot for years; Hamish had only just learned her real name.

Glenna walked in, stopping short at the sight of them. Her gaze flicked between them. "Is somethin' amiss?"

Hamish met eyes with Miss MacMorran. "Nay. Nothin's amiss."

Glenna didn't seem sure whether to believe him, but she made her way to the table. "I took the liberty of welcomin' the man who just arrived. He fancies a piece of pie and a dram."

"I'll see ta the dram," Hamish said, eyes still on Miss MacMorran.

She sent him an expression that was a strange mixture of gratitude and grimace then went to cut the pie.

"And then I'll have a word with ye, Glenna," Hamish said. "Perhaps ye can postpone tonight's writin' lesson."

Her brows were raised when she looked at him, but she nodded as she took the plate in hand and went to give it to the newcomer.

It was nigh on eleven o'clock when the last of the guests left the bar and Hamish was able to speak with Glenna. She followed him into the office, and he shut the door behind them.

"Have a seat." He motioned to the chair across the paper-filled desk from his, and Glenna complied. She looked at him with a hint of anxiety in her eyes, waiting for him to reveal the purpose of this unusually formal discussion.

"I ken the truth about Miss MacMorran," he said.

Her mouth opened in a small *o* shape.

So, he had been right. The two of them *had* been in one another's confidences. And he the dupe. "How could ye keep it from me, Glenna?"

Her brows drew together in an expression of deep apology and guilt, and she scooted forward on her chair. "I never wished ta do so, but . . . well, she was adamant about no' tellin' anyone else, and then"—she gave a little shrug—"over time, I suppose I thought it mattered less. She's helped so much with bringin' more guests that I think I convinced meself ye wouldna mind—that it wasna important."

"But it *is* important, Glenna," he said. "Do ye ken what it means ta have her here? What she's doin' is against the law, which means that what *we're* doin' keepin' her here is, as well."

"But ye didna ken," Glenna said. "I was hopin' ta protect ye by no' tellin' ye who she was."

He leaned his elbows on the desk and covered his mouth with a hand. "Do ye ken why I took this position, Glenna?"

She shook her head.

"Ta be close ta Sir Andrew."

Her brows drew together. "Why?"

"'Tis he who manages Dalmore House—the home I grew up in, the one that was taken from my family. I've been workin' ta reclaim it, but I canna do it without him."

Her eyes widened, and her head shook from side to side. "I didna ken. I swear it, Hamish."

"I ken, for I didna tell ye. But do ye see why 'tis no' just a matter of employin' a different cook than I thought? Or even just a matter of Miss MacMorran's dishonesty?"

She swallowed and nodded. "Aye. She willna be here much longer, though. She expects that—"

"Aye. Dermot. I ken." The question he hadn't dared ask Miss MacMorran hovered in his mind. "She means ta marry him, I assume?"

"I believe so. Though . . . ." Glenna pinched her lips together, as if to keep herself from talking.

"What?"

She lifted a shoulder. "I *had* wondered if perhaps she had reconsidered by now."

He frowned. "Why would she?"

Glenna's mouth twisted to the side, and she looked to be debating her response. Finally, she shrugged. "Because of the way she looks at ye."

Hamish's mouth went dry. "I dinna ken what ye mean."

One of Glenna's eyebrows went up. "Do ye no'? For 'tis the same way ye look at her."

Hamish didn't know what to say or what to think, but his heart thumped against his chest, betraying him to himself, while the heat in his neck and cheeks must have betrayed him to Glenna.

"What'll ye do?" she asked. "'Tis a difficult situation, ta be sure. If Sir Andrew kend she was here . . . ."

Hamish took in a deep breath and rubbed his cheeks and chin. "I dinna ken. What *can* I do? I canna abandon her ta Angus. Neither can I let her go on her own ta Glasgow. Besides, if her father is the type of man ta force her inta such a marriage"—he shook his head—"I dinna reckon he'll be an easy man ta win over for my own purposes."

Glenna frowned. "I had always thought Sir Andrew a decent man, but ye're right. No decent man would allow Angus ta marry his daughter—ta say nothin' of compellin' her ta do so. Miss MacMorran said she hardly kens her father anymore. I wonder if his wife's death broke him. As for yer own wishes, I reckon the biggest obstacle will be yer father's reputation. Sir Andrew is staunchly against the Jacobites. I'm sure ye ken that."

Hamish sighed. He wasn't a Jacobite. He had served in His Majesty's Army for nearly a decade, after all, and he had done so with honor and valor. He even had a medal to prove it. But for some men, it would never be enough to counter the stain on the past. "Well, we can certainly use the extra help. It seems our work has only grown since hirin' her on. Once she leaves, I reckon we'll need ta look for someone ta replace her."

Glenna gave a rueful smile. "Perhaps two people."

Hamish tried to smile back. It didn't feel possible. Someone might be able to do the work she had been doing, but they couldn't ever replace her.

16

By the light of the flickering candle in her room, Ava lowered her chin to tie the kertch behind her head. She hoped it did a decent job of hiding her red hair, which was likely to give her away more than anything else if someone spotted her. In any case, people who saw the kertch would assume she was married, and anything that put a barrier between her true identity and the one she had taken on at Glengour was to be welcomed.

Angus's pointed stare in the coffee room flashed across her mind, and she felt the familiar niggling worry inside. Had he forgotten about it? Put it out of his mind? She had a hard time believing that. But had there been enough doubt about what he had seen to make him think he had imagined a likeness where none existed?

She wished she could know. Angus MacKinnon wasn't the type of man to give up easily, but neither could he simply stride into Glengour and demand to see her. What *could* he do?

There was a soft knock on her door, and she whipped her head around, heart skipping a beat.

She forced herself to breathe. Of course it wasn't Angus. He wouldn't take the time to knock if he *had* come to find her. She took a steadying breath and walked to the door, lifting the latch and opening it just enough to get a glimpse of Hamish standing in the dark corridor. The candle he held threw shadows across his face, making him look more menacing than she had ever thought him, this man who had so much power over her now that he knew the truth.

"I thought we might discuss the day ahead—how ta divide the labor amongst all of us." He spoke in a low voice with a glance that flicked once down the corridor. Dorcas MacGurk had taken the room diagonal to Ava's.

"Aye, of course," Ava said, opening the door wider. "Come in."

He nodded and walked in. There was strain between them. She could feel it, and she hated it, even if she understood the reason for it. Hamish was under no obligation at all to allow her to stay at Glengour. Most men would have dismissed her on the spot. But Hamish was not like most men. He was not like *any* man Ava had known. He was slow to anger and kind yet firm. His strength was obvious to anyone who so much as glanced at him, but it was held under tight rein.

His figure—broad shoulders and lofty height—made the room seem much smaller than it already was, and he was obliged to stay near the door where the ceiling was the highest.

"I only want ta be helpful," she said. "Whatever I can do . . . ."

"Whatever ye can do that willna put ye in front of the guests," he corrected.

She grimaced. "Aye, I suppose so."

"The trouble is, ye've given Glengour a reputation now. People are expectin' ta be fed yer pies, and I reckon they'll no' be content with whatever Dorcas"—his jaw flexed—"manages ta make."

"I can teach her," Ava said. "It willna take long ta do if she's skilled in the kitchen. And then I can see ta the washin' and tend ta the fire and whatever else needs doin'."

Hamish held her gaze. "I'm no' entirely certain 'tis fair ta ye ta push ye out of the kitchen. Ye *did* arrive here first."

Ava shook her head and averted her eyes, embarrassed to think the topic of her arrival might bring her deception to the forefront of Hamish's mind again. "Dorcas came ta be a cook, and that's what she should be. Besides, I willna be here much longer."

"Right," Hamish said. There was an awkward silence.

"I believe I have enough practice ta be useful with other tasks," she continued, eager to avoid the topic of her departure. It brought a strange lump into her throat.

"I dinna doubt it. Ye'll be missed when ye leave."

Her heart pattered, and she let out a wobbly laugh. "What, because ye've taken such a likin' ta my pies?"

"Nay, lass. Because I've taken such a likin' ta *you*."

Ava's cheeks warmed, and she found her tongue sticking to the roof of her mouth.

"But I willna say nay ta another piece of pie if ye're offerin'." His half-smile teased her. "Miss MacMorran."

Her smile wavered. "Please. Dinna call me that. If ye wish for me ta stay here, ye'll no' treat me any differently just because ye ken who my father is. Call me Ava."

"Ava," he said slowly, and she couldn't tell whether it pleased or displeased him. "It suits ye better than Dorcas. But I canna go on callin' ye Ava—'twould be ta undo all ye've worked for in hidin'. So, what am I ta call ye when others are near?"

She thought for a moment then shrugged. "Lass? Though, I reckon I'll continue ta answer ta Dorcas out of habit."

"Verra well, then. Lass."

She'd heard that word thousands of times in her life, surely, but never had it made her heart flutter as it did now when

Hamish Campbell said it. It was the last thing she needed when she was leaving so soon.

"'Tis only for a few days," she said. Every reminder was needed. Soon, Dermot would arrive, and her short time at Glengour would become a strange and distant memory.

"When do ye expect he'll arrive?" Hamish didn't need to specify who *he* was. They both knew.

"Any day, I reckon. I sent the letter a week ago now."

He tipped his head from side to side. "If he left immediately, he might be here tomorrow or the next day, I suppose. But . . . ."

"But what?"

He looked hesitant to speak. "What if he wasna home when it arrived? Perhaps ye ken he was—perhaps ye correspond regularly."

Ava swallowed nervously. The thought had crossed her mind, but she had written it off. The McCurdys rarely left their home—or at least they hadn't used to. But what if she was wrong? She had no doubt Dermot would come to her immediately when he received the letter, but what if it had never made it into his hands? What if the messenger had never bothered to take it?

At some point, Ava would have to leave Glengour, with or without Dermot. She couldn't stay here indefinitely—she couldn't ask Hamish to hide her indefinitely.

"I'm sure he'll be here soon," Hamish said, but his words didn't reassure Ava. "Shall we go down and start the work? I reckon I hear Dorcas wakin'."

Ava nodded, and Hamish opened the door. She stepped toward it then stopped, remembering something. She turned toward the bedside table and reached for the small pouch that contained the spices she had taken from home. There was a fair amount less than there had been when she had first arrived at Glengour.

Hamish's brow was furrowed when she came to face him. "What's that?" he asked.

She raised the satchel slightly and smiled a bit. "The secret ta Glengour's recent success."

He reached a hand for it, and she allowed him to take it. He put it to his nose and inhaled slowly, and his lips turned up at the corners. "Aye. I recognize it. Smells like"—he inhaled again—"well, it smells like you."

There went her heart again. She hadn't realized she had a distinct smell, or that Hamish had noticed.

He rubbed the satchel between his fingers. "Is that cinnamon I smell?"

"Aye, amongst other things."

"Why do ye keep it up here instead of in the kitchen?"

"It belonged to my mother. 'Twas the only thing of hers I had time ta take with me from home."

His gaze fixed on hers, and he held the satchel still. "And ye've been usin' it for the pies?"

She nodded. "She never made a pie without it—and neither will I."

He handed it back to her gently, shaking his head. "Keep it for yerself, lass. We can get some for Glengour from Craiglinne. I can send Mark for it today if ye tell me all the spices and the proper measurements."

Ava nodded, feeling a burning at the back of her eyes for Hamish's compassion about something as silly as a bag of spices. "I'll use this for today."

Dorcas MacGurk—the real one—was an amiable, rosy-cheeked woman Ava liked immediately. She had plenty of experience in the kitchen, but she was not too proud to take instruction from a girl half her age on the making of the pies the inn had become known for in such a short time.

When Ava confessed to her ruse—admitting that she had assumed Dorcas's identity for a time—Dorcas had listened with a frown that made Ava more nervous with every passing word. At the end, though, the woman had laughed heartily at the situation, a reaction which perfectly encapsulated her jovial personality. She brought a merriness to the kitchen that couldn't help but make Ava smile—and feel little stings of jealousy at the thought of the joy continuing without her once she left.

Hamish had managed to secure an agreement with two of the nearby farmers regarding a regular purchase of mutton, and the inn was flourishing. Everything seemed to be falling into place. Except Ava. She would soon be falling out of place.

She could feel it in Hamish's manner. Since his visit to her two days before, he seemed more aloof, too busy to spare more than a quick, polite smile when they happened to encounter one another on the occasion that his tasks required him to come to or pass through the kitchen.

Ava shouldn't mind it. It would make it easier to leave when Dermot arrived. She should be applying her mind to what came next, not worrying over Hamish's manner toward her. With all the strange events of the past two and a half weeks, she had nearly forgotten that, with the arrival of Dermot would come the arrival of her future: marriage. She was no longer certain how to feel about the prospect.

She turned the crank on the well, bringing up the bucket which sloshed slightly as it emerged from the black depths, remembering when Hamish had shown her how to operate it. She glanced at her hand on the crank, still able to feel the ghost of his touch there.

She was a fool for entertaining such thoughts. He could

never respect her, to say nothing of loving her, after the lies she had told.

With a sigh that turned into a small puff of white air before her face, she unhooked the heavy bucket and lugged it toward the kitchen door, which opened as she approached.

Glenna was there, and the expression on her face told Ava something was amiss.

"What? What is it?" Ava asked.

"Yer father," Glenna said. "He's here."

Chilly wet crept into her shoes, and Ava looked down. She hadn't even realized she had dropped the bucket. She turned away, looking for the best entry into the trees, but her hand was taken by Glenna's.

"He didna come for ye, Ava," Glenna said. "He's sittin' with Hamish in the coffee room, eatin' and drinkin'."

Ava could hardly think, but her breath came quickly, forming a fast-dissipating cloud around her face in the chill March air. Had Hamish called for him to come? Had Angus told him to?

Glenna held her hand firmly. "Hamish willna betray ye, Ava. Ye need no' worry for that. I only came ta warn ye so ye wouldna come in and reveal yerself unwittin'ly."

Ava's eyes flitted from Glenna's face to the kitchen and back, over and over, as though at any moment, her father's face might appear there.

"My father doesna come ta Glengour," she said. "He goes ta The Maidenhead in Craiglinne." She shook her head. "He kens I'm here. He must."

"I dinna think he does, Ava."

"Why else would he come? 'Tis the only explanation. I must go."

Glenna held her back yet again. "Nay, there *is* another explanation." There was a strange look on her face—tight-lipped, hesitant.

Ava lifted her shoulders, impatient to be released but curious what Glenna could possibly mean.

"I only learned of it a few days ago meself," Glenna said.

"Learned of what?" Ava felt her foreboding grow again.

"Have ye heard of Dalmore House?"

Ava nodded. "My father sometimes has business there."

Glenna nodded. "It belonged ta Hamish's father. He's hopin' ta reclaim it. Has been wantin' to for years, as I understand it. I dinna ken much more about it, but he says yer father is the man with the power ta give it back ta him. That's why he's come today. Ta discuss Dalmore."

Ava's heart plummeted. Glenna seemed to think her words would provide reassurance, but they did anything but that. Ava remembered her conversation with Hamish out here behind the inn—he had spoken of wishing for a true home. He had meant Dalmore House.

If Hamish needed something from her father, and if her father had any suspicion she was at Glengour, would Hamish betray her?

17

Hamish kept his gaze covertly on Sir Andrew as he poured them both a glass of whisky. The man's arrival had been a complete surprise, and Hamish was vacillating between hope at what it might mean for Dalmore House and his own future, and worry for what it might mean for Ava. Was it pure coincidence that he was here just days after Angus had come? Hamish had begun to think he would never hear from Sir Andrew.

He carried the glasses over to the table, setting one before Sir Andrew, who smiled at him politely. He wore a wig, tied in a neat queue at the base of his neck by a small, black ribbon. Unlike Angus MacKinnon, Sir Andrew had a generally pleasant countenance, though there was a pulled look to his eyes, and his square jaw seemed to Hamish evidence that he could be a determined man. It was clear where Ava had come by her own stubbornness.

"I apologize for the tardiness of my visit," Sir Andrew said. His piece of mutton pie sat untouched, but once Hamish sat down, he picked up his fork. "I have been much occupied of late."

"Ye need no' apologize ta me, sir," Hamish said. "Ye must be a busy man."

Sir Andrew looked around the coffee room. "It seems you, too, have been busy. I can see a bit of resemblance to the last time I was here—it has been nearly two years—but you have made a number of changes, have you not?"

"Aye, we have. We're hopin' ta divert some of the traffic this way from Craiglinne."

"And I understand you are having success in that." He cut a piece of pie, and his fork hovered in the air as he spoke. "I admit, I was anxious to try this fabled pie I have heard so much about." He looked at it, turned the fork from side to side to inspect it, then slipped it into his mouth.

Hamish could feel the stiffness of his muscles at the topic of conversation, and he took the opportunity to eat a piece of the pie on his own plate. It was delicious as ever, and the smell reminded him of Ava.

Sir Andrew chewed his bite slowly, eyes slightly narrowed. He pulled the napkin from beside his plate and wiped at his mouth. "What a unique flavor."

He was right. It *was* unique. And that comforted Hamish not at all. He thought of the bag of spices Ava had shown him. *She never made a pie without it—and neither will I.*

"What is that I taste?" Sir Andrew asked. "Nutmeg?" His gaze settled on Hamish.

Hamish tried to look thoughtful. "Perhaps? I canna rightly say. I'm no expert on these things." He gave a little chuckle. "That's why we have a cook."

From the corner of his eye, a movement caught Hamish's attention, and his heart dropped. But it was only Glenna, seeing to the three other men in the coffee room.

"And who *is* this cook?" Sir Andrew asked. "I understand she is a recent addition to Glengour."

"Aye, that's right," Hamish said, grateful he could respond

truthfully. "Her name is Dorcas MacGurk."

Sir Andrew's gaze remained on him, and Hamish forced himself not to squirm under it. He was being watched for any sign of dishonesty. Thank heaven the real Dorcas had arrived so he wasn't obliged to tell blatant untruths.

"I should like to compliment her. She has achieved something laudable with this pie."

Hamish wasn't fooled. He knew what Sir Andrew was doing. But he gave a little nod and called to Glenna, hoping she had been able to speak with Dorcas about the situation so she wouldn't betray them to Sir Andrew.

Glenna came over, wearing a smile, but Hamish could see that, like him, she was not at her normal ease.

"Would ye send Dorcas out?" he asked. "Sir Andrew would like ta speak with her—about the"—he glanced at Sir Andrew, feigning thought—"nutmeg, was it? Well, whatever spices she's used ta make such a fine pie." He held Glenna's gaze pointedly, hoping she would understand the danger the conversation could put them in. On the other hand, if it was handled well, it might serve to put Sir Andrew's suspicions to rest.

Glenna glanced at Sir Andrew and nodded. "Of course. I'll fetch her right away."

There was an uncomfortable silence as they waited. Sir Andrew seemed disinclined to speak, and Hamish began to doubt that they would manage to discuss Dalmore House at all. The man was preoccupied with his suspicions, and it was unlikely that his mood would be conducive to helping Hamish—particularly if he believed Hamish to be concealing something about his daughter.

Dorcas emerged, and Hamish wasn't sure whether to be relieved or worried to see her looking as merry and unconcerned as ever. Either she was confident in her abilities to manage this interaction, or she was on the verge of saying something they would all regret.

Hamish made the quick introduction, noting how Sir Andrew's eyes flicked from Dorcas around the room, as though he was looking for any sign of his daughter.

"I understand you are the person responsible for making this distinctive and savory pie?" Sir Andrew asked.

Dorcas's hands were clasped in front of her, flour graced her cheeks, and the cap she wore on her head was slightly askew, giving the impression that she had been hard at work. She nodded. "Aye, sir."

"Did I correctly detect nutmeg?"

She smiled and nodded again, this time more quickly and excitedly. "Ye've a discernin' palate, sir."

He smiled politely. "I do not think nutmeg is very commonly used, being somewhat expensive, as you undoubtedly know."

Hamish gripped the seat of his chair with one hand.

"Och," Dorcas said, "terribly expensive. But my last master always kept it on hand—French, he was—and he liked it in everythin', so I've grown accustomed ta usin' it. Couldn't leave it out of my special spice blend."

Sir Andrew inclined his head. "I see. Well, my compliments to you for a very fine dish."

Dorcas made a small, ungainly curtsy that made Hamish's mouth twitch, then left the men to their food and drink. She had done better than Hamish could have anticipated, and he made a mental note to heap praise upon the new cook.

"Perhaps you have heard," Sir Andrew said as Dorcas disappeared into the kitchen, "of my eldest daughter's recent disappearance."

Hamish considered pretending complete ignorance, but he guessed Sir Andrew would never believe that of someone who worked at an inn so near Glenlochan. "Aye, sir. I had heard it mentioned in passin'. I'm verra sorry ta hear it."

"You haven't happened to have any word of her, have you?" His eyes bored into Hamish, who shook his head.

"Nay, sir. I canna say I have."

"It was my understanding she passed through Glengour and left with a tinker."

Hamish's lips turned down in a frown. "'Tis possible, certainly. He and his wife take on a passenger every now and then."

Sir Andrew picked up another piece of pie, and his eyes rested on it, suddenly pitiful and sad. "I worry about her, wherever she is."

Hamish's conscience writhed. Whatever Sir Andrew's failings, whatever his intentions were for Ava and Angus, there was no doubting he was sincere in those words, at least.

He sighed and set down the fork, as though he didn't have the appetite for something that reminded him of his daughter. "Forgive me. You wished to speak of Dalmore."

Hamish swallowed. This was what he had been waiting for, and yet the situation was not at all what he had hoped.

"Aye, sir," he said. "'Tis kind of ye ta meet with me when ye've so many other concerns at present."

"I am always full of concerns these days." Some of his sadness lingered in the words, giving Hamish pause yet again. But this might be his only opportunity with Sir Andrew.

"Perhaps ye ken this already," Hamish said, "but I've only recently returned from servin' in His Majesty's Army—in August, I set foot on Scotland's shores again for the first time in nearly ten years."

Sir Andrew gave a polite smile in acknowledgement. "Allow me to welcome you home."

"Thank ye, sir. 'Tis good ta be back." Hamish took in a deep breath. "I was hopeful that there might be a reconsideration of . . . the situation with Dalmore House. Ye mentioned the debts left when 'twas taken over by the Crown, and I thought perhaps they'd be willin' ta allow me ta make payments on those now that I've"—he pressed his lips together, suddenly realizing how pretentious his request sounded and how much a bit of practice might have aided him in this conversation—"now that I've . . . well, proven my loyalty ta king and country."

Sir Andrew held his gaze, saying nothing for a moment. "It is a highly unusual request, to be quite plain with you. As you are perhaps aware, the majority of the attainted estates were auctioned off in order to pay off the heavy debts acquired under the Jacobite lairds and leaders. Those remaining have been, for the most part, under the management of the Board of Commissioners for the Forfeited Estates, of which I am a part."

Hamish knew all this, but he let Sir Andrew speak despite it. He was eager for any bit of information about Dalmore.

"Once I took up residence at Glenlochan, the management of Dalmore House was given over to me, as it is within a near enough distance that I can visit every now and then to oversee the improvements."

Improvements. The word was full of mysterious and frightening possibility. How much had Dalmore changed since Hamish had been there as a young man?

"What you are asking is quite complicated, in fact," Sir Andrew continued. "There are hurdles and obstacles of all sorts which would require a great deal of work on my part. The success of it all would depend upon a number of things."

Hamish nodded, feeling the last bits of his hope deflating. Whether Sir Andrew was making more of the difficulties than they merited because his own goals at Glengour had failed, Hamish didn't know.

"I can only imagine the burden the Crown took on with all the debts of the estates under the management of the Board," Hamish said. "I thought they might be eager ta ensure they made some of their money back."

"Perhaps," said Sir Andrew noncommittally. "I will have to

gauge the interest of the others on the Board—I am but one man, you know."

Hamish nodded, but he wasn't fooled. From what he had understood, Sir Andrew's opinion was given special weight, given his presence in the Highlands and proximity to the estate. If he vouched for Hamish, the others were likely to yield to his perceived expertise. Most of the men on the Board were from the Lowlands—solicitors, government workers, peers who spent most of their time in London or Edinburgh, many who never bothered attending board meetings at all, from what Hamish's acquaintance, Mr. McCabe, had told him.

Sir Andrew surely had more power than he was letting on.

Glenna emerged from the kitchen again as the three other men in the room rose from the table, flicking a few coins onto it and bidding her farewell. She glanced at Hamish, and he tried to keep his expression impassive, as he guessed Sir Andrew was watching him carefully.

Sir Andrew looked around the room, his gaze settling on Glenna for a moment as she gathered up the glasses and set them on the tray she had brought. His mutton pie was still untouched but for the one bite he had taken. Hamish felt a flash of annoyance. There were any number of men who would have wasted no time devouring that pie, and Sir Andrew had hardly touched it.

"I am impressed with these improvements you've made," Sir Andrew said. "Would you be willing to show me more? Provide a tour, if you will."

Hamish only allowed himself the briefest of pauses before smiling. "Aye, of course." He glanced at Glenna, but she didn't seem to have heard. "Glenna, would ye mind watchin' over the arrivals and the coffee room for a wee while? I'll be givin' Sir Andrew a tour of the inn." He held her gaze, but he needn't have. Glenna was intelligent, and he could see in her eyes that she understood what this meant.

"Perhaps we can go see the rooms first—those which are no' currently occupied, at least. I think there are one or two."

Glenna nodded. "I'll make sure everythin's in order there." She hurried out of the room and up the stairs, and Hamish was conscious of a feeling of frustration with her. She needed to be informing Ava—hiding her—not fixing up the empty guest rooms. Apparently he had overestimated her understanding.

Hamish led the way as they scaled the narrow staircase to the guest rooms, keeping up a flow of informative, if unsolicited, talk. They reached the top landing, and he turned to the right to guide them down the corridor.

"What is up there?" Sir Andrew indicated the staircase that led to the next floor of the inn.

"Och," Hamish said with a dismissive wave, then he grasped his hands behind his back. "That's just the servant rooms. They havena been changed yet. Hopefully soon, though."

"I should like to see them despite that," said Sir Andrew. "It will give me a good idea of the differences between the inn before you began the changes."

Hamish's hands clenched each other until his nails dug into his skin. "Of course."

He led the way up the next staircase, trying to think back on this morning when he had been in Ava's room and what they would find there that might betray her. She had taken the pouch of spices with her, at least, but surely Sir Andrew would recognize her portmanteau and cloak.

Everything was about to be ruined. Ava would be discovered, and Hamish could say goodbye to any chance whatsoever of reclaiming Dalmore.

He started on the opposite side of the corridor from Ava's room. There was little reason to do so—it was only delaying the inevitable—but he wasn't prepared to answer the questions Sir Andrew would have when he saw his own daughter's belongings there. He took him all the way into the first room, explaining things that needed no explaining—the issues with leaking, the absence of candlesticks since their staff was so few —but he could only postpone for so long, and they finally reached Ava's door. Hamish opened it, teeth clenched, muscles tight.

But there was no sign whatsoever that any person inhabited the room. It looked just as the others had, if perhaps a little less dusty, and Hamish tried to calm his nerves with deep, even breaths. Glenna must have managed to hide Ava's things while they were in the other room. If so, she had done it with mouse-like quiet.

By the time Hamish had opened every one of the doors— Sir Andrew was pretending a great interest in the differences between the rooms, but Hamish understood what he was doing —Sir Andrew seemed to lose his enthusiasm. There was disappointment in his eyes as they descended the stairs to the level with the guest rooms.

In contrast with his interest in the rooms on the floor above, he showed barely any interest at all in the ones meant for the guests.

"Ye seem tired, sir," Hamish said. "Perhaps we should save the rest of the tour for another time."

At the suggestion, Sir Andrew straightened, and his brows drew into a frown. "No, no. I would like to see the rest of the inn. Please"—he gestured ahead of them, inviting Hamish to continue the tour.

Hamish smiled and gave a quick nod, hoping Glenna had taken Ava outside and well away from the inn. At this rate, Sir Andrew was likely to wish for a visit to the stables as well— perhaps even the privy.

He tried to conceal his unease as he guided Sir Andrew through the remainder of the inn.

18

With a candle in one hand and Ava's hand in her other, Glenna hurried them down the stairs to the cellar. Ava hardly had time to ensure her feet landed solidly on the uneven stairs, but they managed to reach the bottom without incident.

"Over here," Glenna said in an urgent whisper, and the candle flickered with her quick footsteps toward the far wall, where several barrels were stacked.

"If they come down," Ava said, "I'll no' be able ta hide behind those without bein' discovered."

"Ye will," Glenna said, setting the candle on the floor. "Help me." She hefted one of the barrels—far too easily for there to be anything inside it— and set it a few feet to the side of where it had been.

Perplexed, Ava followed suit, until the six barrels were stacked just as they had been, though shifted to the side.

Glenna picked up the candle and extended it forward, revealing what looked to be a dark piece of fabric, hanging from the stone wall. She pulled it aside, and a black abyss gaped back at them.

Ava's eyes widened, and she looked at Glenna, who

gestured for her to hurry inside. Ava took in a deep breath, remembering the rat that had scurried over her feet the first time she and Hamish had ventured into the cellar.

"He'll no' find ye there," Glenna assured her, "long as ye're quiet. I'll leave the candle with ye, too. Hurry. Once ye're inside, I have ta put the barrels back."

Ignoring the pounding of her heart and the crawling of her skin, Ava slipped under the blanket and into the black hole.

Glenna handed her the candle once she was inside then stopped for a moment, her alert eyes settling on Ava. "Never fear. Ye'll be safe here." She gave another reassuring nod then let the fabric fall into place.

Ava listened to the sounds of Glenna's quick work, counting as the barrels were put back into place—one, two, three, four, five, six.

"I'll be back for ye," Glenna's hushed voice sounded, then her footsteps retreated and soon disappeared up the stairs.

The silence that enveloped Ava was so stark and complete that she could hear nothing but the sound of her own heart beating and an intermittent dripping somewhere behind her. It smelled damp, and each drop echoed eerily. Every now and then, a cold draft seemed to whip at her from behind, and only the barrier of her own body kept the candle alight. She was glad for the bit of light it provided, but she didn't know if she wanted to turn around to see what was behind her.

Where *was* she? This had certainly not been part of her tour with Hamish. She could only assume this was where smuggled goods might be hidden, safe from the eyes of excisemen.

Over the next few minutes, her heart began to slow and her eyes to tire of looking at the only thing available to them: the flickering flame of the candle and the slow melting of the tallow. She reached a hand out to her left, and it was quickly stopped by a stone wall, cold and damp. Switching the candle to her other hand, she did the same to her right, meeting with the same sensation and solid barrier.

The space was narrow—not even wide enough for two people to stand abreast—and Ava tried not to pay attention to the increased panic she would feel if she allowed herself to focus on how surrounded she was on all sides. Trapped.

She finally gained the courage to turn slowly, hoping to see how far the wall behind her was, but the candle cast its light for a few feet then was gradually consumed by the oppressive dark. She could see no wall, and she had no intention of going to seek it. What if rats were the least of her worries?

The sound of footsteps on the cellar stairs met her ears, setting her heart racing again. The voices speaking were too muffled for her to make out their words, but she could hear the timbre of her father's short responses which followed Hamish's voice. It brought back memories of hearing her parents muted voices outside the bedchamber she and her sister Bridget had shared as children.

A sudden force constricted her throat, closing in on it just as she feared the walls beside her would do, and her eyes began to sting. She missed her father. She missed the man he used to be.

How had it come to this—to hiding from him with a heart that beat in terror of discovery? She covered her mouth with a hand.

"We're havin' ta adapt ta the increase in business we're seein'." Hamish's words were muffled slightly but clear enough to make Ava realize just how little separated her from the two men. "We dinna generally keep enough whisky, wine, or ale here ta serve the number of people who've been comin'."

"Well, I could certainly be of help there if you were wishful. I have steady access to a supply of plenty of wine and whisky to suit the food you are serving."

"'Tis kind of ye, sir," Hamish responded. "We have a

supplier for the whisky—the Shaw women should be able ta keep up with the demands for now. But we can discuss everythin' more once we're upstairs. Ye can see here the few bottles of wine left ta us."

Ava's father made an assenting sound, and their footsteps drew nearer to Ava.

A squeaking behind her made Ava startle, and she stopped a vocal reaction with the hand to her mouth, turning to face the culprit as a skittering of feet—too many to belong to just one rat—sounded in the invisible depths her candle's light couldn't reach.

Her breath came quickly, and her toes curled in her shoes instinctively, reminded of her last brush with a cellar rat. Then, at least, she'd had Hamish to grab onto. Now, she was alone, unable to move or cry out for fear of betraying her presence.

She shut her eyes, willing herself to stay calm, to remember how much larger and more capable she was than a mere rat.

Giant, connivin' beasties they are.

She pushed Hamish's words from her mind just as a meow sounded, echoing slightly. Ava's eyes flew open, and Mary stepped into the light of the candle, her flashing eyes settling on Ava.

"What was that?" It was her father's voice, and Ava froze at the sound of it so near. She didn't even dare turn back toward the piece of fabric that separated her from a life with Angus MacKinnon.

"What?" Hamish asked.

Mary reached Ava's skirts and brushed up against them, mewing again, a bit more softly this time.

"That," Ava's father said.

With her free arm, Ava scooped the cat into her arms, unsure how else to keep her from revealing their whereabouts.

"Och," Hamish said. "'Tis only Mary, our cat. She's probably hidin' somewhere in here. 'Tis a favorite haunt of hers."

Ava tried to stroke Mary with her fingertips, a task made difficult by the fact that one hand held the candle and the other arm held the feline in place. But the effort was enough. Mary began to purr, and her eyes closed.

"I imagine you hear a great deal of gossip here at the inn and see any number of people over the course of a day," her father said. Footsteps were followed by the subtle scraping of glass, and she imagined him inspecting a bottle of wine.

"Aye, sir," Hamish said. "Though, I dinna pretend ta take much heed of the former."

"Well"—the bottle clanked again—"I hope you will keep an ear out for word of my Ava. My daughter means a great deal to me, and I would be forever indebted to the person who brought her to me safely."

Ava swallowed, turning slowly and carefully toward the fabric enclosure again. Her father's words sounded so sincere, so harmless. Had he rethought his insistence on marrying her to Angus? Had her absence acted as a glass of water over his head, bringing him to his senses?

"It goes without saying," he continued, "that there would be perquisites for anyone who had any information about my daughter's whereabouts."

Ava's stomach and teeth clenched. Any tenderness she might have been feeling when her father had first come down into the cellar fled, quickly replaced with indignance and hurt. Glenna had said her father had come to speak with Hamish about Dalmore House, which made the inference impossible to avoid. He was dangling Hamish's hopes and dreams in front of him in exchange for information about Ava.

Would Hamish take the bait? The silence lengthened, and Ava stopped scratching Mary, listening as intently as she could.

"I'll keep an eye and an ear out, sir," Hamish said.

"I would appreciate that," he replied. "Of course, my own worries for her are of foremost importance. It is my duty to protect her, and you can understand how grievous it is to be burdened with the knowledge that I cannot do that at the moment. But the truth is, she is a fugitive from the law, and she may be found guilty of breach of promise, as she is set to be married to Angus MacKinnon."

Bile rose in Ava's throat. He had *not* come to his senses. How could he speak of protecting her in the same breath as he talked of marrying her to Angus? Had he truly managed to convince himself that the match was desirable for anyone but him and Angus?

It made her sick—sick with anger and hurt to be used so ill by the man she had depended upon for so long. She could only be glad her mother wasn't here to listen to him. Her disappointment would have been crushing. She had always meant for Ava to choose her own husband.

"That must be difficult, indeed," Hamish said, and their footsteps retreated toward the stairs.

Tears—angry, hurt tears—spilled over onto Ava's cheeks as she stood in her hiding place, alone but for Mary and whatever rat the cat had been chasing. She couldn't yet leave, that much was clear. Her father obviously suspected her presence at the inn, and she would wait in this miserable hole in the wall for hours if it meant protecting herself from the future he had in store for her.

A va's tears had since dried, and Mary had left the comfort of her arm for the excitement of whatever rodents were scurrying across the floor in the dark. Ava's feet ached from standing for so long, but she hadn't been able to bring herself to sit down—to bring herself any nearer the rats' domain. She kept herself away from the walls, too, having seen enough evidence to know they could climb those, as well. More than once, her candle had nearly been extinguished by the little drafts that came from behind.

Finally, she heard footsteps on the stairs. The fact that it was only one set reassured her that she had nothing to fear, and that assumption was borne out as the barrels scraped across the floor and Hamish's voice came, saying, "Are ye there, lass?"

"Aye," she said in a tired voice that rasped from disuse.

The blanket was soon pulled aside, and the candle she held —only a few inches tall by now—cast light across Hamish's worried face. He put out a hand, and she took it reluctantly.

She was feeling exhausted in every way, depleted, and hopeless. Hamish didn't want her at Glengour. He couldn't possibly. She had taken advantage of him, lied to him, and now put him in the position of lying to her father to protect her.

His brows furrowed even more deeply as he inspected her by the light of her candle, searching her face. He touched a hand to her cheek. "Ye're freezin'." He pulled his hands to his mouth and blew into them, setting them back on her cheeks.

Ava hadn't realized just how chilled she had become in the dark, damp hiding place, but the warmth of his hands brought a humiliating rush of tears to her eyes again. She blinked hurriedly, turning her head so that his hands dropped.

"Lass? What is it?"

She shut her eyes. How to explain it all? That she had just spent what felt like hours hiding from her own father? That everywhere around her, there seemed to be men for whom she was merely a pawn—or an obstacle—to obtaining the future they desired? She had never felt so alone.

"'Tis nothin'," she said. "Is my father gone?"

Hamish didn't respond right away—he was looking at her intently, and she could only hope the candlelight was too dim for him to see evidence of the tears she had managed to keep from spilling over. Finally, he nodded. "Aye, lass. He's gone. Ye need no' fear."

Was that true? Did she truly have nothing to fear from Hamish? "Glenna told me, Hamish."

He looked at her in confusion. "Told ye what?"

"Of yer hopes in regards ta my father and Dalmore House."

He nodded slowly.

"Ye should have told me."

Hamish grimaced, shaking his head. "I would have. Truly, I would have. But I didna wish for ye ta . . ."

"Ta what?"

He lifted his shoulders. "I didna wish for ye ta trouble yerself over how yer presence here would affect things. I didna wish ta give ye another reason ta worry—or ta leave."

"But I *should* leave," she said. "I must."

"Nay," Hamish put a hand on her arm, as if he feared she would go right then.

"I'm only makin' yer life more difficult."

He smiled wryly. "It wouldna be my life if it wasna so. Difficult is all I've ever kent."

His words hardly consoled her, for he had a choice here between difficult and easy, and he was choosing the difficult path because of her. At some point, though, would he not reconsider that choice?

A little chill draft swept around them, and Ava shivered, rubbing at her arm with her free hand. She looked up at Hamish and into his eyes. "Why did ye no' tell my father the truth? He may well give ye what ye desire if ye do."

The muscle in Hamish's jaw tightened, and he shook his head. "I'd be no better than Angus if I did such a thing. I told ye ye'd be safe here, lass, and I meant it. So, please. No more talk of leavin'. I'll no' let ye go."

"Ye couldna stop me," she said.

"Is that right?" he asked.

It wasn't right, of course. Her gaze raked over his wide

shoulders and thick arms. He could stop her in a second if he wished to. "Ye canna keep me here. Or at least, ye willna."

He folded his arms across his chest, and a challenging glint entered his eye. "If ye do leave, I expect ye ta repay me the sixpence I gave the messenger."

She pinched her lips together. She had the money to repay him, but it would cripple her attempt to make the journey toward Glasgow.

He lowered his head a bit, forcing her to meet his gaze. "I dinna mean that. And ye're right. I willna force ye ta stay, lass. But I *want* ye ta stay."

He put a hand to her cold cheek, and her heart sputtered along with the candle, which was growing dangerously low. Why would he want her to stay when she was keeping him from everything he wanted? It was his chivalry, nothing else.

"We agreed ye'd stay until Dermot arrived, did we no'?"

She bit the inside of her lip. Would Dermot ever come? Would she be found by her father before he could? What if his feelings for her had changed? What if he was married?

Dermot aside, the situation was unfair to Hamish. He was promising to keep her safe, but could she ask him to do so when it was at such a cost to himself? How could she complain about being a pawn in men's hands if she was making Hamish a pawn in her own?

"Is that still what ye wish for? Ta go with Dermot?"

She swallowed, holding his gaze, her mind a hum of contradictory thoughts. It was impossible to think clearly with his warm hand on her cheek. She couldn't say no, though. This had been the plan all along. She couldn't and wouldn't tell him that she was beginning to doubt everything—especially the future she had planned for herself.

It seemed strangely bleak now. Going to Dermot had been an escape from the awful and ever-more-imminent specter of marriage to Angus, and nothing had changed about that—she was still willing to do anything to avoid that fate. Dermot was still the kind friend she had always been able to trust, too, even if she felt none of the spark or pull she felt toward Hamish. Marriage to Dermot would be safe, even if it could never be the marriage she had begun to wish for—something full of laughter and safety and twinkling blue eyes that found hers at all the right moments.

Marriage to Dermot was the sensible thing.

"Aye, 'tis what I wish for." She put her hand over the one he still held at her cheek and gently pulled it down. Her aching heart belied her words, though, and for a moment longer than was necessary, she kept his hand in hers.

He gave a slow nod. "'Tis decided, then. Ye'll stay until he comes."

"It should be any day now," she said, though her nerves betrayed her uncertainty. She was still haunted by the possibility that Dermot had never received her letter.

"I'm certain ye're right," Hamish said.

Ava took in a deep breath. She needed to believe Dermot would come. She couldn't doubt him—he was dependable and loyal. He would not have changed so much in the time they had been away from one another. She would show a face of confidence to Hamish. Otherwise, she might lose her resolve.

He glanced behind her. "I'm sorry ye had ta stay in there so long alone."

"Och, I wasna alone," she said.

"Aye," Hamish said, shaking his head. "I heard Mary. She nearly betrayed us."

"She and the rats."

His eyes narrowed suspiciously. "Nay, then, lass. Ye're havin' a laugh, surely. If there were rats with ye, ye'd have screamed."

"No' all of us scream at the sight of rats, Hamish." Teasing helped her feel lighter, and she desperately needed that.

"What, ye dinna believe me?" She gave him a little push toward the hole in the wall. "Go on, then. See for yerself."

He resisted easily, driving home again how powerless she would be if ever he decided to use his force against her. "Nay, I believe ye. But I dinna understand what business Mary has here if no' catchin' the wee beasts. What else could she be doin'?"

"Perhaps ye've made her hesitant since ye scolded her the last time she caught one."

Hamish shot her an unamused look and made to take the candle from her, but she pulled it away and out of his reach. "I'll keep the candle this time."

He looked at her with twinkling eyes. "Ye'll never forgive me for that, will ye?"

"I can forgive, but I'll no' forget."

He chuckled softly. "Fair enough, lass. Let's get ye upstairs and by a fire."

She led the way, feeling better and more capable of facing the future than she had just ten minutes ago. Hamish seemed to have that effect upon her. She couldn't help but smile in his presence, and heaven knew she needed reason to smile today.

Here he was, caring for her, calm and collected, despite the fact that he'd just been offered his dream in exchange for betraying her. Unlike her father and Angus, Hamish did not seem eager to throw her to her terrible fate for his own gain.

Perhaps he was content to wait until Dermot came to spirit her away. Then the time would be his to pursue Dalmore. She had no dispute with his desire to reclaim the home of his father and ancestors—indeed, she would have helped him if she saw the path to do so. But she didn't like that he would be anxious for her departure.

Whatever, the case, her father could never know Hamish had hidden her here, for that would be the end of his bid for Dalmore House, and she owed him more than that.

19

Hamish poured a glass of ale and set it before the man sitting at the bar—a man making a short stop on his way north. He seemed disinclined to talk, a fact Hamish was grateful for, as he himself was in no mood for civil conversation.

Ever since Sir Andrew's departure two days ago, he hadn't slept well, nor had he been able to relax for fear that either Sir Andrew or Angus might appear suddenly. Angus had nearly gone into Hamish's quarters unnoticed, and Hamish suffered under no delusions that Sir Andrew had left Glengour convinced Ava was not there—or hadn't been there at some point, at the very least.

He glanced at the window, and through the warped glass, he saw a figure running toward the inn, short and slight enough to indicate the person's youth.

Hamish excused himself to the man drinking his ale and slipped out from behind the bar, smiling civilly at the men he passed on his way to the front door. He opened it just as the boy ran up to him, extending a folded paper toward Hamish without saying a word.

Hamish took it and opened it, trying not to show his unease

at who it might be from, and the boy fled back the way he had come. Apparently no response was expected.

He looked down at the short note.

Tonight. Be ready at midnight.

Fowlis

Hamish took in a deep breath. Tonight. He had begun to think Fowlis had decided to dispense with his services without informing him.

Hamish folded up the note. He was struggling to sleep at night; he may as well make use of himself rather than staring at the ceiling and tossing and turning. By midnight, the guests would be asleep. His main concern would be keeping any potential late arrivals ignorant of the goings-on. Thankfully, Glengour was suited for that quite well.

He turned back inside and made his way to the kitchen, asking Glenna to join him when she was at liberty to do so. Dorcas was cutting up mutton, while Ava knelt before the fire, adding peat to it and leaning away to avoid the subsequent gush of smoke.

Dorcas was turning out to be a valuable addition to Glengour, loyal and joyful as she seemed to be. It was fortunate, for if Hamish had been in any doubt of her trustworthiness, it would have made the night ahead very difficult indeed.

Once Glenna came in, Hamish told them all what news he'd had from Fowlis. "I dinna expect any of ye ta take part in tonight's activities. I only ask ye ta keep everyone clear of the cellar and listen for late arrivals."

Dorcas and Glenna nodded in tandem.

"Ye can rely on us, sir," Dorcas said.

"We're ready ta help however we can," Glenna chimed in.

Hamish nodded, feeling grateful for the strong and loyal women he was able to work with at Glengour. He didn't doubt their abilities to do just what was required. He left the kitchen, threading through the larder and into the laundry.

"Hamish."

He stopped and turned. Ava had followed him.

"I mean ta help," she said. "With the goods."

Hamish shook his head. "Nay."

"Hamish, ye're breakin' the law, hidin' me here. I mean ta return the favor."

"Nay, lass, there's no favor ta return," he said.

"Dinna be ridiculous. But even if that were true, do ye mean ta say ye couldna use the help?"

Hamish rubbed his beard. He *could* use the help, of course. But it was too dangerous, and Ava was too precious. "These are Angus's men, lass. Ye might be recognized."

She nodded. "I've thought of that. 'Twill be dark, will it no'?"

"Aye, but—"

"I'll make certain there's no recognizin' me. And I'll keep quiet. I want ta help, Hamish." She folded her arms. "I *intend* ta help."

He looked at her face, lit by the light coming through the window. She was beautiful, but she was stubborn. And, aggravating as it could be, he admired her all the more for it.

She was of little use doing what Glenna and Dorcas would be tasked with, since she needed to keep out of the eye of any potential late arrivals. At least he would be able to keep an eye on her if she was with him.

Or perhaps he was merely finding excuses to spend more time with her. It was a silly goal. She would be gone soon, nothing but a memory.

Somehow, that thought only made him more determined to take advantage of the little time they had left.

"Verra well," he said. "But ye'll stay by my side."

She nodded.

"And away from Fowlis."

"I'll make certain he wouldna recognize me even in full daylight."

Hamish's brows knit together, but he nodded. There would be little enough light to worry about. Their time would be spent in the dark—outside and then in the tunnel. With the rats.

"Meet me in the cellar at half-past eleven, then," he said.

H amish descended the stairs to the cellar with the lightest feet he could manage for a man of nearly seventeen stone. He did so with the hum of nerves and excitement running through his veins, reminiscent of his days in the army.

The inn was quiet, with Glenna and Dorcas seated by the fire in the kitchen. Mark was in the office, ready to alert Glenna to any possible arrival and to listen for any activity on the stairs. It would be out of the ordinary, to put it lightly, for any guest to make their way into the cellar, but Hamish would take no chances, not given the events of the past week.

He hadn't seen Ava for a few hours. She had been busy with laundry while Hamish had been occupied with guests, ensuring there was nothing left undone that might interrupt them later on.

When he opened the door to the cellar, the light of his own freshly lit tin lantern was the only thing illuminating the area. The abundant but miniscule holes in the tin allowed little beams of light to spill down the stairs, and the broken lantern door clanked softly with each step Hamish took. The rest of the room was still bathed in black, untouched by the light.

He made a sound of annoyance and opened the lantern door more widely, hoping it would stay in place. The last thing they needed was the clanking of tin to betray them. He started as a large, dark figure emerged from the back of the room. He pulled out his *sgian dubh* and held it out.

"Och, ye mean ta kill me?"

Hamish's brows snapped together, and he stepped forward, holding out the lantern. The light illuminated the person more fully, from the knee-high boots and breeches to the jacket, cravat, and Scotch bonnet. The face, though, was still dark but for whites of the eyes and teeth.

He squinted and stepped closer, and the person's smile grew wider. There was no mistaking it now.

"Ava?" he said in bafflement.

She laughed and nodded.

He chuckled and lowered his *sgian dubh*. "Ye're lucky I didna attack ye. What are ye doin' here in the dark?"

She bent over and picked something up from the ground— a candlestick. "I blew it out when I heard ye open the door. I wanted ta see if ye'd recognize me."

"Recognize ye? Ye hardly have a face ta recognize." Her hair, too, must have been darkened and concealed, for the grey bonnet she wore almost seemed to float above her head.

"Soot," she said, answering the question he hadn't asked. "I'm covered in it a great deal of the time anyway. Thought I might as well put it ta use." She lit her candle using his lantern.

"And ye dinna think it'll make the men *more* curious of yer identity?"

"No' if ye wear it, too. I brought some for ye." She picked up yet another thing from the ground, this time a mug.

He shot her a look, but the idea was a good one. He himself had considered it, but half past eleven had crept up too quickly, and he hadn't wanted to keep her waiting.

"We'll have ta hurry," he said, taking the mug from her.

Together, they covered his face in soot, and Hamish tried to ignore the touch of her fingers as they brushed his forehead and cheeks. He repeated the name in his mind: Dermot McCurdy. Dermot McCurdy.

She stepped back after a bit and admired him with an amused smile. "Shall I dump the rest on yer hair?"

He put the mug out of her reach. "Nay, no time for that, lass."

"Lass?" she said. "Ye're mistaken. I'm Harold. New ta Kildonnan—and no' one ta talk much."

Hamish laughed. "Pleased ta meet ye, then, Harold. Where *did* ye come by yer clothes?"

She looked down toward the floor and stuck out one of her boots. "Mark was kind enough ta lend them ta me."

"Well," Hamish said, "'twill certainly be dark enough ta keep ye from bein' recognized—provided ye dinna speak. Or smile. Ye're too bonnie ta make a good man."

"I'm blushin' under the soot," she said.

Was she serious or teasing? Sometimes he thought she returned his esteem and affection, but inevitably, he was reminded of two things. Ava was waiting for Dermot McCurdy to take her and marry her, and even if she hadn't been, she was the daughter of Sir Andrew MacMorran. She was meant for better things than life with Hamish Campbell, lowly innkeeper and son of a treasonous Jacobite.

"Are ye certain ye wish ta do this?" he asked.

She looked him in the eye, but a little smile lingered on the edge of her lips. "Aye, Hamish. I'm certain."

"Verra well, then, *Harold*. Let's go. They may be waitin' for us already."

She nodded. "Where *do* we go?"

"Through the tunnel." He led the way toward the far wall.

"That's a tunnel?"

He glanced at her over his shoulder. "Aye. What did ye think it was ye were hidin' in the other day?"

"A wee room. But that explains the draftiness. Where does it come out?"

He set down his lantern and started moving the barrels, and she joined. "Just past the tree line. Ye'll see. Or perhaps ye won't. 'Tis especially dark tonight."

Once the barrels were out of the way, he picked up both light sources and handed Ava her candle. Pulling back the plaid that draped over the entrance to the tunnel, he stepped aside. "After you."

She passed by him, and Hamish couldn't stop a smile at the strange sight of her in breeches, with no trace of the bonnie ginger hair that was such a distinctive part of her.

"Ye failed ta mention this part of the inn when ye gave me the grand tour," she said in a whisper as Hamish followed behind her, letting the plaid drop into place.

"My apologies," he said. He kept a hand on one wall and the other holding the lantern, all while ducking his head to keep from scraping it on the ceiling of the narrow, short tunnel. "I didna ken at the time how enthusiastic ye'd be about smugglin'."

The squeaking that echoed throughout the tunnel made Hamish cringe, as did the pockets of gathered water they were obliged to navigate as the ground began to incline. Every now and then, Hamish felt a drip of cold water land on his face or bonnet.

Splashing and chittering converged for a moment nearby, and Hamish's hand was seized as a rat skittered away through and then out of the candlelight.

He stopped and held Ava's hand in his, pressing it lightly to reassure her, even though his own heart thundered in his chest —whether for the rats or for the hand he held, it was hard to say. It was a good thing none of the men they would be working with would be holding Ava's hand, for they would find it hard to believe she was a man, so slender and soft was it.

"Ye've made a coward out of me," she said with a laugh full of nerves. "I didna used ta be afraid of rats."

"I've faced down a line of angry French soldiers on the battlefield," he said, "but I reckon my heart beats as fast now as it did then."

She laughed and pulled her hand away, and Hamish turned back toward their path, forbidding himself to dwell on how it felt to hold her hand—to know she looked to him to protect her, even if it was only from rats.

Dermot McCurdy. Dermot McCurdy, Hamish reminded himself.

"Enjoy that candle," he said. "There'll be no light allowed once the work begins."

As if on cue, a gush of air swept through, sprinkling them with water from the stone ceiling as Hamish's light extinguished. He stopped, and Ava's laugh echoed in the tunnel.

"Ye were sayin'?" she teased.

"Och. Here." He reached for the candle she held, and she hurried to draw back from him.

"I think no'!" she said. "Ye've a spotty history with them down here at best."

"'Tis just ta relight it," he said, keeping his hand out expectantly.

"I'll hold it, then," she said, and she allowed him to hold the wick close to her flame, which flickered with the small drafts that were coming with increasing frequency the farther they walked into the tunnel.

He held the lantern in place, keeping the door open, but nothing happened, and he clucked his tongue impatiently. "It willna light. The wick must be too wet, and there's too strong a wind."

She gave an exaggerated sigh and handed him her candle.

"That's a good lass." He traded the guttered candle for the lit one and turned to guide them the remainder of the way. He kept the lantern door facing him to prevent the wind from extinguishing the flame, forcing them to make do with the light that came through the punched holes.

"Well," Ava said after they had walked a few feet in silence, "if ye insist on takin' my candle, at least give me yer hand, for I canna see where I'm steppin' with yer hefty frame blockin' all the light." She reached out her hand expectantly, and he took it with an inevitable stuttering of the heart. He had done his heart no favors by allowing her to accompany him tonight.

The path became steeper and less even as they approached the end of the tunnel, and all the while, a chill gust tried to push them back the way they came. Ava's warm hold on his hand was in stark contrast to the cold, and part of him hoped the tunnel would never end. She was quiet—unusual for her—and he wished he could know what she was thinking.

Two minutes later, they reached the exit, emerging under a crooked stone arch and into the darkness of the Kildonnan woods that skirted this part of the coast. The smell of trees, wet dirt, and sea salt blended in the wind. It was cold and smelled as though it might begin raining soon.

Hamish expected Ava to let go of his hand once they left the confines of the tunnel, but she kept her hold on it. He glanced at her, unable to help himself, and blinked. He had forgotten her disguise, but the whites of her eyes were large as her gaze searched the darkness around them. The snapping of twigs informed them of someone's approach, and she let his hand drop. Hamish put his arm to his side, ready to pull out his *sgian dubh* in the event that the new arrivals were not friendly toward them.

But he soon recognized Fowlis and Warnock, flanked by two other men.

Fowlis's eyes went to Ava, and there was a nerve-wracking moment where Hamish feared she might be recognized, despite the pains she had taken with her appearance.

"Any more comin'?" Fowlis asked.

Hamish shook his head, and Fowlis' mouth drew into a sort of grimace.

"We dinna have many workers," Hamish explained, "and we couldna leave the inn unwatched."

Fowlis gave a shrug. "The women would have been no use."

Hamish forced himself not to look at Ava.

"And who's this?" Warnock asked, thrusting his chin to indicate Ava.

"This is Harold."

Warnock grunted, not looking overly impressed with Ava.

"Harold," Fowlis said, looking at Ava over by the light of Hamish's lantern. Hamish casually switched it to his other hand, hoping there would be less light for Fowlis's inspection. "How old are ye, lad?"

"He canna speak," Hamish blurted out, heartbeat racing. Ava's appearance might not betray her, but her voice was another matter.

All four gazes of Fowlis and his men transferred to Hamish.

"Had his tongue cut out." Hamish didn't allow himself to look at Ava's reaction to his improvisation. "For lyin' and blasphemin'."

"Poor lad," said one of the men, apparently moved by the falsehood.

"Canny choice, Campbell," said Warnock. "Canna inform on us even if he wanted to."

Hamish gave a nod. He was sure to have an earful from Ava later.

"Time ta go, then," said Fowlis. His interest in Harold seemed to have dissipated. "Put out the lantern and leave it here. I ken the way well enough."

They trudged out toward the sea in a mist of darkness. Hamish kept close behind the man in front of him, while Ava brought up the rear. Every now and then, he felt her hand brush his back, as though she needed something to assure her he was still there. He wished he could have held her hand.

Two small boats waited in the waves at the shoreline, attended by two men, and the six of them who had just arrived began to heave the casks out of the boats. Hamish was relieved to see their size. Ava would be able to carry them.

The casks were connected in pairs by a rope, which allowed the men to sling them over their shoulders so that one cask sat in front and the other against their backs. As Hamish arranged his own load, he knew a growing fear. The casks were heavy for their size, packed with salt as they were, and they would be obliged to carry them to the tunnel and then over the uneven ground within. As far as Hamish could tell, it would require perhaps three trips to empty the boats of their burden. This was no small effort that would be required of Ava.

He glanced at her, but she was not looking at him. She was busy fixing the casks over her shoulder. He felt a rush of affection and concern over her, soot-covered and unrecognizable as she was.

She seemed to sense his eyes on her, for she looked up and sent him a reassuring smile.

He discovered he had underestimated her fortitude. The task required not three but four journeys to and from Glengour in oppressive darkness, but not by a single word did Ava betray the hardship of the undertaking. Hamish had deprived her of such an option in his attempt to save her from speaking, and his guilt lay as heavily on his shoulders as the casks of salt. Only by her increasingly heavy breathing and two stumbles in the tunnel did Hamish know how taxed was her strength.

On the fourth and final approach to the boats, Hamish said to Ava in an undervoice, "I'll take yer load this time. We can delay a moment at the opening to the tunnel, and I'll move them ta my shoulders."

She shook her head, and, at the archway when he attempted to do just what he had said, she simply slipped past him, breathless but stubborn as ever.

"Well done, lads," Fowlis said when they had stacked the last of the casks. He, too, was out of breath, and the others stretched their necks and shoulders in the dark of the tunnel. "Tomorrow night, they'll be taken on—some ta Fort William, some ta Darnock. There'll be horses waitin' back at the end of the tunnel tomorrow night."

Hamish nodded, silently swearing to himself that he would keep Ava from helping with the second part of the ordeal.

Fowlis looked at Hamish. "Ye'll have yer money once all of this has been loaded safely. And ye can decide then how much ta give wee Harold here." His gaze moved to Ava. "Ye did well, lad. I didna expect ye ta last."

Ava gave a nod to accept the compliment, and Hamish only wished Fowlis could know that it was a woman who had just accomplished a task taxing the strength of five sturdy men.

The way into the cellar was blocked now, and Hamish and Ava would be obliged to walk back to the inn and through the front door. The other men bid them a quiet farewell, some disappearing into the trees while two headed back in the direction of the boats, leaving Hamish and Ava to make their way to Glengour.

Hamish led the way, and they walked in forced silence. Hamish was too wary that they might be followed or watched to allow any conversation between them—not with the lie he had told about Ava's tongue.

When they reached the side of the inn, Hamish put a hand out to signal for Ava to wait while he verified there was no one nearby to witness their return. It must have been nigh on two o'clock, though, and it was silent and the inn dark.

They walked toward the front door with light footsteps and ears alert to any sound, and Hamish opened the front door, blessing the work Glenna had recently done to ensure it wouldn't creak loud enough to rouse every guest in the inn.

Glenna seemed to have heard them all the same, though, for she emerged from the kitchen, lit by the glow of a dying fire, into the dark and empty coffee room.

She seemed not to be surprised by Ava's disguise. "Did ye manage?" She yawned as she asked the question.

Hamish nodded. "It'll all be gone by this time tomorrow night." His body was tired, but his mind was too alert for him to feel a pressing need to sleep as Glenna apparently did.

She smiled sleepily. "I'm glad ta hear it. I think I'll be off ta bed if ye dinna mind—only a few hours till mornin'. I let Dorcas go upstairs ta sleep an hour ago."

"Aye, of course," Hamish said. "Go on."

Glenna yawned again and left the two of them in the entryway. When her footsteps were no longer audible, Hamish turned to look at Ava, who was rubbing her neck.

He let out a gush of air through his nose. "I should never have let ye come."

"As if ye could have stopped me," she said, and her teeth glimmered even in the dark against her soot-covered skin. Her eyelids hung heavy, though, belying her humorous words.

"Stubborn lass," he said without rancor.

"Well, when ye cut out a woman's tongue"—she looked at him churlishly—"she has ta find ways ta make certain she's no' underestimated."

He chuckled. "I *didna* cut out a woman's tongue. 'Twas Harold's tongue. And 'twas his master who did it, no' me. There's a whole story—I came up with it as we worked in case anyone asked more questions."

"*I* am Harold," she said dryly, "and ye're my master. So"— she looked at him significantly—"ye cut out my tongue."

"And yet ye dinna seem ta have any trouble usin' it."

"Och, ye havna heard the half of it, Hamish Campbell. I have a great deal ta say after all that time." Her words were severe, but she was smiling, and her tired eyes twinkling.

"I'd expect no less," he said. "Ye can finish yer scoldin' tomorrow, though. I swear ta sit silently as ye do it. Ye should get some sleep while ye can, though. Mornin' will come quickly."

She sighed and looked down. "I suppose ye're right. And I canna sleep in those sheets covered in all this. Glenna would never forgive me." She wiped a hand on her cheek and looked at it with an expression of mixed amusement and distaste.

Hamish felt a twisting, an aching in his chest looking at Ava just then. She would be gone soon, and he was dreading it. How would he say farewell to this extraordinary woman—strong, beautiful, and able to make him laugh as no one else could? How would he hand her over to a man he didn't know, one he couldn't be sure would treasure her as she deserved to be treasured?

"Goodnight, then, Hamish," she said, meeting his eyes. The humor was gone now, and they seemed to search his in the dark.

Was it possible to miss someone who was standing right in front of you? Hamish certainly missed Ava. He wanted desperately to pull her into his arms.

"Ye did well, lass," he said. "Goodnight."

20

Ava woke in the morning, heavy-eyed and with a neck and shoulders that ached as she turned over in bed. She moved to put a hand under her cheek only to realize she held something—a rag.

Her eyes opened. She had never finished wiping the soot from her face. She had covered the pillow with her cloak when she'd reached her room after saying goodnight to Hamish, promising herself to rest her legs for but a quick moment while she wiped at the soot, but she had been too tired to keep sleep at bay, apparently.

It was still too early for the sun to have risen fully, but even in the dark, Ava could see the shadowed part of her cloak where the soot from her hair and face had rubbed onto the fabric.

Her feet were only somewhat rested from the sleep, still tired and swollen from last night's work. Once or twice during the ordeal, she had been worried she might collapse. She touched a hand to each shoulder, wincing slightly. The rope, pulled taut by the weights on each end, had dug into her shoulders all night long. When Hamish had offered to take her burden on, she had wanted more than anything to say yes, but she had been too afraid of the potential questions and comments it would occasion when the other men inevitably noticed.

Then, too, she had wanted to show Hamish she was strong and capable. She had insisted on coming, after all. She refused to let herself become a burden rather than a help. But, more than anything, last night had shown her how much she craved Hamish's approval and forgiveness. She wanted to repay him for the kindness he had done by hiding her, contrary to the law, despite what he stood to gain from doing otherwise.

Seeing his face had given her the strength she needed to put one foot in front of the other when she had thought it impossible moments before.

She hurried to wash her hair and face from the remnants of soot still there, and the small water basin in her room sloshed with black water by the end of her efforts. Her face was clean enough, but her hair would likely bleed soot when she next washed it, too.

When she saw Hamish in the late morning, she stated her intention of helping with the coming night's task. Only the prospect of having Hamish with her to keep her strong could make her look upon it without pure and unadulterated dread.

Hamish shook his head, though, once she stopped speaking. "Nay. 'Tis kind of ye, lass, but Fowlis has enough men ta see ta things tonight. We're no' needed—and I think it best that Harold's presence be a one-time occurrence. If Fowlis discovers no one's heard of a Harold lackin' a tongue, there's like ta be questions."

Ava wasn't even certain she believed him that their help wasn't needed—she knew an inkling he might be saying that to save her the work. She suspected she would find him in the tunnel if she bothered to go there and check at midnight, but she couldn't regret his chivalry if that was the case. She didn't think her shoulders could bear another night like last night's.

It hadn't been all agony, of course. There had been something special and memorable about the time they'd spent alone before joining the other men. Words had escaped her as she'd followed behind him, her hand in his. And even after, the knowledge that they guarded a secret from the others had made her feel closer to Hamish than ever. He somehow made her feel both strong and precious.

Whatever the truth was, the next day, Hamish informed her that everything had gone according to plan and the tunnel had been emptied of its contents. "Well, of the contents *we* put there," he said wryly as Ava hung up a freshly laundered sheet in the laundry. "Mary and the rats can now return ta their usual habits."

Ava shot an amused glance at him as she reached for another sheet. He was leaning a shoulder against the wall, as though he meant to stay for some time, and his eyes watched her absently. It made her smile. He took his duties as innkeeper seriously, so to know that he would choose to spend the few spare moments available to him in her presence was flattering. Besides, she liked the company. It could be lonely, staying out of the eye of the guests when the others were coming and going, walking freely about the inn.

"Do ye mean ta stay here and watch me work?" she said teasingly. "Or would ye care ta lend a hand?"

He pursed his lips thoughtfully. "The former, I reckon." But he pushed off the wall and came to her side, taking a corner of the sheet and helping her drape it over the line to dry.

She tugged the side closest to her to even out the sheet then looked up and found Hamish's eyes on her and a little smile playing at his lips.

"What?" she asked.

His gaze flicked to her hair, which was mostly covered by

her kertch. "Still havna managed ta rid yerself of the soot?" He reached a hand to a piece of hair which had managed to escape and was hanging onto her forehead. He rubbed it between his finger and thumb.

She grabbed his wrist and pulled his hand away, shooting him an annoyed glance, which was met with one of mirth as he revealed the streak of gray upon his fingers.

"Alack," she said, letting go his hand and turning to her work with a sigh. "I've a cruel master who works me inta the ground and doesna allow time for washin' anythin' but the laundry."

He looked at her with faux-sympathy. "A woeful tale, lass. Perhaps I can be of assistance with that." He reached for the bucket of water she'd fetched from the well earlier that morning, and his expression turned mischievous as he picked it up, looking at her meaningfully.

She took a wary step back, looking at him with wide eyes.

Quick footsteps sounded, and Glenna appeared in the doorway, breathless. "Gaugers!"

Hamish dropped the bucket onto the floor.

"And the sheriff, too," Glenna added. "I was out sweepin' when I saw them on the road. They'll be upon us any moment."

"The sheriff?" Hamish said bemusedly.

"Aye," Glenna said, lifting her shoulders. "He's never been opposed ta free tradin'. I reckon . . . . " She looked to Ava with a grimace, and Ava's heart plummeted.

"Ye reckon they're here for me."

"'Tis my suspicion, aye. Angus has the sheriff under his thumb, ye ken. But there's no time—"

Ava made for the door leading behind the inn— her father, too, was close with the sheriff—but she was stopped with Hamish's firm hand.

His eyes were on the window, and he pulled her away from it. "Ye canna go that way. They'll be watchin' the inn from outside. Stay with Glenna in here. I'll take them to the office and my own quarters then through the coffee room ta the kitchen. When ye hear me close the office door, come around the back of the stairs and hide yerself in the office."

Ava and Glenna nodded, and with a final glance at Ava, Hamish left the kitchen.

Ava's fingers trembled with nervous energy as she stared after him. She shut her eyes and forced a deep breath, though it shook on the way in and out. Was this what everything had come to? Would she be discovered by the revenue men and taken by the sheriff back to Glenlochan? Would she be forced to marry Angus MacKinnon after all?

21

Hamish cooperated willingly with the men's demand to search the premises, hoping his friendly face effectively concealed the fear he was feeling. He didn't know what he would do if Ava was discovered, but even the thought made him feel desperate.

He tried to use a gentle hand in guiding their hunt first to his own quarters then toward the kitchen. He would have to trust Glenna to hide Ava's things as she'd done when Sir Andrew had insisted upon seeing every corner of the inn.

It was simple enough to tell by watching the excisemen and sheriff that it was not just smuggled goods they were after. The way their eyes wandered, settling on each one of the guests in the coffee room and on Dorcas when they reached the kitchen, told Hamish they were every bit as interested in the people at Glengour as they were in what items they might find concealed there.

If Angus had sent them, as Glenna had suggested, he would be well aware that the goods had already been taken. This was nothing but an excuse to search out Ava.

When they reached the end of their search a full hour later,

Hamish suppressed a sigh of relief and refused to let his gaze wander to the office door as it insisted upon doing.

"Thank ye for yer cooperation, Mr. Campbell," said the sheriff as they stood at the edge of the coffee room. "The information we received gives us ta think there may be illegal activity this evenin'. For that reason, Paterson here"—he nodded at the exciseman beside him—"will remain. He willna bother yer guests, so long as they're law-abidin', of course, and he'll make himself comfortable in the coffee room, so ye dinna need ta sacrifice one of yer rooms."

Hamish held his hands behind his back, and they tightened. "'Tis no sacrifice. We wish for ye ta be comfortable, Mr. Paterson, if ye're ta stay with us."

The tall, somber man shook his head and walked to the table in the middle of the floor—the one with a clear view to the kitchen door as well as the stairs and office door. "Right here will suit me fine, Mr. Campbell."

Hamish smiled and nodded. "If ye change yer mind, ye need only say as much." How would Ava ever manage to get out of the office?

The sheriff conferred for a moment in an undervoice with Paterson then took his leave of Hamish, but not without a final, sweeping glance over the coffee room, the stairs, and the corridor that led to the cellar.

Once the sheriff was gone, Hamish offered Paterson a dram, which the man accepted with a stone-faced expression. Hamish procured it for him, asked if there was anything else he could get for him, then went to the kitchen, where both Dorcas and Glenna were. They looked at him expectantly.

"Gone?" Glenna asked.

Hamish shook his head, keeping his voice low as he responded. "We have company for the night—one of the gaugers is stayin'. Intends ta remain at a table in the coffee room all night."

"And just what does he think ta see?" Dorcas asked, arms akimbo. "A few bags of smuggled salt sittin' down for a dram at the table next ta him?"

"Nay," Hamish said. "They're no' here for smuggled goods."

Glenna worried her lip. "And Ava trapped in the office."

Hamish's eyes widened. "She willna come out now, will she?"

Glenna shook her head. "I told her ta stay put till one of us came ta get her."

Hamish breathed a sigh of relief and tapped a fist against his mouth thoughtfully. "She'll have ta stay there. For now, at least. Perhaps if Paterson has a likin' for whisky, we can manage ta distract him long enough ta move her. He accepted the dram I offered him."

The women nodded in assent.

"I'll see if I can fill his belly ta burstin'," Dorcas said, "so he'll no' be able ta resist noddin' off."

But Paterson was made of sterner stuff than they had expected. He drank his dram slowly, and while he accepted a piece of mutton pie, he refused the second helping Dorcas offered him of both food and drink. He was not a man likely to fall asleep on the job. Whatever Angus had offered him, it was more enticing than what they had to offer at Glengour. He asked for a cup of coffee and assured them he would need nothing else.

The one activity he *did* seem interested in was carrying on a long and aggravating conversation with Hamish. The few times Hamish attempted to get up in order to greet new guests, Glenna was inevitably there to do it on his behalf. She seemed to think that Hamish occupying the exciseman's time was preferable to the alternative. And perhaps she was right.

But Hamish was anxious to speak with Ava. She had been in the office for hours now with only a brief visit from Hamish to acquaint her with what was happening. He had promised her then to bring food and drink as soon as he was able. At least she was safe.

It was late indeed when he finally managed to shake the conversation of Paterson. He asked Glenna to bring him mutton pie and ale—"If 'tis all the same ta you, I'll take them with me and turn in early tonight." He held her gaze a moment longer than necessary, hoping she would understand his intent.

"Aye, sir," she said. "Ye must be starvin'. I'll be sure ta bring ye plenty."

Hamish sent her a grateful glance then turned back to Paterson and manufactured a yawn. "Ye certain ye dinna wish for a room? We've one unoccupied, and I reckon ye're as tired as I am."

Paterson shook his head. "Thank ye, sir, but nay. I've my duty ta tend to. I'm well enough where I am."

Hamish smiled civilly and rose from the table to accept the tray Glenna brought. He couldn't help but raise his brows. There were three pieces of pie, an entire jug of ale, and a set of utensils.

"I ken yer appetite, sir," Glenna said as she noted his reaction.

Hamish rubbed his belly, hoping sincerely that the enormous amount of food wouldn't cause any suspicion on the exciseman's part. "'Twill be my downfall. Good night, Mr. Paterson."

The man nodded, apparently unconcerned by the display of food. His eyes were on Glenna, and Hamish felt a twinge of guilt leaving her to his unending conversation. But not guilty enough to stay.

Ava was not in the office when he slipped in with the heavy tray in hand. The door to his quarters was latched, and Hamish gave the lightest of taps with his knuckle, glancing over his shoulder as if Paterson might suddenly appear.

The door creaked, opening just a hair's breadth—enough

for him to see a bit of Ava and the glow of the fire behind her. He gave a nod to assure her he was alone, and she opened the door wider to allow him in.

"Brought ye a bit of food," he said once the door was safely closed behind him. His eyes went to the gorse on the table. It was amazing what such a small thing had done to make his quarters more cheery.

She glanced at the tray, and her brows went up. "A bit of food, ye say?"

"Och, well, 'tis for both of us. Ye're no' the only one who's had a tryin' day. I havna eaten, either. Paterson nearly talked my ears off my head."

She laughed, and the sound was music to his ears after the stress and danger of the day.

"Shall we go ta the table?" he suggested.

She shrugged and glanced at the fire. "I've come ta be rather comfortable over here." On the small couch, his plaid was in a heap, as though she had thrown it aside to come answer the door. He liked the thought of her wrapped up in the plaid he had worn for so long.

"By all means, then." Hamish put out a hand to invite her to take her seat. He glanced at the chairs by the table, but Ava seemed to read his thoughts.

"Nay, ye'll come sit here." She patted the place beside her. "I've no wish ta wait ta eat or take turns handin' the tray back and forth, and I reckon ye'd say the same."

He gave a little chuckle, eyes on the small space available to him. Sitting in such close proximity to Ava was the last thing his heart needed. But it was certainly what it *wanted,* and he made no argument.

"Do ye have another cup in here?" she asked, picking up the one Glenna had sent with him. "And a fork?"

He sucked in a breath through clenched teeth and shook his head. "A short time ago, the answer would have been *aye.*

But with all the people comin' recently—and with my failed attempt at porridge—I took everythin' I had here ta the kitchen."

She picked up the sole fork. "Looks as though we'll be takin' turns after all."

"I dinna think Glenna felt she could give us two without givin' rise ta suspicion."

She shrugged apathetically and took a slice from the end of one of the pies, handing him the fork once she'd taken her bite.

The fire crackled, warming their bodies, while the pie filled their bellies.

"Dinna tell Dorcas, but"—Hamish poked at the pie with a fork—"they're no' quite as good as the ones ye make." He glanced at Ava, and she was looking at him through narrowed eyes.

"Are ye flatterin' me, Hamish Campbell?"

He chuckled and poured a cup of ale. "Is it flattery when 'tis the truth?" He handed her the cup, and she took it with a quick *thank ye.*

"If only ye'd tried my mother's pies," she said. "My sister Bridget always said they were better than mine." She took a sip of ale, and Hamish had the smallest inkling that she had done so in a timely way so as to hide her face.

"I canna speak ta that," he said, cutting another piece, "never havin' tried yer mother's, but I canna imagine a mutton pie tastin' any better than the ones ye make." He offered her the fork. "Perhaps 'tis the memory of yer mother which makes them taste better ta yer sister."

Ava took the fork slowly, and he could see the thought in her eyes. "I hadna thought of it that way. After my mother died, I made the pies for a time, but my father would never even take a bite, and Bridget . . . well, ye ken already what she thought." She smiled wryly and ate a forkful of pie.

He was reminded of watching her father eat the pie and

wondering if that had reminded him of her. "Do ye miss them? Yer family?"

She chewed the food in her mouth, and he wondered if he had crossed a line with his question. It was only one of many he had.

"Aye, I do. My siblin's in particular." Her mouth twisted to the side. "Mostly, I miss what we once were."

"Afore yer mother died?"

She nodded, and she nudged at the food on the plate with the fork. "We had less money, but we were happier." She looked up at him and smiled, though it still held a hint of sadness. "After Ma fell ill and we moved ta Glenlochan, things began ta change. And when she died"—her throat bobbed, and she shrugged again. "My da has never been the same. 'Tis almost as if he canna bear my mother's absence, so he throws himself inta everythin' else ta keep his mind from it."

"Must almost feel as if ye lost them both."

She met his gaze. "Aye. 'Tis exactly how it feels."

The food and drink sat forgotten for a moment as they held one another's gazes. "I always wondered what 'twould be like if I hadna lost both my own parents," Hamish said. "If I'd really kent my mother. But perhaps 'tis easier never ta ken someone than ta ken 'em and lose 'em."

Ava shook her head. "There's no such thing as easy when it comes ta losin' someone. Just different types of hard, I reckon."

He couldn't keep his gaze from her—the radiance of her hair in the firelight, uncovered for once; the small freckle just beside her right eye; the depth to her brown eyes that were as beautiful now in their somberness as ever they were in laughter. She would leave him—it was only a matter of time. Would it be easier if he had never known her at all? To never know what it was like to look into the face of the woman he wanted more than anything but could never have?

She finally turned her eyes from him, handing him the fork. "Do ye have no other family?"

He tilted his head from side to side. "Properly, aye. A cousin of my father's took me in after my father died, but I was always a burden ta them, no matter how hard I worked ta be otherwise. The only real family I ever had was my father at Dalmore."

"Is that why ye want ta return there?"

His hand slowed as he moved to cut the pie. He had never truly asked himself why it was he was so set on reclaiming Dalmore, and her question took him off guard. "I suppose so."

She gave a slow, understanding nod. "The heart always longs for the place it was most at peace." There was a moment of silence, then she snatched the fork from him with a little, teasing smile that seemed to say, *ye took too long*. "What of the soldiers ye served with? Did they no' become family ta ye?"

"Aye, in a way. But I was always different."

She handed him the fork again. "What do ye mean?"

He frowned slightly as he scooped up the last bit of the second piece of pie. "They all had families back home—letters and news ta look forward to, a place ta return to. They longed for the end; I dreaded it."

"Dreaded the end of the war?"

He smiled wryly. "It meant I had nowhere ta go anymore—nowhere ta belong, I suppose."

She watched him for a moment, and he felt suddenly anxious at his confession.

"Ye belong here," she said. "Dealin' with a nuisance like me." Was it a trick of the firelight? How did her eyes manage to twinkle so captivatingly?

"A slovenly nuisance, no less." He reached to the crumb at the side of her mouth and swept it away.

"Ta equal her slovenly master." She put a hand to his chest, taking him by surprise, but she merely brushed at a collection of crumbs that had fallen onto his shirt.

"Och," he said. "Been spendin' too much time with ye. Yer slovenliness is contagious."

She nudged him with an elbow, and they shared a laughing glance as both of them tended to any residual crumbs from the ones pointed out.

Ava looked toward the small box that sat on the kitchen table, and her expression became thoughtful. "Ye earned that medal in the war?"

Hamish glanced over at the open box on the table. He had forgotten he had left it there this morning. He poured more ale into the cup and cleared his throat. "Aye."

"Yer whole company received it?"

"Nay." He took a drink, feeling suddenly uncomfortable.

Her eyebrows went up. "Just you, then?"

"Aye."

She had the fork now, but she made no move to use it. She was watching him. "The box was already open. I'm sorry if I've upset ye. I didna mean ta . . . ."

He shook his head. "Ye've no' upset me. 'Tis only . . . I've no' really talked about it."

"Oh," she said. "Well, ye dinna need ta do so if ye prefer no' ta do so. 'Twas no' my place ta look, only 'twas open, and I grew a bit bored after a few hours. Ye've still no' carved yer name inta any of the beams nor hung any tapestries ta keep yer visitors entertained."

He chuckled. She always managed to make him feel lighter. "Ye're the only visitor I've had, lass. And I dinna blame ye for lookin' in the box." He paused. Receiving a medal for a day when so many men lost their lives had always been a source of confusion for him. "I mentioned starin' down a line of enraged French soldiers the other night."

She nodded, listening.

"My company was surprised one day by an attack by the French. We were woefully outnumbered, and they managed ta wound many of our men afore we could escape." He shook his head, remembering the conversation with his superior in the cold woods. "I kend a few of them had survived, but ta return for them was dangerous—foolish, perhaps—and the officers didna wish ta endanger those who remained. But I couldna leave them there."

There was silence, punctuated by the cracking fire.

"So, ye went back?" Ava asked.

"Aye. Once dark fell."

"Were they alive?"

He swallowed, trying to blink away the memory of the scene, stumbling around in the dark over bodies. "A few of them, aye."

"And those men survived?"

"All but one."

The silence resumed, and Hamish stared into the fire. He could feel Ava's eyes on him.

"And ye keep the medal in that box?"

He shrugged. "I've never kent where ta keep it—nor do I ken how ta feel about havin' it at all."

"Ye saved the lives of those men, Hamish. Ye're a hero."

He shook his head. "I'm no hero, lass. I did what I hoped someone else would do for me. Besides, for those who hate my father, a medal will change nothin'."

"No' if ye keep it in that box, certainly," she said.

He looked at her, finally. "What am I meant ta do? Wave it in the face of everyone I meet ta persuade them I'm worthy of their notice? A medal for the innkeeper at Glengour?"

She said nothing.

He let out a breath through his lips. He had never felt deserving of the medal, and he would never wear it, as some men did. It belonged in a place like Dalmore House, not at Glengour Inn.

"Ye deserve it, though, Hamish. Innkeeper or no." She took his hand. "I'm glad ye've been recognized for yer courage." Her mouth turned up at the side. "Though, they might take it back if they saw ye with the rats here."

He chuckled and looked down at her hand holding his. Her touch warmed him through, and he let his thumb slip along the edge of hers.

Her hand went more rigid in his, and he looked up at her. She was staring at their hands, though, a look of alarm on her face. He had gone too far.

He let go of her hand. "I should be lettin' ye sleep." He rose from the couch and took the tray with him.

"Lettin' me sleep?" She put aside the plaid and rose. "I'm the one who's invaded *yer* quarters."

"Nay, no' invaded, lass. Ye're welcome here." He walked over to set the tray down on the table then went to the bed, trying not to think too much about the fact that Ava would be sleeping there. "'Tis no' the finest bed ye'll ever sleep in, but . . . ." He straightened the blanket.

Ava walked over, a frown on her brow. "And where do *you* intend ta sleep?"

He lifted his shoulders in a careless gesture. "In the office."

She stared at him. "What? On the floor?"

His mouth curled up at one corner. "Aye. Now, get some sleep."

He walked to the door with Ava following close behind and opened it, turning back toward her. "Secure the latch, just as ye did afore," he said in a low voice. He couldn't let Paterson know he was sleeping in the office. "Only open if ye hear three taps."

"Three taps," she repeated.

His gaze raked over her face. He was reluctant to bid her goodnight. His eyes landed on her lips for a moment, and he forced them away, though he was nearly certain she had noticed. He had no right to wish to hold her or kiss her. She would be Dermot's soon, and he hers.

The thought made his stomach clench and his heart feel wrung and empty. "Good night, Ava."

"Good night, Hamish."

He took a step back into the office, and she slowly closed the door, eyes on him. He thought he saw a sliver of reluctance in her gaze, too, but a moment later, the latch fell into place.

Hamish shut his eyes, taking in a deep breath.

The heart always longs for the place it was most at peace.

Hamish was becoming far more familiar than he had ever thought possible with the longings of the heart.

22

Ava's hand lingered on the latch, and she stared at the grains of wood in the door for a moment. She had spent so much of the day alone in Hamish's quarters, with nothing but her thoughts and worries to keep her company—wondering if all their efforts would be for naught. She had been unable to escape visions of a future with Angus, haunted by his face and the thought of sharing anything with him: food, a home, and especially a bed.

Hamish's presence had been a welcome distraction and a comfort. She was reluctant to lose it, and as though of its own accord, her hand lifted the latch slightly.

She gave herself a shake and lowered the latch soundlessly into its proper position, turning her body away from the door.

Her eyes went to the gorse. It still sat on the table in the kitchen, though it was beginning to look faded and droopy. How had she been at Glengour long enough for such a thing to happen?

What was meant to be a short stop at the inn had turned into three weeks—she could hardly credit it. It was nearly the ides of March. She had thought to be married to Dermot by now, but here she was. And Dermot nowhere to be found.

Her eyes moved to the plaid, still draped on the couch, and she went to it, picking it up in her hands and inhaling softly. It smelled mostly of smoke, but there was a subtle hint of something beneath that—something that reminded her of Hamish.

Hamish. She looked to the door to the office. He had nothing but hard floor to sleep on, unless he decided to sleep in the chair. She looked back to the plaid in her hands.

Certainly he should have *something* to warm him. There was no fire in the office, after all.

She walked back to the door, quietly lifted the latch, and tapped with a soft knuckle.

Once.

Twice.

Thrice.

The taps were barely audible. Her heart raced. Perhaps Hamish hadn't heard it—there was no sound of movement or shuffling within. And perhaps that was for the best. The plaid was merely an excuse to see him again—Ava knew th—

The door opened, and she blinked in surprise. She hadn't even heard him come to the door. The office was completely dark behind him—not even a candle lit. He was looking at her intently, eyes alert and waiting for an explanation. Her eyes flicked down. He had removed his neckcloth, but the button at his throat was still fastened. Ava knew an impulse to undo it.

"I thought ye'd want this at least." She held out his plaid.

He smiled slightly and took it from her. "Aye. Thank ye."

"For takin' yer bed and offerin' ye yer own plaid as consolation?"

He looked down at her with affectionate amusement. "I didna earn that medal sleepin' in King George's bed with silk sheets and pillowcases, lass." He looked behind him into the dark. "'Tis better than most of the places I slept for the last decade." He tossed the plaid behind him.

"But ye're no' a soldier anymore, Hamish. Ye're an innkeeper—surely, ye deserve a bed in yer own inn." She pursed her lips. She was tired of asking others to do so much for her, tired of being a burden, even if Hamish was not one to complain of it. "I suppose ye've grown used ta bein' inconvenienced by me, but I dinna like it." Her head came up. "I never meant ta be such a nuisance, Hamish—ta cause such trouble."

"Och, lass." He put a hand on both of her shoulders. "Ye're no' a nuisance. Never think it."

"But I do think it."

He tipped her chin up with a knuckle so that she was looking into his eyes. "Then, stop. If I truly thought ye a nuisance, I'd have thrown ye out of the stables the first night I met ye."

She managed a small smile, but the way his soft touch lingered beneath her chin made her heart race. Such a strong reaction for such a small touch. "Nay, Hamish. Ye said it when ye first met me—ye kend I'd bring ye trouble. And I have."

He was shaking his head before she had even finished speaking.

"Aye, Hamish. Admit it. I *have* brought ye trouble."

He wrinkled his nose and dropped his hand from her chin. "Perhaps a wee bit of trouble, aye, *but*"—he said it before she could interrupt him—"ye've brought a great deal more than that, Ava."

"Aye," she said wryly. "Gaugers and the sheriff."

Hamish waved them away with a dismissive hand. "Ye ken that's no' what I mean. I'm fond of Dorcas, and I'm glad she's here. But I'm even more glad she didna come when she was meant to, for otherwise I wouldna have mistaken ye for her that night in the stables. I hardly kend then how fortunate I was."

Ava shook her head. She hadn't meant to put him in a position where he was obliged to reassure her. "Always so kind. Forgive me. I think all of it is beginnin' ta take its toll on me— all the hidin', no' kennin' what will happen ta me."

He set his hands on her shoulders again, lowering his head and forcing her to meet his gaze. "Nothin' will happen ta ye, lass. I willna let it. I'll be in the office all night, ensurin' ye're safe. No harm will come ta ye; no one will find ye." He stared her in the eye as though to ensure she knew he meant what he said.

She nodded, swallowing with effort. His words meant more to her than he could know.

"Ye willna be in here tomorrow," he said. "I'll rid us of Paterson, and ye'll be free ta go on as ye have been until Dermot arrives."

Until Dermot arrives. He *would* arrive. Ava had to believe that. It was a question of how soon—and of what she wanted to happen when he did. Dermot was a good, respectable man, and he had been a friend to her for most of her life. But she couldn't stop comparing how she felt with Dermot to how she felt with Hamish right now, his hands on her arms and looking at her as he now did. Dermot, Ava was discovering, was more like a brother to her than a lover, even if he had come to regard her more as the latter.

"All will be well, lass." Hamish pulled her closer and lowered his head, setting a kiss upon her hair—a gentle kiss that sent shivers down her back and warmth all the way to her fingertips.

She swallowed. That was what she needed to know—that all would be well. It was only that, somehow, what she had seen as *well* before—escaping to Dermot, avoiding marriage to Angus—now seemed so much less than well, for that future lacked the person she had come to so depend upon and care for. It lacked Hamish.

Ava shut her eyes, forcing herself to stay in the present, not to allow herself to be wrapped up in the worries of the future. Just for a moment, she wanted to forget her worries, to believe that all *would* be well. She focused on the warmth of Hamish's breath on her head, the firmness of his strong hands on her shoulders, and the security of his presence. She put her hands on his arms, breathing in the smell she had recognized on the plaid.

The soft pressure of his lips on her hair disappeared, and his breath left a trail of warmth as his mouth grazed over her hair and onto her forehead. Ava's hands grasped at the fabric of his loose shirtsleeves and, slowly, he kissed her forehead. Then her temple. Then her cheek. His lips lingered in the last place, as though hesitant to continue to the only reasonable final destination. Ava's lips tingled with anticipation.

With only a heartbeat of vacillation, Ava turned her head and brushed his lips with hers, an invitation for him. His grip on her shoulders tightened for a moment, and Ava waited, unable to breathe, to see whether he would accept the invitation.

His hold on her arms loosened, and a sick thud of disappointment filled Ava's stomach. She let go of his sleeves and dropped her hands only to find Hamish setting one hand on her cheek and the other at her waist, taking the air from her lungs as his lips met hers.

Softly, his lips explored hers while his hand cradled her cheek as it would something precious. After so long feeling pushed and controlled and used, the gentle way Hamish touched her undid something inside her. Never had she felt she needed anything more than she needed him now.

She wrapped her arms around his neck and pulled him closer. The hand at her waist slid toward the small of her back, and the one holding her cheek moved into her hair, enveloping her in his hold as he deepened the kiss, making Ava feel she would never be the same again.

Finally, their lips broke apart, their quickened breath mingling in the small space between them as their foreheads touched and rested against each other.

His hold on her back loosened slightly, and Ava responded by tightening her hold on him. "Dinna leave me." The words escaped her without permission.

His hand caressed her cheek. "I dinna wish to, lass. Surely ye ken that." His hand slid down under her chin, and he tipped it up, kissing her again. She felt the same fire that burned inside her in his touch. She should shy away from the danger of such heat, but this one, she felt to embrace. She *wanted* to be consumed by it.

He pulled back and looked at her, his eyes searching hers. "But I have ta leave now while I've a shred of willpower left ta me."

Ava's heart stuttered at the implication of his words but she gave a nod—a nod that went against everything she wanted.

He took her hand in his and looked down at it as his thumb slid along her knuckles. "I'll be just beyond that door. Sleep well, lass."

She could almost believe him less eager than she was for him to stay, but the final glance he sent at her before he closed the door was so full of reluctance, it set her heart at rest.

E ven though her mind and body were alive with what had just happened, once she did fall asleep, Ava slept more soundly than she had in some time, knowing Hamish was so near, so ready to protect her.

When she woke, the fire glowed faintly, and a little thrill ran through her body at the memory of the night before. She pulled the blanket closer around her, feeling content to know that it had been wrapped around Hamish every night before this one. It felt like a bit of him was present, holding her.

Somewhere in the back of her mind, the thought of Dermot pressed itself on her awareness, but she pushed it aside as she rose and added another peat brick to the dying fire. She held the blanket from the bed about her shoulders, but her exposed ankles tingled with the cold in the room.

She hurried to put on her stays, stockings, and petticoats, then replaited her hair, which was the worse for the night of sleep. Just as she tied her cap in place, three soft knocks sounded on the door.

Her heart raced, and she took a moment to smooth her petticoats and ensure all was in order before walking toward the door and lifting the latch.

Hamish looked down at her from eyes that evidenced that he had been sleeping not long ago. The edge of his nose was pink from the cold. The plaid was draped around his shoulders, held close to his body by his hands, and a few locks of his hair had come undone from his queue. For some reason, the sight of him so unkempt brought her joy—it felt intimate in a different way than their kiss.

"Good mornin', lass." His eyes seemed to ask the same question running through her mind: what now?

"Cold, are ye?" she asked, touching a finger to his nose.

He smiled at her, and all the feelings from the night before flooded into her chest and body anew.

"My time at Glengour has weakened me, I reckon," he said.

"Well, I'd invite ye in ta warm yerself by the fire, but"—she gave an apologetic shrug—"'tis no' my place ta do so. Ye'd have ta ask the master."

His eyes twinkled. "I'll have ta force my way in, then." He opened the plaid with his arms, took a step forward, and grabbed her, wrapping her into the blanket and picking her up so that her feet left the ground.

She muffled her laughs with his shoulder as he walked into the room and used his foot to shut the door behind him. Sitting down on the couch, he set her beside him so that her legs draped over his lap. He wore a smile that made her feel a flood of contentment.

"Would ye look at that?" he said. "I'm warmer already."

Their smiling gazes connected and held for a moment, then he leaned in toward her. She met him in the middle, catching his lips eagerly. His hand found hers, and he held it tightly, surprising Ava with how much feeling could be expressed by such a small gesture.

She pulled away with a contented sigh, and he took the end of one of her plaits in hand, thumbing the end. "We've only a few minutes before the day starts."

She nodded. "And I promised Glenna ta help her with her writin' tonight." She looked around. "That's only if I ever manage ta leave this room."

"Ye're a kind lass," he said, kissing her again. "And I wouldna mind if ye never *did* leave this room. But I'll go see what Paterson is about. When we spoke yesterday, they made it sound as though 'twould only be for the night. I reckon they thought they'd catch sight of ye after so much time."

She moved her legs to allow him to rise and watched him as he re-tied his neckcloth and donned his jacket, admiring his broad figure and how handsome he managed to look even with disheveled hair and wrinkled clothing.

"I'll return with news—and perhaps some food," he said, and with a smile that set her heart aflutter, he left the room.

Ava remained on the couch, reluctant to move from the warmth of the space. When Hamish returned some time later, it was with a bannock in hand, though a bite had been taken out of it.

She raised her brows when he handed it to her, and he

looked at her with wide-eyed innocence. "A necessary action ta prevent Paterson's suspicions."

She shot him a look to show how little she believed his story.

"Ye shouldna look at me so, lass. 'Tis that sort of attention ta detail"—he pointed to the bite mark on the bannock—"that has Paterson gatherin' his things. He means ta leave after he's had a bit of food and drink."

Hamish soon left her to eat the remainder of her bannock in peace, only to return an hour later with news of Paterson's departure. "I reckon he'll be back soon enough with one excuse or other, but for now, we're free of him, and ye can finally go."

"Ye mean ye expect me ta get back ta work?" She feigned disappointment. In truth, though, she *was* reluctant to leave. Not because she was eager to avoid work but because the time she had spent in Hamish's quarters felt like a sliver of something she would find impossible to recapture once she left. An abundance of problems were waiting to be faced outside the two doors separating her from the rest of the inn.

"Aye, lass." He gave a playful tug to the string of her kertch. "Ye ken we canna manage without ye."

He led the way into the office and then out to the entry way. Just as they emerged, the front door opened, revealing Mrs. Shaw and her daughter. Their eyes immediately went to Hamish and Ava, and, to her dismay, Ava felt her cheeks go red at the thought of what assumptions the women might make from their simultaneous exit. For all the Shaws knew, they had only been in the office, meeting about business matters. But Ava knew the truth, and her cheeks betrayed it.

Mrs. Shaw's eyes widened as they flitted from Hamish to Ava and back.

"Mrs. Shaw," Hamish said in surprise. "I didna expect ye till tomorrow."

Her eyes lingered on Ava, slight contempt evident in the lift of her lips. "We've seen the number of people passin' through of late—people of all sorts"—her eyes flicked to Ava again, making a pass from head to toe—"and we thought ye might need more than usual. We've brought three casks today."

Cheeks still burning, Ava excused herself. Once she was out of view, she pressed a hand to her hot face, taking a moment before going into the laundry. She had no reason at all to care what Mrs. Shaw or her daughter thought, but their presence had been unexpected, and Ava's reaction had certainly not been under her own control.

She went about her duties in the laundry, larder, and kitchen, trying not to betray herself again when Glenna and Dorcas inquired after how she had fared during Paterson's presence. The encounters, while innocuous, began to breed an unease in Ava.

What *would* happen now? Should she write a letter to Dermot and advise him against coming? What if he had already left? What would happen when he arrived?

Even setting aside Dermot's potential arrival, it was not as though she and Hamish had come to any particular understanding. There were still hurdles to be reckoned with, Ava's own father being foremost amongst them. She couldn't keep her presence at Glengour a secret from him forever, and if there *was* a future with Hamish, her father would inevitably discover that Hamish had lied to him.

And what of Hamish's own aims? What of Dalmore House? Ava had seen how unreasonable her father could be, and he would never be content to trade a marriage between Ava and Angus with one between her and the son of a known and reviled Jacobite, to say nothing of allowing Hamish to take back the property once he realized how Hamish had lied to him.

Ava couldn't see the way forward at all.

The obstacles followed her around all day, niggling at her and driving away the contentment she'd been feeling since

Hamish's visit. She only saw him a few times throughout the day—always in passing—and when the inn quieted for the night, Glenna pulled her into her room, eager to practice more writing.

Ava tried to conceal her anxiousness to be done with the night's lesson. She could never have stayed at Glengour without Glenna's cooperation, and she wanted to show her gratitude for that, even if her heart longed to be with Hamish and speak with him about the challenges before them. Did he see a way forward for them? Was it what he wanted?

When she finally left Glenna's room, a candle in hand, Ava's first glance was toward the door to the office. It was closed, though, and there was no trace of light underneath to give any hope that Hamish might still be awake.

How would they ever manage to find the time to speak? Keeping her feet light on the old, wood floors, she turned the corner to the stairs and nearly cried out at the sudden view of a dark figure sitting on the stairs.

"Shh," Hamish said, rising and putting a finger to his lips. "I didna mean ta frighten ye," he whispered.

Her heart thumped against her chest, but she smiled in spite of it. He *had* stayed up waiting for her.

"Tired?" he asked in the same whisper.

"Nay," she said, though her body chided her for the untruth. It would have been glad for more rest, but her mind and heart were forces to be reckoned with, and they would not sleep soundly until she'd had some time with Hamish.

He took her hand in his and led her through the office and into his quarters. Ava pushed away the memory of the accusatory gaze of Mrs. Shaw as Hamish closed the door behind them.

He turned toward her and, as though he had been waiting to do it all day, swept her into his arms and a warm embrace. She yielded to it gladly, letting the fears and worries that had been building all day while they had been apart give way to the familiar sense of peace she felt whenever she was with him. It was strange to feel such calm when everything about her life was still in turmoil.

When they pulled away, Hamish led her to the couch and spread the plaid over their legs. He took her hands in his once he'd sat down beside her.

"Long day?" he asked.

"The longest." It wasn't that it had been much busier than the days before, but the anticipation of speaking with Hamish and the muddle of thoughts occupying Ava's mind had drawn out the minutes and hours, making every task feel like an annoyance.

Hamish was looking at her, concern in his eyes, but he dropped his gaze and played with her fingers for a moment. "I've been thinkin', lass."

"Never a good idea," she said, and he smiled at her. She needed that smile. She had been missing it all day. "What have ye been thinkin'?"

He looked somewhat reluctant to speak, and Ava knew a sudden worry in her heart.

"What if ye spoke with yer father? Tried ta help him understand?" He held her gaze.

Her brows drew together. "Understand what?"

He shrugged lightly. "Why ye've been hidin' here."

She searched his face. "He kens why I've been hidin' here, Hamish." She frowned more deeply still. "Do ye think I didna try that already? Talkin' ta him?"

"Nay, I'm certain ye did, but . . . perhaps things have changed since then."

She shook her head. "I heard him when he came here, Hamish. He told ye I'm a fugitive—that I'm in breach of promise ta Angus. He's no' changed. He's still usin' threats ta have his way."

He held her hand more firmly. "But ye werena there ta hear or see him when we sat in the coffee room together. I saw it in his eyes, lass. Yer absense pains him. He worries for ye. Perhaps he's merely doin' whatever he can ta get ye back so he kens ye're safe."

Her nostrils flared slightly. "My absence pains him because it keeps him from gettin' what he wants. And if he worries for me so much, I wonder he tried ta marry me ta Angus MacKinnon—a man with a reputation for abductin' women and attempted murder." Her jaw tightened. "Nay. He only worries for himself anymore."

There was a small silence, but she could see Hamish's thoughtful expression—the little *v* in his brow, the tinkering with her fingers, the frown to his lips. "Is it no' worth a try?" He looked up at her.

"Nay, Hamish. The last time I saw my father, he threatened ta drag me ta the kirk. I'll no' give him the chance."

"I could go with ye ta see him," Hamish said, scooting closer to her. "I'd never let anythin' happen ta ye, lass."

She opened her mouth only to close it again. The entire conversation was perplexing to her. "Why are ye pressin' this?"

His lips drew into a thin line, and he seemed to struggle with how to say what he was thinking. "Ye've said yer father wishes for yer marriage ta Angus because of how 'twill benefit him."

Ava nodded, waiting for him to continue, to explain this sudden idea, which he seemed loath to let go of.

"He'll no' abandon such a plan easily, but"—he shifted again so that he was facing her more directly, one of his knees resting on the edge of the couch—"if the two of ye mended things, perhaps he'd be more willin' ta entertain the idea of givin' me the chance ta reclaim Dalmore House. I wouldna blame him for refusin' my request ta marry ye when I have nothin' ta offer, but if I had Dalmore House . . . ."

Ava was silent, her muscles suddenly stiff. He wanted her to make peace with her father so he could take back Dalmore House. The knowledge made a weight settle in her stomach. How much of his desire to be with her stemmed from such an aim?

"What is it?" Hamish asked.

She gently pulled her hand from his grasp and shook her head. "Nothin'."

"Lass." His gaze was on his hand, now empty. "I've upset ye."

"Nay. I'm tired. That's all."

He nodded slowly, though his eyes watched her with careful concern. "Get some sleep, lass. We can talk more tomorrow."

She gave a stiff nod and rose, displacing the plaid from their legs. He rose with her, taking her hand up again. She allowed it, but her stomach and heart weighed her down with uneasiness. Had she truly escaped her father's machinations only to find herself being used by another man for his own goals? Did he expect her to grovel before her father? She had done nothing wrong.

Perhaps she was being overly sensitive—too suspicious. She needed time to think, for it was true—she *was* tired.

"Good night," she said, and she turned toward the door before Hamish could try to kiss her. The last thing she needed was a mind and heart more clouded than they already were.

She left his quarters and made her way through the dark, up both sets of stairs, and into her room. Her stomach was a tight knot of emotion, her heart consumed with confusion and loneliness as she climbed under her blanket and stared up at the ceiling.

Hamish's words had been unreasonably hurtful to her. Of course he had not given up his dream of taking back the home of his childhood and his ancestors. And why should that fact bother her? She had been feeling guilty ever since discovering she had inadvertently become an obstacle to his goal, had she not? She had wished she could find a way to help him achieve what he wanted, so, why did it pain her to hear him ask her to do just such a thing? Was it so wrong for him to wish for something from her in return after all he had done for her?

She wished she could see into his mind and heart to decipher everything—to rid herself of the terrible suspicion that she was being used again as a pawn. But no matter how well she felt she knew Hamish Campbell, she hadn't known him long at all. Could she truly trust him? Things between them had shifted so suddenly and unexpectedly—she'd barely had time to search her heart and understand what it wanted.

A future with Hamish was full of unknowns. Dermot, on the other hand, was reliable and familiar. She had known him most of her life.

And yet, her heart longed for Hamish.

23

Hamish slept ill. He had been too impatient to see Ava, too anxious to hold her again to wait until morning, so he had stayed up, knowing she was occupied in teaching Glenna her letters. Every spare moment of the day, his mind had been taken up with the problem staring him in the face: how to keep his hold on the sudden and blessedly welcome change in his relationship with Ava. It seemed too good to be true—a dream—and he foresaw a multitude of ways it might disintegrate before his very eyes.

When Ava had finally left Glenna's room and come with him into his quarters, her response to his embraces had lacked something, and he had worried that perhaps she had seen the same obstacles to a future together. But his suggestion—the only path forward he had been able to see—only seemed to push her farther away. Her reaction had struck within him a cold, gripping fear: he was going to lose her.

After a night of restless sleep, he woke early and threw himself into work he had been putting off in the stables. For weeks now, he had been delaying it, finding excuses to avoid it so he could spend his time in the inn where he was more likely to see Ava. Today, though, he could use the distraction and distance. He would not pressure her again. He couldn't bear to see what would happen if he did and to wonder if his mishandling of things was what had pushed her away. He would give her time to make her own decision.

Together, he and Mark cleared away the years of discarded supplies—broken bridles, bent horse shoes, rotted wood, rusty nails—that sat in a pile behind the stables, taking breaks only to see to arriving travelers and guests. Mark was not gregarious, and Hamish wasn't sure whether to be glad for it or lament it. The working silence gave his mind plenty of time to conjure up arguments Ava might find against pursuing any sort of future with him. Dermot McCurdy was foremost among those arguments. He was a looming threat—a name without a face; a man who, unlike Hamish, possessed an estate to take Ava home to; a presence in Ava's life far longer than Hamish had been.

But Dermot was only one of many reasons Ava might be thinking better of things, and Hamish could have easily written a long list for her perusal after his hours in the stables.

He pushed up his sleeves and wiped at his forehead with his arm. He had long since shed his neckcloth. It was only the middle of March, but the weather was milder than any of the ones in recent memory, enough so that he had become warm early on in the day. His clothes and skin were generously sprinkled with dirt and bits of rust, and his queue had, as it so often did, come loose enough that a few strands tickled his neck and brushed at his cheek when he moved.

He glanced at the sky which, while sunny for a good part of the morning, had since turned gray and cloudy, promising rain. The weather here in the Highlands was changeable—the best and worst thing about it. A downpour might turn to glowing, columnar rays of sun in less than an hour, or, which seemed more likely, a morning of blue skies might turn to a fine, misty smirr and then a deluge that went on for days.

Ava was his morning of azure skies and warm sunshine, but there were threatening, dark clouds on the horizon.

The sound of an approaching wagon reached Hamish's ears. "I'll see ta it," he said to Mark, who nodded.

Hamish's stomach growled, and he licked his dry lips. He hadn't eaten since the somewhat stale bannock he'd taken from the kitchen as Dorcas had begun lighting the fire there, and he was parched.

The carriage he had heard emerged from the trees that lined the road, and Hamish's brows went up. There were plenty of carts and wagons that passed through Glengour, but a carriage always caused a stir, and this one was bound to do so, pulled as it was by two strong bays and in such good condition, despite the dust and dried mud that coated the bottom few inches of the body. The likes of it had perhaps never been seen in Kildonnan.

Hamish went to the horses' heads as the coachman stepped down from his seat and opened the door. He couldn't help but watch intently, curious who would be traveling in such an equipage on the road Glengour sat upon. Perhaps it was a visitor to Dunverlockie. Alistair Innes had been long-awaited by his sister, but it was unlikely he would stop at the inn rather than traveling the rest of the way to the castle. Besides, it would have surprised Hamish indeed to find Innes with enough money to afford such an equipage.

A man emerged—a gentleman, to all appearances—and set a cocked hat atop a well-groomed, brown wig. His eyes swept over the inn yard, landing upon Hamish. He was good-looking, with dark brows and the shadow of stubble on his jaw. His clothes, while inevitably wrinkled from the journey in the carriage, were of good quality and fine tailoring.

An unwelcome thought accosted Hamish.

"Good day," said the man, stepping down. His gaze again took in the inn, and while there was no outright disgust written upon his face, there was an obvious look of resignation that raised Hamish's hackles. If only the man could have seen the state of Glengour a few months ago.

"Ulrick," the man said, "help this man take the horses to the stables to be brushed down and given their hot bran mash."

Hamish raised a brow. "I'm afraid we dinna have hot bran mash, sir."

"Oh," said the man with a slight frown. "Very well, then. Just do your best, Ulrick. Sir"—he directed himself to Hamish —"where can I find the innkeeper, if you please?"

Hamish put out his hands, palms up to display himself. "Ye've found him, sir. I am the innkeeper."

The man's eyes flicked to Hamish's clothing, and Hamish wished he'd had the chance to clean up a bit before seeing to this particular guest.

"Oh, I see." The gentleman smiled politely and looked to his coachman, who seemed to be waiting for instruction.

"Mark will meet ye in the stables," Hamish said, and the coachman led the horses back.

Hamish knew an impulse to straighten his clothing and unroll his sleeves, but he fought it. "Ye'll have ta excuse me— I've been workin' in the stables all day. But I hope ye'll allow me ta welcome ye ta Glengour Inn, Mister ... "

"McCurdy," the man replied cordially. "Dermot McCurdy."

Hamish ignored the constricting feeling in his chest. His suspicion had been correct. *This* was the man Ava had been waiting for—this fine gentleman whose horses and carriage gave a fair picture of just what he could offer as a husband.

"Hamish Campbell," Hamish said, "at yer service."

"Thank you. Pleased to make your acquaintance. I am looking for someone here." His eyes went to the door of the inn. "MacMorran is the last name."

Hamish glanced around to ensure there was no one within

earshot. "Perhaps 'twould be better if we discussed things inside. I've an office we can speak privately in."

"Yes, perhaps that *would* be for the best."

Hamish led the way to the inn, but his thoughts and feelings were a whirl. Something very much like humiliation was sweeping over him. All the arguments he had constructed against himself all day seemed confirmed with Dermot's arrival. How had he ever thought he merited a chance with Ava MacMorran when the man behind him was the alternative?

For the last three weeks, Hamish had worked beside her, and it had been so easy to forget that they came from different worlds. Had things been different, had Hamish's father not been apprehended and Dalmore House taken by the Crown, perhaps they would have met, not in an inn like Glengour, but at a dinner or a *ceilidh*. They might have danced and laughed together, and Hamish would have asked Sir Andrew for permission to pay his addresses to Ava with the knowledge that he did so as an equal.

But he was an innkeeper, covered in dirt and the smell of horse manure, with nothing to offer Ava but a position as a servant in an inn and the money he had managed to acquire through smuggling.

He invited Dermot into his office and offered him a seat.

"Would ye like a dram? Or somethin' ta eat perhaps?"

Dermot seemed to debate for a moment. "No, thank you. I would rather see to my business first."

Business. Was that how he saw his purpose here? Was Ava business?

"Is Av—is Miss MacMorran here, then?" Dermot asked.

"Aye, sir, she is. Though, it'll be best if ye dinna call her that. No doubt ye ken she's tryin' ta hide her presence here."

"Yes, of course. I will take the utmost care. Perhaps you could direct me to her room—and provide me with one near it."

Hamish opened his mouth then clamped it shut. Was Dermot not aware . . . ?

He seemed to note Hamish's hesitation. "Just for the night. We will be on our way tomorrow. You *do* have a room available, I hope?" His eyes darted around the office, apparently taking stock again of his surroundings.

"Aye, sir. We've a room for ye, but it willna be next ta Av— Miss MacMorran's."

He gave a nod. "I will make do with whatever you have. Perhaps you can take my things to the room you speak of and show me to hers." He began to rise.

Hamish cleared his throat. "Ye'll no' find her in her room, Mr. McCurdy."

"Oh," he said, halting his progress to stand. "Where *will* I find her?"

Hamish hesitated. "In the laundry, I reckon."

Dermot's brows flew up, and his wig moved with them.

"Or perhaps the kitchen."

"The kitchen?"

It was wrong of Hamish to take pleasure in shocking the gentleman, but he couldn't help himself. Dermot McCurdy was amiable enough, but his confidence and subtle condescension irked Hamish. Had Hamish not identified himself as the innkeeper, Dermot would likely never have paid him any heed at all.

It was strange, that. This was the man whose arrival Ava had been awaiting and Hamish dreading for nearly two weeks. But Dermot had no care for Hamish other than to acquire information from him regarding Ava's whereabouts. Hamish was a means to an end, nothing more. What would Dermot think if he knew all that had passed between Ava and Hamish since her arrival there? It would shock him far more than the discovery that he might find her in the kitchen.

"Will you take me to her, wherever she is? I should like to ensure she is well."

"She *is* well." Hamish couldn't help himself. Dermot clearly intended to take on the role of protector to Ava, undoubtedly to save her from the squalor he saw her to be living in, but she needed no protecting. "I've done my best ta see ta that since her arrival."

For the first time, Dermot seemed to look at Hamish as though to truly take stock of him. "Allow me to thank you for your care of her, Mr. . . . Campbell, was it? But I should like to see for myself. I have known her some fifteen years now. I will know if she is well or not."

Hamish's jaw clenched, but he gave a deferential bow of the head. Dermot's words smarted because they were true.

"Right this way, then, Mr. McCurdy."

24

Ava poured the water from the bucket into the washbasin in the laundry room. Her arms ached just looking at the washboard. She had been scrubbing and wringing out sheets for the better part of the day, with respites every now and then to fetch more water from the well or help Dorcas in the kitchen.

While the task kept her hands busy, her mind had been free to roam—and her heart to wish for Hamish's company. She had not seen him all day. He had gone to the stables before the sun had risen and had not come inside except to show travelers to their seats in the coffee room. He had not even come to the kitchen for his regular bowl of porridge.

At first, Ava had been relieved. She was still so unsure what to think of their conversation from last night—unready to confront him when her heart longed to give him what he wanted even as her pride recoiled at the thought. Would he want her without the path he assumed she would provide to Dalmore House?

By midday, she was fairly certain he was avoiding her, and the thought made her heart twinge. Had her hesitation to talk to her father made him realize that he did not, in fact, wish for a future with her? That she was too selfish to do just this one thing for him, after all he had risked for her? She could hardly blame him if that was the case.

She swallowed and sat down, taking the next dirty sheet in hand and setting it in the fresh water. The water crept up the fabric, slowly soaking the dry areas until she pushed it down to immerse it entirely.

Footsteps approached from the direction of the cellar, and she looked up to see the door open and Hamish appear there.

Her heart skipped and stuttered, and she turned her body so that it faced him. "Hamish."

His gaze only rested on her for a moment, but what she saw there unsettled her—the somberness. "Ye've a visitor, Miss MacMorran."

Ava's eyes widened, and she was vaguely aware of the way his form of address confirmed her fears, putting distance between them. She was *lass* no more.

But there was a more pressing problem—the visitor. Had he brought her father? Did he expect her to speak with him now, as he had suggested last night?

Hamish held her gaze for a moment then stepped out of the way, and Dermot appeared in the doorway, cocked hat in hand, gaze intent on Ava.

Her jaw dropped open. "Dermot." She rose and pulled her hands from the water.

"Ava." He walked over to her and wrapped her in an embrace.

Still blinking with surprise, she submitted to it, not knowing what else to do. Her eyes went to Hamish, who gave her a curt nod and turned away.

She watched his figure disappear, hardly aware that Dermot still held her.

"I have been so worried for you." He pulled back, putting

his hands at her elbows and looking over her evaluatively, then at the basin of water where the sheet floated.

"What are you doing in here?" His tone was one of incredulity, and he spoke as he had written. His Scots had been shed for a more refined accent—perhaps one to match his clothing. Neither thing was meant for a place like Glengour.

She lifted her shoulders and wiped her wet hands on her apron, resisting the urge to speak as he did—to match his refined manners. She wouldn't pretend to be other than she was. If Scots had been good enough for her mother, it was good enough for her. "Laundry."

"Yes, I can see that." He smiled, though his brows were bent in a bemused frown. "But... why?"

She stared at him, uncomprehending. "'Tis part of my duties. I work here, Dermot."

He blinked.

"I had ta find a way ta support meself until ye came." She felt a flash of annoyance at him. What *had* taken him so long? His arrival had come at the most inconvenient of times.

"Well," he said, "you work here no longer. I thought to stay the night, but"—his mouth frowned as he looked about the small, cramped room—"I think it best if we leave as soon as we can. Ulrick will have to have my horses sent on home when they've had a chance to rest. I hope the inn has two of their own on hand we can take. Where is the nearest kirk? Perhaps we can persuade the minister to see to things right away."

"The kirk?" Ava couldn't keep pace with the rapid changes she was being confronted with.

"Yes. We cannot journey to Glasgow until we are married— things must be done properly, of course—or as properly as they can be, given the situation."

Ava's heart thudded. This was what she had wanted, wasn't it? This had been the option she preferred—marrying Dermot.

Why, then, was she feeling swept up on a wave taking her to a destination she didn't wish to go to?

"Ye only just arrived, Dermot," she said evasively. "And I have work ta finish."

His mouth drew into a thin line as his eyes went to the sheets hung on the drying lines. "It pains me—and I know your father would agree—to see you debase yourself with this work."

"Debase meself?" She gave an incredulous laugh. "Ye think I'd never done the wash afore comin' here? Ye ken better than that, Dermot, for all yer fine clothes." She sat down in her seat again and set to grinding the sheet along the ridges of the washboard.

He stepped beside her, setting a hand on hers to stop it. "Yes, but that was *before*, Ava. You are the daughter of Sir Andrew MacMorran now. Things have changed—for both of us."

She stared at his hand on hers, her jaw working. "And what if I prefer how things used ta be?" She looked up.

His expression told her that he understood what she was saying not at all.

"I canna leave right away, Dermot," she finally said. "Ye must be tired from the journey. Ye should go have somethin' ta eat and drink. We can talk once ye've settled in."

He let out an exasperated breath and let her hand go. "I did not come here to *settle in*, Ava. I came to find you and take you with me—as you asked me to do. Where is the urgency now that you conveyed in your letter?" The irritation in his voice surprised her. He had never used to be sharp with her.

She turned the wet sheet over and rubbed it against the ridges harshly. "Perhaps ye'll find it hidden away with yer *own* urgency—or lack thereof."

She saw him rear back slightly out of the corner of her eye. "What do you mean?"

She stopped and looked at him again. "I wrote ye when I first arrived, Dermot. 'Twas nearly three weeks ago. I began ta think ye might no' come." She shrugged. "I work here, Dermot, like it or no'. And I canna simply leave the obligations I've taken on."

He frowned. "You might have said something of that in your letter, then. It did not come at a particularly convenient time for me, either, Ava." He was not the type of man to show anger easily, but the resentment in his voice was evident, and it struck a chord of guilt in Ava. He had traveled for days to come to her, evidently ready to marry her without delay. His exasperation at her reluctance to leave was entirely warranted.

And yet, her reluctance remained.

"I've inconvenienced ye a great deal." She rose to a stand again and dried her hands on her damp apron. "I ken that, and I'm sorry for it. Ye were the only one I could think ta call upon."

His eyes held hers, troubled but understanding. He shook his head and took one of her hands in his. "No. You are right. I was delayed in coming by"—he grimaced, and there was something in his eyes Ava couldn't pinpoint—"some matters that needed attending to. But surely you did not doubt I *would* come?" His jaw grew firm, and his chin lifted. "I promised you I would come for you if ever you called, and I should not complain that you, too, have things to take care of before you can leave." He gave her a tight-lipped smile. "I *am* tired from the journey—and hungry. I will go see that the horses have been properly taken care of and then rest for a while. Then we can decide what to do."

She nodded, though a movement caught her eye behind him. Hamish was in the doorway again, and his gaze flicked down to the hand of Ava's which Dermot held.

His face was impassive as he said. "Yer belongin's are in yer room, Mr. McCurdy. I can show ye there whenever ye're ready."

"Thank you, Mr. Campbell." Dermot let Ava's hand drop

and turned to Hamish. "I must speak with Ulrick, but I would be grateful if you would show me to my room once I've returned." He turned back toward Ava, whose eyes shifted between both men, feeling as torn about whom she should focus her attention on as her mind was about the two paths before her.

"Perhaps once you've finished with this, you can join me for some food and drink in the coffee room?" He turned his head to Hamish. "If Mr. Campbell agrees to it, of course."

"I've no objection," Hamish said in a voice void of emotion. Did he truly feel that way? Was he relieved to see Dermot had finally arrived—someone to free him of the burden he had taken on and any false hopes he might have raised in Ava's heart? Or was it pain behind the emotionless expression he wore?

"Perhaps we could sit down in the kitchen instead?" Ava said. "I've been stayin' away from the coffee room, ye ken. Dinna wish ta be recognized."

Dermot frowned a bit. "But now that I am here, surely you need not worry about that."

Ava's gaze flicked to Hamish. Dermot seemed not to understand the situation. It was little wonder. Her note to him had been brief, of necessity.

"If ye prefer ta sit in the coffee room," she said, "ye dinna need ta worry about doin' so without me. I have work enough ta occupy me for some time." She couldn't keep her eyes from Hamish, desperate to understand what he was thinking and feeling. He met her gaze for a moment, but his expression was still inscrutable.

Dermot's eyes seemed to follow the unspoken interaction, and they lingered on Hamish for a moment before returning to Ava. "No, no. I will be glad to sit down with you in the kitchen, of course, if you prefer it."

"I do," she said. "I'll do my best ta finish this quickly"—she nodded at the wash—"and will meet ye in the kitchen afterward."

"Settled, then." Dermot smiled at her then disappeared.

Hamish lingered for a moment then gave Ava a quick nod and turned to leave.

"Hamish," she said, unable to stop herself. But as he turned back toward her, she found herself at a loss for what to say. "I . . . ."

"He came," Hamish said, and the stale bit of a smile he managed struck at her heart. "Just as ye said he would."

Ava swallowed. "Aye, but . . ." Why could she not find any words? None at all?

The muffled clopping of horse hooves sounded, and Hamish glanced behind him toward the front door. His gaze returned to Ava. "There's a guest ta see to."

Was he so eager to leave her? To avoid conversation? She couldn't very well blame him, for what had she said to him so far but stuttered nothings?

She nodded, and he disappeared.

Ava shut her eyes and dropped back onto the stool, covering her face with her hands. For weeks now, she had been waiting for the chance to leave Glengour, but now that the opportunity was before her, she couldn't bear the prospect. What was she to do?

25

Hamish had rarely felt so reluctant to leave his bed. Normally, the cold was what kept him the extra minutes under his blanket, but today, it was simple dread. The thought of another day in the company of Dermot was enough to make Hamish pull the covers over his head and try to seek peace in the oblivion of more sleep.

There wasn't anything particularly unlikable about the man. He seemed reasonable and concerned with Ava's safety, which Hamish could hardly fault him for. It was his apathy toward Hamish and his subtle disdain for Glengour that irked him. If Dermot had treated him with pointed insults borne of jealousy, it would have been less bothersome. The indifference, though, served to drive home Hamish's suspicions: he was so far below Ava that he didn't even register to Dermot as someone who might compete with him for her affection.

But there was no avoiding getting out of bed. Dermot and Ava would leave today, and Hamish could at least begin the work of forgetting her, forgetting that he had ever allowed himself to envision a future with her.

At least with her gone, he and the others would have plenty

of work to occupy their time. Little comfort *that* was.

When Hamish arrived to the kitchen after dressing and making a few notes in the inn's record books, he found Dorcas, Ava, and Dermot there and a pot of water already boiling over the fire. The three of them were speaking, but they turned at his entrance.

"What is it?" he asked, keeping his eyes on Dorcas.

"The spices," Dorcas said, holding up the satchel they had acquired from Craiglinne. "There's only a wee bit left. Enough for today, perhaps, but no' for tomorrow. I meant ta say somethin' yesterday, but it slipped my mind."

Hamish's gaze flicked to Ava.

"I have some," she said. "Enough left for three or four days, perhaps. 'Tis upstairs."

Hamish shook his head. "Nay. We'll no' take yers, lass. I'll go ta Craiglinne later today."

Dermot's expression was full of confusion. "Can the pies not be made without it? Surely they are not an essential ingredient."

"Here at Glengour they are," said Dorcas with an amused smile. "If there's one thing I've learned since I came here, 'tis that."

"I'll go with ye," Ava said.

Hamish's gaze flew to hers, searching. Why would she suggest such a thing? He didn't know, but the thought of driving to Craiglinne with her made his heart thump and little flickers of hope light his heart.

"What? In the wagon?" Dorcas said. "Ye'll be seen, miss."

Ava hesitated. "I'm the only one who kens the right mixture, though."

Hamish said nothing. She had written the amounts needed of each component of the mixture for Mark when he had gone to Craiglinne the first time, so her reasoning sounded to Hamish like a flimsy excuse to go with him. Not that he minded that. It added another spark to the hope trying desperately to find its hold.

"If you are determined to go, Ava," Dermot said, "I will take you. I know little of spices and such, but I can lend my carriage and my escort. You can tell me what to get, I imagine, and I can carry out the task with no one the wiser about your presence. Then, too, we need not deprive Glengour of two of you. Mr. Campbell, you are needed here most of all, I imagine."

He was right, of course, but Hamish could only manage a quick nod and a tight jaw.

Dermot turned to Ava, who smiled at him. "'Tis kind of ye, Dermot."

Hamish looked away from the exchange that made his chest feel as though it was gripped in some sort of vise. "Thank ye, Mr. McCurdy." He gave a quick nod and left the room.

He was outside, providing a passing traveler who was in too much of a hurry to come inside with a cup of ale, when Dermot's carriage rolled into the yard from the stables, ready to leave for Craiglinne. The coachman tipped his hat at Hamish, giving the reins a little toss. The two horses attached to the equipage belonged to the inn. Undoubtedly, Dermot was trying to save his own horses for the journey with Ava.

Hamish tried not to think of them sitting in the confines of the carriage together right now and what they might be doing there, but images of them holding hands—among other things —insisted upon pestering him until the sound of the carriage wheels had long since dissipated.

He threw his mind and body into his work, forcing himself to greet guests with a smiling face, accompany them to their seats, and spend time speaking with them. Anything to keep his mind from the other thoughts crowding in. After an hour of such activity, he found himself looking eagerly for any sign of Ava and Dermot's return, though it was still much too early to look for such a thing.

All he knew was he could no longer keep silent. He had to tell Ava how he truly felt, even if he faced rejection. At least he would know he had done all he could do.

Finally, in the late morning—and nearly three hours after their departure—a carriage came around the bend. Hamish kept his demeanor calm even though there wasn't a calm inch of his body as he stepped outside to go meet the equipage. His eyes narrowed at the sight of the horses, though. They were not the ones Mark had hitched to Dermot's carriage. And it was not Dermot's carriage, either. It was Sir Andrew's.

Mark appeared from behind Hamish, hurrying to the horses' heads and leaving Hamish to greet the unexpected— and unwelcome—visitor. Sir Andrew stepped down once the door had been opened by the driver, and behind him followed Angus MacKinnon and the sheriff, Mr. Brodie.

Hamish struggled to master his surprise and the dismay that followed. An errand that brought these three men to Glengour could be nothing but highly undesirable. Thank heaven Ava was not here.

"Mr. Campbell," said Sir Andrew with a smile that belied the threat of the company he kept.

"Good day, sir," Hamish said with a deferential nod. "Mr. MacKinnon. Mr. Brodie."

Unlike Sir Andrew, the other two men didn't make the effort to show anything but grave expressions as they greeted him. Mr. Brodie did offer a little grunt of acknowledgement.

"Can I get a table for ye?" Hamish asked as Mark led the horses away. "Some food and drink?"

"I was hoping to speak with you first," Sir Andrew said, "but I imagine Angus and Mr. Brodie would appreciate that."

"Of course," Hamish said as he opened the door. "My office is just ta yer right. I'll be with ye in a moment, sir."

Hamish's mind and body were abuzz as he led Angus and the sheriff to their seats and poured both a dram. Glenna came out at the sound of their voices, and he saw her eyes widen with the same surprise he had felt. She covered it quickly, though, and, after a quick word with Hamish, returned to the kitchen to retrieve two plates of food.

As Hamish walked toward the office, he shut his eyes for a moment at the door and pulled in a deep breath, asking the powers that be for help navigating whatever was in front of him. As he took a seat across the desk from Sir Andrew, he noticed for the first time the paper clasped between the man's hands.

"How can I help ye, sir?" Hamish asked.

Sir Andrew shot him a polite smile. "The last time I was here, I was impressed with the refreshments you offer your guests. You mentioned that you acquire your whisky from the Shaws. Is that right?"

"Aye, sir." This was not at all the conversation he had expected to have.

Sir Andrew held his gaze. "I took the liberty of calling upon Mrs. Shaw the other day, hoping she might be willing to supply Glenlochan with the fine whisky she distills, as well."

Hamish couldn't find anything to say to this bit of information, so he merely waited, but Sir Andrew took his time, holding Hamish's gaze. The good-natured expression he had been wearing seemed to fade slowly.

"I know my daughter is here, Mr. Campbell."

Hamish's muscles tightened.

"Mrs. Shaw and her daughter were able to confirm it to me, so I beg you will not try to persuade me otherwise. I hope we can come to an agreement here without the involvement of the sheriff. I can overlook your dishonesty and perhaps even help you"—he thumbed the paper in his hand—"if you are willing to help me ensure my daughter is protected—and returned to me."

"With respect, sir," Hamish answered, keeping his gaze

228

away from the mysterious paper, "she came here *seekin'* protection, and we've done our best ta provide her with that. I think we've succeeded."

"And yet, she is *my* daughter. Her protection is my responsibility, Mr. Campbell. Not yours. The sheriff would agree with me, I am certain you will acknowledge."

Hamish was quiet for a moment. He had no doubt the sheriff would agree with Sir Andrew, but that meant little to Hamish. Having a legal responsibility for someone did not always equate with acting in their best interests.

"Ye're right," Hamish finally said. "She's no' my responsibility, Sir Andrew. And because of that, I have no power ta force her ta do anythin' against her will, includin' agreein' ta go with ye. Ye ken Ava well enough ta understand she's no' one ta be bullied."

"You have chosen to employ her here, Mr. Campbell. She remains an occupant of Glengour at your pleasure. You could easily change that."

Hamish frowned, searching Sir Andrew's face. "Why do ye need *my* help?"

Sir Andrew inclined his head in acknowledgment of the question's validity. "I could take her by force, of course. It is within my rights. But I prefer not to make a scene—and I imagine you are reluctant to do that, as well, given the number of guests in your coffee room in this moment. If you will agree to see that she is in the yard at a pre-appointed time, we can avoid any of that."

Hamish scrubbed a hand across his jaw. "Sir Andrew, I've developed a deep admiration for yer daughter while she's been here. Her happiness and well-bein' matter ta me—greatly." He felt an unexpected constriction in his throat and cleared it away. "I canna turn her away when she's asked for my help. I willna betray her in such a way."

Sir Andrew searched Hamish's face. "And what of Dalmore?

I come prepared to offer you a means of taking it back—of making it a Campbell estate once again." He unfolded the string on the papers he had been holding and set them down on the desk, turning them so they faced Hamish. "In exchange for your cooperation, I am willing to be a voice for you to the Committee and ensure the forgiveness of half of the debts connected to Dalmore House."

Hamish swallowed, and his eyes flicked to the paper. Half the debts. That was thousands of pounds. If he continued helping Fowlis, he might have enough to pay the remaining debts within the year.

And what would he be left with if he refused to help Sir Andrew? If Ava chose to leave with Dermot, as Hamish assumed she would, he would be left without her *and* without Dalmore House, for a refusal would anger Sir Andrew to the point that he might well go out of his way to see that Hamish could *not* reclaim Dalmore, no matter how much money he had to his name.

Ava no longer required Hamish's protection now that Dermot was here. It was for that very reason she was with him now.

But what would be the victory of winning back Dalmore House if Hamish complied with Sir Andrew's request? He might have a home, but he would have no one to share it with —*a pile of stones*, Ava had once said. His father would not be there. His mother would not be there. Ava would not be there. He would sleep, eat, and work there alone. And he would do it knowing he had betrayed the woman whose good opinion and well-being mattered more to him than anyone else's.

He shook his head and pushed the paper away. "Nay, sir. I canna agree ta what ye ask."

Sir Andrew held his gaze. "There has been discussion amongst the Committee of selling Dalmore House to the neighboring laird—MacPherson, as I imagine you remember. He hopes, I believe, to raze all the buildings on the property to make way for agricultural improvements that are of interest to the Crown."

Hamish clenched his teeth and hands. Dalmore House, while not the grandest of Highland estates, had been standing for two hundred years, and the Campbells had always taken care of their tenants and kin. He had little doubt the agricultural improvements Sir Andrew referred to would transform the farming property into pasture for sheep. It might bring in revenue for the Crown, but it would put the tenants out of work and force them into poverty, as such changes had already been doing to so many.

"I regret hearin' that," Hamish said, trying to keep his voice level. "But I still canna agree ta the terms ye've set out. I'd no' be worthy of Dalmore House or the Campbell name if I held my honor so cheaply."

Sir Andrew's jaw hardened. "I have attempted to be understanding and generous in this discussion and am disappointed in your choice. You understand, I imagine, that by harboring my daughter here against my will, you are in violation of the law? She is a fugitive, and you are enabling her—indeed, who is to say you are not holding her here against her will?"

Hamish's jaw tightened, and he thought of the sheriff sitting at the coffee table outside. "Ye can threaten me, Sir Andrew, but 'twill no' bring yer daughter back ta ye. 'Twill no' regain ye her trust. I've no doubt ye love her—that ye take yer responsibility for her seriously, but"—he frowned deeply—"do ye truly wish ta cede that responsibility ta Angus MacKinnon? Surely ye ken him well enough ta understand why Ava would leave her home and family and work at an inn rather than agree ta such an arrangement? Ye betrayed her trust, sir."

Sir Andrew sat back, staring at Hamish evaluatively, a hard light in his eye. "Do you propose yourself as an alternative to Angus?" He raised his brows. "Mrs. Shaw was kind enough to inform me of the relationship she has witnessed between you and Ava. Allow me to disabuse you of any notion you may have taken up regarding my daughter. She is meant for greater things than the Glengour innkeeper, Mr. Campbell."

The words struck Hamish in the heart. "I dinna pretend ta believe meself her equal, sir—I've come ta ken her too well ta think such a man exists—'tis certainly no' Angus MacKinnon. Perhaps I dinna have the influence Angus has, but I would care for yer daughter in a way that man never could. And if ye'd agree ta help me, I wouldna be the Glengour innkeeper but the laird of Dalmore, as I was meant ta be."

Sir Andrew shot up from his seat, setting a clenched fist on the desk. "You've harbored my daughter here against my will for weeks—an unchaperoned young woman living with a bachelor—forcing her to engage in work below her station, and you have the audacity to champion yourself as a candidate for her hand? You are fortunate I do not run you through for the suggestion. Ava will never marry an innkeeper. She will never marry a Jacobite." He spat the last word.

"I'm no Jacobite, sir," Hamish said, rising to a stand. "I'm loyal ta the king, and I spent the last decade of my life provin' it."

Sir Andrew let out an incredulous scoff. "You think no other Jacobite has served His Majesty's pleasure when it suited him to do so?"

Carriage wheels sounded outside the window, and Hamish glanced over to see the approach of Dermot's carriage through the undulating glass of the window pane.

"Your father sullied the Campbell name irreparably," continued Sir Andrew. "It will not be associated with the MacMorrans."

Hamish hardly heard his words. Unless Dermot and Ava went through the back entrance to the inn, they would soon be confronted with Sir Andrew, Angus, and the sheriff.

26

The carriage wheels rumbled and jostled over the uneven road that led into the inn yard. Ava's eyes instinctively searched for Hamish. It had been a long few hours in Dermot's company, and she couldn't help but compare the experience with the easy terms she and Hamish enjoyed when they were together.

Those terms had certainly not been present between Ava and Dermot today. Neither of them had been terribly inclined to talk. Ava hadn't been able to find the words to speak with Dermot about her feelings, her confusion—not after he had traveled so far and was so clearly expecting for them to be married—and quickly. She had expected him to bring up the matter, but he, too, had seemed disinclined to talk and had spent a great deal of the journey staring out of the carriage window.

At one point, he had asked her questions about Angus. Her description of Angus—her experience with him, her knowledge of his reputation—had been received with due horror by Dermot, but he had quickly fallen silent again after receiving the information.

How had the good terms that had always flourished between them given way to such silence and awkwardness? Was this how it would always be between them? Polite but stale? Ava hardly knew what to do with this fine man he had become, but it made her nervous. She knew how her father had changed as his wealth and connections had increased, after all.

Perhaps, inside Dermot was the same as he had ever been, but it was difficult to see past the appearance he presented now. None of the dirty-faced young boy who had gotten up to mischief with her in the streets of Glasgow. He was neat, tidy, and sophisticated now—far more than she was, especially in her sooty, smoke-saturated clothing.

While the future Dermot came expecting was ever on her mind, Ava hadn't been able to bring herself to start the conversation addressing it. What would she say? She didn't know the right thing to do, but she felt an obligation to Dermot now after all his trouble on her account.

Regardless, she couldn't continue to use her work at Glengour as an excuse to put off the future.

The coachman opened the door and helped Ava down, and she breathed a sigh of relief to be out of the uncomfortable and stifling carriage, well-sprung as it was. Dermot offered her his arm once he had stepped down, as well, and Ava set her jaw as she took it, managing a polite smile which was returned by him, every bit as civil as hers. Had her own behavior made him so stiff? Was he regretting coming?

Ava watched for Hamish to emerge from the inn as he always did with the arrival of guests, but she looked in vain. Perhaps he thought Ava and Dermot not worth greeting. Or perhaps he was angry. She couldn't blame him. She had done nothing but mislead him since arriving.

Dermot opened the front door for her, and they stepped inside.

"I should go see ta things in the kitchen," she said, holding the bag of spices in her hand. She glanced into the coffee room and went rigid.

Angus MacKinnon stared at her intently, as did the sheriff beside him. She grabbed Dermot's hand, and he looked a question at her.

"Angus," she said in a strangled whisper, never pulling her gaze from him as he stared at her from the table.

"Ava."

She pulled her gaze from Angus and looked at Dermot. He stared intently into her eyes, taking her hand between his for a moment, then setting it on his arm with a reassuring look.

The door to their right opened, and Ava glanced over to find herself facing her father and, behind him, Hamish.

Her eyes widened, as she looked between them, then to Angus. A choked feeling took hold of her. What was happening? Had Hamish betrayed her? She found it impossible to believe such a thing of him, but how else could she explain her father's sudden appearance following on the heels of Hamish's suggestion that she speak with him and then his distant behavior toward her?

"Ava," her father said, and his gaze rested on her for a moment. It moved on to Dermot, and his brows contracted slightly. "Dermot."

The sound of a chair scraping against the floor brought Ava's gaze around to Angus, who had risen and was walking toward them. His eyes settled on the way Ava's hand held Dermot's arm. Seeing him approach, she stiffened, and Dermot laid a hand over hers, pressing it lightly.

"Who is this?" Angus asked no one in particular as his gaze rested on Dermot, full of challenge and curiosity. "Whoever you are, be good enough to unhand my betrothed."

A chill ran along Ava's neck and arms. It was finally here— the thing she had been dreading and trying to escape since leaving home.

"I will not," Dermot said.

"Not willingly, perhaps," Angus said with a contemptuous lift to his lip, "but the sheriff will be more than glad to assist you if you require such a thing." He nodded at the sheriff, who took a purposeful step toward them.

Dermot pulled Ava away from the man. "Sir, you will not touch her."

"Dermot," said Ava's father in a stern voice. "I haven't the slightest idea what has brought you here, but you must let Ava go."

"I came here, sir, for one purpose only, and I have fulfilled it. Ava has just done me the honor of becoming my wife."

Every muscle in Ava's body constricted as a strange silence fell over the company. Her eyes darted to Hamish, who still stood behind her father, silent so far. His eyes, though, were intent, his mouth parted slightly as he looked between her and Dermot, hurt and betrayal written there, plain as day.

"What?" thundered Sir Andrew.

"You lie," snarled Angus.

"No, sir," Dermot replied. "I do not. The responsibility for Ava now falls to me. If you wish to discuss anything relating to her, I will gladly do so with you."

Hamish's throat bobbed, and he turned his frowning eyes away from Ava.

Her heart cried out, demanding she tell him that it was not true, that she and Dermot were not married. But she couldn't, for if she did, the sheriff would be free to take her—by force—and she had little doubt what would happen next. Her father was not here to apologize. He had brought Angus, after all.

Ava looked to her father, who was staring at her, eyes still full of surprise and betrayal. Now, at least, he understood what it felt like to be cruelly disappointed by someone he loved, just as he had disappointed her.

"You," Angus said, staring at Hamish. "This is your fault."

Ava whipped her head around to look at Hamish, whose brows snapped together as his head came up.

"My fault the two of them married? Or my fault that the mere thought of marryin' ye was enough ta send the lass runnin'?"

Angus's lips trembled in a snarl, and he took a menacing step toward Hamish. The sheriff and Dermot both shot out a hand to stop him.

Angus's face screwed up in frustration, but the emotion disappeared quickly, and he held his chin high. "Arrest this man, Sheriff."

The sheriff dropped his hand and looked a question at Angus. "The writ I have depends upon the lass bein' an unwed minor, sir. I canna take her now that she's married, and I certainly canna take *him*." He pointed to Dermot.

"Not him," Angus said with a dismissive glance at Dermot. "*Him*."

Ava followed the direction of his gaze and found him to be looking at Hamish. Her heart plummeted.

"Angus?" Ava's father said in questioning surprise.

The sheriff frowned, looking uncomfortable. "Arrest him for what, sir?"

"He has been involved in the purchase of illicit whisky and defrauding the Crown of revenue by way of the free trade. The Shaw women can testify of the first charge and multiple other witnesses of the second," Angus persisted.

"Aye," Ava said. "None of us struggles ta believe that! Why do ye no' arrest Mr. MacKinnon while ye're at it, Sheriff? For 'tis under his direction that the free tradin' happens. A quick search of Benleith would tell ye as much."

Angus's eyes settled on her, taking her in from head to toe with something between anger and indifference. "Mr. Campbell has also been involved in harboring a fugitive of the law."

Ava broke her arm free of Dermot's grasp, desperation

flooding her. She couldn't allow Hamish to be taken when the fault lay with her. "Me. *I'm* the fugitive. So, why do ye no' arrest me? Hamish didna ken who I was when I arrived. 'Tis my fault."

"Ava." Dermot reached for her hand again. "You are not a fugitive. You are my wife."

Angus sneered slightly at Dermot. "You might have had so much more, Ava."

Ava spat in Angus's face, and he doubled back, blinking in surprise as he put a hand up to wipe it away. His jaw clenched, his nostrils flared, and he raised a hand in the air as though he meant to slap Ava.

In a rush, Sir Andrew, Dermot, and Hamish all sprang to action, both Dermot and Sir Andrew reaching for Angus's wrist. There was a shuffling to Ava's right, and before she knew what was happening, there was a *thump*, and Angus was stumbling backward as Hamish clenched and unclenched a hand, his chest rising and falling.

"Get out of my inn," Hamish said, his voice hard and raspy.

Angus wiped his nose, and his fingers came away bloody. He looked to Dermot. "I wish you joy of the wench, whoever you are. You have quite a task before you with a wife like that." He looked to the sheriff. "What are you waiting for, Brodie? Arrest Mr. Campbell. You saw him assault me."

Ava's father took a step forward, his brow wrinkled in a frown. "Angus, really—"

"*Now*, Brodie," Angus said, ignoring her father.

Harried footsteps sounded, and Dorcas and Glenna emerged, both wide-eyed and confused.

The sheriff gave a nervous nod. "If ye'll excuse me, sir," he said to Ava's father, who moved out of the way. "He *did* strike Mr. MacKinnon."

"To spare my daughter the same fate," he replied hotly.

"Arrest him now, Brodie," Angus said.

The sheriff glanced at Sir Andrew briefly but followed orders.

Hamish stood tall and steadfast beside Dermot, his expression impassive as the sheriff took him by the arm.

Ava's heart beat wildly, and she broke free of Dermot's hold. "Ye canna arrest him! He hasna done anythin' wrong!" She went over, pulling the sheriff's hand from Hamish's arm.

She was grasped by both arms, her father on one side, Dermot on the other, and she tried in vain to pull herself free.

"Ava," her father said.

She ripped her arm from his grasp, her anger at hearing his pleading voice sparking a blaze of anger inside her. "Dinna touch me, ye tyrant! This is all yer fault!" She turned from her father, looking to Hamish.

He met her gaze, and the calm resignation there troubled her more than anything. "Let it be, lass." His voice was soft, and his eyes held hers for another moment before the sheriff yanked him toward the door.

Glenna and Dorcas peppered Ava with questions, but she hardly heard them. Hamish was going to gaol, and the punishment for the crimes Angus had accused him of was hanging.

27

Dermot must have informed Dorcas and Glenna of what had passed, for Ava certainly did not do so, and by the time she had gathered herself enough to be aware of what was happening, they had left, undoubtedly obliged to see to the guests—some of whom had witnessed the events from their place in the coffee room, others who had come down the stairs to see what the fuss was about.

Ava became aware of Dermot holding her hand, and the sensation made her churning stomach roil even more. It was not Dermot's hand she wished to be holding.

She turned to her father, and her body shook with anger. "How could ye?"

His brows snapped together. "How could *I*?"

"All ye did was stand there! Stand there and watch an innocent man be taken ta gaol."

"Innocent! He lied to me, kept my own daughter from me, employed you as a lowly maid, tarnished your reputation! He is anything but innocent."

"Come, Ava," Dermot said softly. "Let us not argue."

She ignored him. "'Tis only thanks ta Hamish that I'm alive

and well rather than stranded alone somewhere on the road ta Glasgow."

"Were it not for him and his meddling, you might be mistress of Benleith even now!"

It took a moment for Ava to reply to this, flooded as she was with anger. "Aye, that would be a welcome thing for ye, prideful as ye are. *I* would rather die. But since when did ye take any thought for what I wanted? Or for anyone but yerself, for that matter!"

Her father shook his head, turning his gaze from her, and his energy seemed to have fled, for his shoulders sank, and his voice was soft. "He should not have interfered."

Ava felt the tears beginning to come, and she brushed the first one away. "Ma would be ashamed of ye."

Her father's jaw tightened, and his lips drew into a crease. "*Do not speak of her.*"

Ava stared at him, challenge in her burning, blurry eyes. "'Tis yer conscience that makes it so hard ta hear what ye ken ta be the truth."

Her father took a few breaths then addressed himself to Dermot. "And now you go to Ardgour?"

"Aye," Ava said before Dermot could respond. "Far away from here. Far away from *you.*" She couldn't help herself. The knowledge that her father had brought the sheriff here, meaning to take her by force and marry her to Angus—it tore at her confused and tender heart.

"Come, Dermot," she said, pulling him away and toward the front door.

He gave an awkward nod to her father and allowed himself to be pulled outside. She led him toward the back of the inn where she could be certain she would not have to see her father again. Her cheeks were hot, but the cool air outside chilled the tears sliding down.

"Ava," Dermot said as she pulled him along behind her.

"Ava." He stopped once they were out of view of the stables, and Ava let out a gush of aggravated breath through her nose before turning around and facing him.

His eyes raked over her face, dwelling for a moment on the tears. "What is happening?"

She didn't respond. She hardly knew what had happened over the past twenty-four hours. It was too much for her to think through clearly. Just three days ago, she had been imagining a future with Hamish. Now, he was being taken to gaol while she was staring at the man who had convinced everyone that they were married. *Married.*

He stepped toward her. "I understand you are upset. But all will be well."

"How can ye say that, Dermot? How will it all be well?"

He lifted his shoulders. "Your father will come around to things with time, of course. He loves you too much not to."

"I dinna care about my father." She said the words, but the pain that they caused inside her belied them. Why did her heart insist on caring for a man who cared for her happiness so little?

Dermot stared at her, visibly confused. "Then, what is it?"

Another tear slipped over her eyelashes and onto her cheek. "They've taken Hamish, Dermot. Taken him ta gaol."

"For smuggling, was it?"

She folded her arms and looked to the side, shaking her head. Dermot had no idea what he was talking about. How could he? He had only just arrived—landed in the middle of a complex situation.

"Well?" Dermot said. "*Was* he smuggling?"

"Aye," she looked at him again. "And so was I. Just as everyone here does when given the chance—includin' yer own family. The sheriff himself turns a blind eye—until today." Her nostrils flared. "The free tradin' was only an excuse. Hamish is

bein' taken ta gaol ta be taught a lesson—a lesson about inter-
ferin' with those with more power and money. People like my
father and Angus MacKinnon."

Ava squeezed her eyes shut as she thought of him going to
trial. She couldn't help remembering the outcome of the last
trial Angus had been involved in. It had ended in his favor,
despite a great deal of evidence to the contrary. He had the
influence to guide things the way he wanted them to be.

"Ava," Dermot said. "Is there . . ." He shifted his weight and
looked at her fixedly. "Is there something between you and Mr.
Campbell?"

She held his gaze, not responding immediately. If she told
him the truth, what would happen? Hamish was in gaol and
her feelings for him not completely sorted out. What if the
truth sent Dermot running? Where would she be then?

But she couldn't lie any longer. She hadn't the energy for it.

She swallowed. "Aye. At least . . . there *was*. I dinna ken what
he feels now. I hardly ken what *I* feel now."

Dermot's jaw hung slightly open, and he blinked at her a
few times before speaking. "Then *why* did you ask me to come,
Ava? I do not understand. None of it makes any sense."

"I ken, Dermot. And I'm sorry. I turned ta ye because ye
were the only one I *could* turn to. I didna ken Hamish then."

He rubbed a hand across his forehead and blew a breath
through his lips. "Why did you not tell me as much when I
arrived?"

She took her lips between her teeth gave an apologetic
shrug. "Everythin' happened so fast. I began ta think ye
wouldna come at all, and when ye *did* and ye spoke so quickly
of gettin' married, I didna feel I could tell ye that ye'd come for
naught. Besides, I never thought marryin' Hamish was an
option. 'Tis complicated betwixt us."

Supporting his elbow with one hand, he covered his mouth

with the other, staring at Ava with continued bafflement written across his features. Her stomach writhed with guilt.

"So, you do *not* wish to be married?"

She bit her lip. What *did* she want? She looked into Dermot's eyes. Dermot—her longtime friend, the only person she had ever considered marrying. But that had been before she had met Hamish. And, much as she cared for Dermot and was grateful for what he had done for her, she did not wish to marry him.

"Dermot," she said, "ye came when I called, and ye protected me. I'm grateful for that. Truly, I am. But"—she struggled to find the word—"I dinna wish ta be married ta ye. I love Hamish, and I dinna ken if he wants me still, but I—" She reared back slightly, taken off guard by the chuckle that came from Dermot's lips. She knew not what to make of the strange reaction. "I am truly sorry, Dermot."

He let his head drop back, but there was still a smile on his lips. "Oh, Ava. What a muddle we have made of things."

Ava said nothing, merely watching him with wariness. His eyes were closed and his head still back. It was well, for she couldn't bear to meet his gaze. She wrapped her arms around herself more tightly and stared at the dirt on the ground, where a few blades of grass were attempting to push through the dirt.

Dermot let out a vocal sigh as he brought his head back down. "I have managed to convince everyone that we are married when neither of us *wishes* to be married."

Ava's head snapped up, and she stared at him. "Ye . . . ye dinna wish ta be married, either?"

His forehead wrinkled in a frown, and apology shone from his eyes as he shook his head. "At least, not to you—much as I care for you, Ava, which I do, or else I would not be here. You must know that. But . . . well, I was on the verge of becoming engaged myself when I received your letter."

Ava could find no words to respond. All she could do was stare.

"I had quite a time of it deciding what to do, but"—he took a step toward her and set a hand on her shoulder—"I could never leave you in trouble. Not after all you have been through, and not after . . . ."

"No' after ye told me ye'd marry me when ye next saw me?" She laughed, feeling suddenly light.

He nodded and then smiled—for the first time since he had arrived, it seemed. *This* was why he had seemed so different to her, why he had been so stiff on the way to Craiglinne. It was love in a battle with duty. He had been on the verge of sacrificing his own future for her.

She pulled him into her arms, holding him tightly. "Thank ye, Dermot. Thank ye for bein' so loyal and true. And thank ye for no' wishin' ta marry me."

He laughed and hugged her back.

When she let go and stepped back, he looked at her with a commiserating grimace. "Now what is to be done?"

Her smile faded somewhat. It was a question she had no answer to. "I have ta find a way ta help Hamish."

He nodded.

"And *you* must go marry yer . . . "

"Fiona," he said, and even the name on his lips sounded like a prayer. "But of course I will stay until everything is arranged."

She sent him a grateful smile. She sincerely hoped that everything *could* be arranged. If it was possible, Glenna would know the best way forward.

Ava sought her out immediately, anxious to act. Glenna was eager to be of help in whatever way she could, and her first suggestion was to apply to Lachlan Kincaid for help.

"I sent Mark with a message ta Dunverlockie when I discovered what had happened, so he'll already be thinkin' what can be done," Glenna said as she poured a dram for one of the guests. "He and Hamish served together in the army. 'Twas he who gave the position of innkeeper ta Hamish. He hasna been laird of Dunverlockie for long, but admiration for him has increased rapidly since he arrived. He'll have more power than anyone else who's concerned for Hamish's well-being."

Ava sincerely hoped that power would be sufficient to counter that of Angus and her father, but she had her doubts.

Dermot agreed to go with her to Dunverlockie Castle, and they left as soon as could be managed. The air in the carriage was in stark contrast to their earlier journey that day. It was anxious yet simultaneously more relaxed now that the weight of a future neither of them wanted hung over their heads. Ava asked Dermot to tell her of Fiona in an effort to distract her and pass the time more quickly. As he attempted to describe what he felt for Fiona, his polished speech gave way to stumbling frustration.

Ava reached a hand across and took his. "I ken just what ye mean, Dermot." Her throat constricted. Dermot would return to his Fiona; he would feel all those things again. But Ava . . . .

Upon their arrival at Dunverlockie, they were welcomed in by a servant, who left them in the entry hall as she went to discover whether her master was at home to visitors.

Ava had never been inside Dunverlockie, and she looked around her with a distracted interest as they waited for the servant to return. It wouldn't be long before night fell, and she felt an urgency about rescuing Hamish from gaol. He shouldn't have to spend a night in such a wretched place. He deserved to be rewarded, not punished, for his protection of her.

"Mr. Kincaid must think it an impertinence to be called upon by two people he does not know," Dermot said.

Ava couldn't care less about appearing impertinent. "I dinna think it. He'll ken me by name and by sight, even if we havna been properly introduced. Besides, he doesna seem the type ta set much store by such things."

The servant returned and invited them to follow her to the drawing room. Ava's eyes darted around the large, high-windowed room, but there was no sign of Lachlan, only his wife, Christina, who held a baby in her arms.

She rose at their entrance, graceful despite the small load she carried. "Miss MacMorran," she said with a smile and a small curtsy. "And, was it Mr. McCurdy?"

Dermot nodded and executed a bow—showcasing the refinement he had gained since Ava had last seen him. No doubt Fiona was his equal there.

"I regret that my husband is not home at the moment," Mrs. Kincaid said, inviting them to take a seat.

Ava sat on the edge of the couch, fingers fiddling in her lap. While she was curious to know Mrs. Kincaid better—this was the woman who had been abducted by Angus and his men, after all—today was not the day she would have chosen for a social call.

"Forgive us for callin' on ye uninvited," Ava said. "Glenna Douglas suggested I speak with yer husband about an urgent matter at the inn. Do ye ken when he'll return?"

Mrs. Kincaid's shrewd eyes searched Ava's. "Is this about Hamish?"

Ava nodded.

Mrs. Kincaid's mouth pulled into a lamenting grimace. "My husband has gone to see him in the Craiglinne gaol. Mark brought a message earlier, and Lachlan did not feel he could delay." The baby in her arms fussed a bit, and she raised it so that its head rested on her shoulder. The baby had a head of dark hair, and her head wobbled slightly as she tried to look around the room with wide, blinking eyes.

Mrs. Kincaid stabilized the baby's neck with a gentle hand. "I can have him call upon you at the inn when he returns—in fact, I would not be surprised if he stopped there on the return journey. I am certain he wishes to ensure all is well."

Ava nodded quickly. "'Twould be appreciated, ma'am. I dinna wish ta take him from ye when he's needed, but—"

Mrs. Kincaid waved a hand. "No, no. Hamish is a brother to Lachlan. My husband is anxious to see things arranged."

He could hardly be more anxious than Ava, and Ava sincerely hoped he had an idea of how to make it happen.

28

The Craiglinne gaol was a small building with only a few cells—each too short to stand up straight in, as though defying its disgraced occupants to stand erect. Hamish rubbed his eyes and shifted his weight, letting one leg stretch out on the floor while he bent the other and let his elbow rest upon it.

The other man in the cell—a thief, as Hamish understood it —snored softly, stretched out along the dirty stone floor and using his arm as a pillow. Hamish was not looking forward to sleep, but consciousness was hardly better.

He looked up at the only point of natural light in the cell—a small square window up near the ceiling, overlaid with thick iron bars that blocked most of the light being let in. That light was quickly dissipating as day turned to evening, but the torches had not yet been lit, leaving the cell particularly dim.

A rhythmic clanging sounded, accompanied by shuffling footsteps, and the guard soon appeared, holding a lantern. Hamish paid him no mind until he stopped in front of the cell and another dark figure emerged from the corridor behind him.

"There," said the warden, pointing to Hamish. He turned

toward the figure, and the light from his candle illuminated the face of Lachlan Kincaid.

Hamish scrambled up to his feet as the guard shuffled away, leaving them in dim gloom once again.

"Lachlan," Hamish said, stepping toward the bars and wrapping a hand around one.

Lachlan's brow was drawn into a frown, and his dark eyes swept over the cell before coming to rest upon Hamish. He put a hand on Hamish's and let out a breath through his nose. "I came as soon as I heard."

"Who . . . ?"

"Glenna sent Mark ta the castle with word that you had been taken."

Hamish nodded.

"What happened, Hamish?"

Hamish turned his face away and shrugged a shoulder. How could he explain what had transpired over the past few weeks? "I ran afowl of Angus and Sir Andrew."

"But how?"

Hamish tapped a finger on the bar. He could be honest with Lachlan. He knew that. But it didn't change his embarrassment. "Do ye remember the cook I hired?"

"Aye, of course. More than a few of the men at Dunverlockie have mentioned the likin' they've taken ta the fare there since she arrived. Dorcas, was it no'?"

Hamish's stomach growled softly. He would have given anything for one of Ava's pies right now—or a bowl of her buttery porridge. He brushed away the thought of the taste of her kiss and the smell of her hair. He would have taken them both over an offer of food, empty as his stomach was.

But that option was long gone.

"Aye, I *thought* 'twas Dorcas," he said. "But I discovered no' long ago that the woman I'd been employin' as a cook was, in fact, the daughter of Sir Andrew—Ava MacMorran."

Lachlan stared at him. "Ye mean the one meant ta marry Angus?"

"Aye." The mention of marriage made him feel heavy again. But at least she wasn't married to Angus.

"But . . . but why would she come ta Glengour and act as cook?"

"She meant ta go on toward Glasgow—ta take refuge with a friend, but . . . well, there were a few mishaps, and when I mistook her for Dorcas, she didna correct me."

Lachlan blew out a breath through his lips, shaking his head slowly. "But I still dinna understand how ye come ta be here? Ye didna ken all that, ye said."

"No' at first. But when I did, I couldna betray the lass—I couldna send her ta be married ta Angus MacKinnon."

Lachlan raised his brows in acknowledgement of Hamish's argument. "Nay, of course no'. So, ye let her stay, and ye've kindled the wrath of Sir Andrew *and* Angus as a result."

Hamish didn't answer, letting his forehead rest against the cold iron. He had certainly made a mess of everything.

"We'll get ye out of here, Hamish. Dinna fash yerself."

Hamish shook his head against the bar. "'Twill no' be so easy as that. Officially, I'm here for smugglin'."

"Smugglin'?"

"Aye." He brought his head up and looked at Lachlan. "I meant ta tell ye, but I didna wish ta worry ye with it—no' with the new bairn and all yer other worries." He lifted his shoulders. "I thought 'twould provide me with the means ta pay off Dalmore's debts."

Lachlan grimaced. "They'll never convict ye. No jury would."

Hamish tightened his hold on the bar. "This is Angus MacKinnon and Sir Andrew MacMorran we're speakin' of. If they wish for my head, they'll have it. Of all people, ye ken that." His hand slid down the bar, and he stared at the dirt-filled cracks between the stones on the floor. "It doesna matter. What's done is done. Even if I did walk free, I'll never have Dalmore back."

"Dinna lose hope, Hamish," Lachlan said.

"Nay. Hope only leads ta pain and disappointment." He looked up, holding Lachlan's gaze, clenching his jaw. "I had the chance. I had the chance ta take Dalmore back, and I didna take it. And now I've lost everythin'." He turned away, reluctant for Lachlan to see the emotion gathering like pools in his eyes and filling his throat so that he could hardly swallow.

"Nay, then, Hamish. There *is* hope. I'll find a way ta get ye out of here. Ye may no' have Dalmore, but life is still worth livin'."

Hamish said nothing. He knew that Lachlan was right, but he didn't *feel* it—not in his heart.

"I wasna so different from ye when I returned from the war," Lachlan said. "I was so determined ta see justice done—ta have Dunverlockie back."

"And ye did." The envy tasted bitter in Hamish's mouth. He didn't begrudge Lachlan any of the happiness he had—he deserved every bit of it. But Hamish couldn't help wanting the same thing for himself.

"Aye, I have Dunverlockie. But do ye ken what I learned?" When Hamish didn't respond, he continued. "I've learned what's most important ta me, and it's no' Dunverlockie, Hamish. Christina and Sorcha—they're what matter most. And ye can have that still. It may no' be at Dalmore, but that's my point. Home is where yer heart lies."

Hamish felt his chin tremble and tightened his jaw in an attempt to control it. "I lost that, too." He faced his friend. "I'd have given up Dalmore House if it meant I could have Ava. Now, I've lost both." He turned away, folding his arms across his chest. Somehow saying the words aloud made them feel more real, and his heart ached unbearably.

"Ye mean she willna have ye? Or Sir Andrew willna allow it?"

"She's married now—married today ta the friend from Glasgow. 'Twas foolish of me ta ever expect anythin' else."

The silence after his words was broken only by the soft snores of the thief.

"I'm sorry, Hamish," Lachlan said softly. "There's no wound like one ta the heart. But ye canna surrender ta Angus and Sir Andrew. There's joy still ta be had, life yet ta live. I'll find a way ta have ye out of here."

29

By the time Ava and Dermot returned to Glengour, the sun had already dipped below the horizon. Her eyes searched the yard and the area around the stables for any sign that Lachlan might already be there, but they searched in vain.

With Dermot's help, she dismounted, and they handed off the horses to Mark. The rumbling of wheels sounded somewhere on the road hidden by the trees, and Ava turned to watch for the emergence of the vehicle with a racing heart. Would Lachlan have taken a carriage to Craiglinne? It seemed more likely for him to have ridden there.

A bent-over donkey appeared first, followed by Mrs. Shaw and her daughter in the wagon.

Anger burned in Ava's veins as they approached. They had betrayed Hamish.

"What do ye want," she asked.

Mrs. Shaw stepped down, chin as high as though she was emerging from a royal carriage, and her daughter followed. "We've come for our property."

"Yer property?"

"The casks," Mrs. Shaw said.

Ava's nostrils flared. "So ye've turned King's evidence." Dermot shot her a warning look, but she ignored it.

"I dinna ken what ye speak of," said Mrs. Shaw, lifting her chin again and looking away. But the guilt in her daughter's face was confirmation enough.

"No doubt Angus offered ye a fine reward for yer betrayal. I imagine ye'll be takin' yer spirits ta Benleith from now on."

The smug look on Mrs. Shaw's face was its own response.

"I hope whatever he offered ye is worth a man's life," Ava said.

Mrs. Shaw's expression shifted slightly, betraying a hint of guilt. "What do ye mean?"

"He's in gaol now, Mrs. Shaw," Ava said. "He'll be tried for free tradin', and ye ken what the punishment is if he's found guilty."

Her eyes widened, but she recovered her composure quickly, along with the haughty lift to her chin. "I ken nothin' of what ye're sayin'. I only wished was ta save that poor man from the clutches of a vixen like yerself."

Ava took a step toward her, but Dermot pulled her back and toward the inn. "Come, Ava." He looked at the Shaws. "We will return with your belongings in a moment."

Ava bit her tongue and swallowed down the bitterness in her mouth, looking away from Mrs. Shaw and allowing herself to be pulled inside.

Anger still racing in her veins, she and Dermot retrieved the empty casks from the cellar and returned them to the Shaws without a word. Mrs. Shaw's eyes seemed to search for Hamish, as though she refused to believe what Ava had said. But Hamish never emerged.

Only when Ava returned inside did she feel the strangeness of being there now—the full force of the changes which had occurred since the carriage had pulled into the yard earlier that day. Hamish was gone, and his absence was palpable for her as

Dermot closed the door behind them. He was not behind the bar, fetching a dram for a customer. He was not in the yard, welcoming a guest with his charming smile. He was not in the office, poring over sums and paperwork. He was not in the cellar, hefting casks or being frightened by rats.

He was in the Craiglinne gaol, awaiting trial.

Ava needed work to keep her hands and mind occupied as she awaited Lachlan's arrival, but she found herself paralyzed with the knowledge that she was no longer confined to the back of the inn, away from the guests. There was no need to hide any longer. She could work anywhere she wished. She had longed for that for so long, but now that it was a reality, there was no joy in it.

"I must go see him," Ava said as the chatter in the coffee room buzzed in the background.

"No, Ava," Dermot said, taking her firmly by the arm as though he worried she might run away right then. "It is late and the road too dangerous. We will do everything we can, but it must wait until morning."

She tried to keep busy as she waited for Lachlan's arrival, helping with the fire and washing dishes in the kitchen. Dermot retired early to write a letter to Fiona. He promised to set his mind to the problem of Hamish's arrest, but Ava had little hope he would be of any help. This was not his world. He had no power here.

It was not until the company in the coffee room had begun to wear thin and Ava was fetching another bucket of water for washing dishes that the sound of hoofbeats met her ears.

Her heart couldn't help but skip as she hurried toward the side of the inn, leaving the well with the bucket at the bottom. Had it taken Lachlan so long to return because he had managed to free Hamish? Would Hamish be with him?

But Lachlan was alone, and his expression brooding as he swung down from his horse and handed it off to Mark. Ava stood a dozen feet away, afraid to speak with him and hear whatever news made him look so grave.

Once the horse was gone, his gaze moved to Ava, and it became less somber and more alert.

"Ye must be Miss MacMorran."

"Aye," she said.

"Forgive me. 'Tis Mrs. McCurdy now, is it no'? I understand I am ta offer ye my felicitations."

Her eyes widened, and, looking around to ensure there was no one near, she stepped toward him. "Nay. 'Tis Miss MacMorran still."

Lachlan's eyes narrowed, but before he could talk, Ava continued. "Perhaps we can speak inside."

He nodded, keeping his eyes intently upon her, and followed her to the back of the inn and to the kitchen door. Dorcas was within, and Ava performed the requisite introduction, feeling anxious for it to be over. But Glenna soon appeared with a tray full of dirty dishes. She stopped at the sight of Ava and Lachlan.

"My laird," she said in surprise, setting down the tray on the table.

"Glenna," he went over and took her hands in his. "Thank ye for sendin' Mark with the message."

She nodded. "Of course. I kend ye'd wish ta be aware of it as soon as ye could be."

He blew out a breath. "I went ta Craiglinne right away. I've just come from there."

"Ye saw him, then? How is he?"

"He's . . . well, his spirits are low, as ye might reckon." His eyes flitted to Ava briefly. "I stayed with him quite a while—longer than I'd planned for. I didna wish ta leave him there alone." The edge of his mouth quirked up in a wry smile. "The only company he has either snores or squeaks."

"Mice?" Ava asked with round eyes.

"Aye," Lachlan replied with a grimace.

"I asked ta speak with Mr. Kincaid for a moment," Ava said, feeling the urgency more than ever. "About Hamish. Ye're welcome ta stay—"

Glenna shook her head. "I've a wee spill ta clean up in the coffee room. But ye ken I'll do whatever I can for Hamish. Anythin'."

Ava nodded, and she led Lachlan into the larder as Glenna left and Dorcas tended to the fire. She turned toward Lachlan, who was watching her with the same interest and intentness she had noticed outside.

"Hamish was under the impression ye'd been married—this verra day."

"I ken," she said, shutting her eyes. "'Twas all a mistake. Dermot only said so ta protect me, and I couldna refute it without puttin' meself back in my father's power, and afore I could find a moment alone ta explain ta Hamish . . . "

"He'd been arrested."

She nodded, biting her lip, wondering how he must have felt. "I've been thinkin' all day what can be done ta set everythin' aright, but . . . ."

Lachlan came forward, putting a hand on her shoulder. "Dinna fash yerself, Miss MacMorran. We'll find a way. We must do what we can ta persuade Angus and yer father ta reconsider. I can attempt ta speak with Angus—he made a promise ta me no' long ago, and I intend ta remind him of it. I canna promise anythin' will come of it, but I mean ta try. I dinna ken yer father well, though. Do ye reckon he'd listen ta me? I can attest ta Hamish's character—ta his valiance."

She put a hand in front of her mouth, fiddling with her lip as she tried to envision how such an encounter would unfold. He *had* tried to stop Angus from striking her, though that was a low bar indeed for a father. There had been one or two moments, as well, when Ava had thought he seemed shocked at how Angus had managed the entire situation. Perhaps there was hope.

"I wish I kend if 'twould help," she said. "My father has changed, though. He doesna listen anymore. 'Tis why I left." She sucked in a large breath and looked at Lachlan. "I'll speak with him meself. I dinna ken if he'll hear me, but I must try."

Lachlan's eyes searched her face. "Forgive me for bein' forward, Miss MacMorran, but"—he shifted his weight, looking as though he was slightly uncomfortable with whatever he was about to say—"do ye love Hamish?"

Ava tried to rid herself of the lump in her throat, but it stuck there persistently, keeping her words inside and making it difficult to breathe. All she could manage was a nod as she bit a trembling lip.

Lachlan sent her a commiserating glance. "Ye couldna find a man more deservin'. If ye wish, I'll accompany ye home tomorrow."

She nodded. A conversation with her father would necessarily reveal that she was not, in fact, married to Dermot, and it was possible he might prevent her from leaving once he discovered that fact—that he would still expect her to marry Angus. She had to be prepared for anything. "I'd be grateful for that."

"We'll go first thing in the mornin'. Perhaps with both of us there, he'll see reason and agree ta help. He has enough influence that it might be enough ta free Hamish—even if Angus refuses ta listen."

Ava certainly hoped so.

———

A s she anticipated, Ava had struggled to sleep. The last time she had gone before her father to counter him, she had been obliged to flee home. There was little evidence that he had become less entrenched in his wishes and demands of her—indeed, she was not even certain he would be willing to see her. She had lied to him, hidden from him, and, as far as he knew, gone against his wishes by marrying Dermot. She had called him a tyrant and told him she was moving to get away from him. Those were harsh words.

For the most part, though, her thoughts had centered upon Hamish. She had tossed and turned, unable to stop picturing him in the Craiglinne gaol, surrounded by rats and violent criminals. It was her fault he was there. If smuggling had been his only offense, they would not have cared. It was the fact that he had hidden her at Glengour, enabling her to marry Dermot that spurred their anger. She had begged him not to betray her presence at Glengour to her father, and now they saw him as responsible for her supposed marriage.

When the time came to rise in the morning, Ava felt as though she had hardly slept. She hurried to dress for the day and went downstairs to see to her duties as quickly as possible. Lachlan had promised to arrive by ten, and Ava didn't wish to leave Glenna and Dorcas with her duties in addition to theirs *and* Hamish's.

She had already started the fire and set the water to boil by the time Dorcas stepped into the kitchen, bleary-eyed and sluggish. Ava checked the laundry that had been hung yesterday and, finding it to be dry, set to folding it, though her fingers seemed disinclined to obey her, full of nervous energy as they were. She feared being too late to do anything for Hamish. What if Angus wasn't content to simply put him in gaol? What if he tried to rush the process in some way?

At half-past nine, she walked to the stables to ask Mark to ready one of the horses then returned inside and went up the stairs to dress. She tried to make herself presentable in a way that might inspire her father with confidence in her and a greater likelihood to listen. With no mirror to guide her, though, it was a difficult task. Her best efforts would have to suffice. She hurried down the stairs, through the office, and into Hamish's quarters. Her restless mind had at least one redeeming quality—it had given her an idea.

She paused in the doorway, struck still by the memory of the last two times she had been here. She tried to feel Hamish's arms around her, his kisses on her head, her cheeks, her lips. But the memory was elusive. It felt so far in the past with all that had since happened.

Her gaze flitted to the couch and the plaid that still sat there, then over to the small box on the kitchen table. The gorse hung limply over the sides of the tankard. The sight was an unwelcome one, for it reeked of unfulfilled dreams and disappointed hopes, and she promised herself to fill it with a fresh batch.

She strode over and opened the box. The medal sat inside, and she took it out, rubbing her thumb over the ridges and the inscription. It did not surprise her to know of Hamish's bravery; she had seen his coolness in the face of being arrested. A medal seemed like a paltry reward, in many ways, particularly if it remained hidden in this box day and night.

She stared at it, remembering when they had spoken of it together.

What am I meant ta do? Wave it in the face of everyone I meet ta persuade them I'm worthy of their notice?

That was just what she intended to do.

Horse hooves sounded outside, and she hurried to shut the box, clasping the medal in her hands and rushing to meet Lachlan in the inn yard.

Together, they rode the four miles to Glenlochan, both of them keeping silent. When they arrived, Ava took in a large breath, trying to quiet her nerves and gather her courage. This was the right thing to do. It was the *only* thing to do.

Her fears that she might be refused entrance from her home were unfounded, and one of the footmen opened the door for Lachlan and her with only a raising of the brows to indicate his surprise at Ava's reappearance. When she asked where she could find her father, the footman directed her to the library.

She led the way, but when they reached the door, she paused. This was where they had last argued, and the memory of her father's stubbornness and her subsequent anger burned bright for a moment.

"Dinna fash, Miss MacMorran," Lachlan said.

She slipped a hand in her pocket, closing her fingers around the cold medal, hoping it would give her the sort of courage it honored in Hamish. She could be brave for him.

She set her shoulders and opened the door. Her father sat behind the desk, a pair of wiry spectacles perched on his nose, and a stack of papers before him, but he looked up at her entrance.

"Ava," he said in surprise. His jaw quickly set, though. "Have you come to say goodbye? I had Taylor gather up your things. They are in a trunk in the drawing room."

Only then did his gaze flick to Lachlan, and his brow furrowed.

"Kincaid," he said.

Lachlan made a quick bow. "Good day, Sir Andrew."

Ava's father looked to her as if for an explanation.

"I've come ta speak with ye, Da. Mr. Kincaid is here ta lend his support." She lifted her chin. "And ta protect me."

His frown turned into displeasure. "Protect you? Is that not your husband's responsibility?"

Ava breathed deeply. Already she would have to confess the extent of her dishonesty; already she would see how far he meant take his threats of force. "I dinna have a husband, Da."

He stared at her, silent, but his eyes searched hers.

"Dermot feared ye'd take me and force me ta marry Angus."

The words brought a flash of anger back. "Just as ye threatened ta do."

The ticking of the clock on the mantel filled the silence. Her father's glance flicked to Lachlan then back to Ava, but his face was impassive. After seven ticks, she continued.

"I'm no' here about that, though. I'm here ta speak with ye regardin' Hamish."

Her father frowned. "What of him?"

"I want ye ta help us get him out of gaol."

His eyebrows snapped together. "The man is a criminal."

"Nay, Da. He's a good man."

Lachlan nodded and stepped forward. "'Tis true, sir. I served with him meself, and ye'll no' find a better or more courageous man."

Sir Andrew shook his head. "A liar is not courageous. He is a criminal and a free trader."

"As am I," Ava said. "If that makes me fit for gaol, then I suppose I should go there meself."

"Do not be ridiculous, Ava," her father said impatiently. "You are neither a criminal nor a smuggler."

"I am, though. I was there, same as him. I helped carry the cargo and hide it meself." She held his gaze, unflinching. "And I'll turn meself in ta be tried beside Hamish if ye refuse ta lift a finger ta help him." If her father thought he was the only one capable of issuing threats, he was wrong.

"Good heavens, Ava!"

She could feel Lachlan's surprised gaze on her as well as her father's, and she held her ground. "Hamish protected me; he kept his word ta me when my own father betrayed my trust. I'd rather be tried beside a man I admire and love than be forced inta marriage with the likes of Angus MacKinnon."

Her father rose, pulling off his spectacles and tossing them onto the desk in frustration. He rubbed at his eyes. He looked older and more tired than she had ever seen him. The image tweaked Ava's heart slightly in spite of herself. In his expression, she saw frustration, but behind it, there was exhaustion and traces of grief. Ava felt all the same things.

When she spoke, it was in a quiet voice. "Ye married for love, Da. Why will ye no' let me do the same? Would ye take that from me?"

He whirled toward her. "I married for love, Ava, and look where that has brought me! I've lost my wife, and my daughter despises me." His chest rose and fell sharply, but his chin trembled. He slumped down so that he sat on the edge of the desk and covered his face with a hand. "Love brings only pain."

Ava glanced at Lachlan, who was looking to her for guidance. She gave him a nod, and he left the room. Once the door had closed, she walked toward her father's side and, with hesitation, put her hand on his shoulder. "I dinna hate ye, Da." She swallowed. "I miss ye."

He kept his eyes shut, but his hand moved down to cover his mouth.

"I ken Ma's death affected ye—it devastated us all. But ye havna been the same since." She felt her emotions rise to the surface and tried with no success to swallow them down. "It's felt as though I lost both of ye."

He set a hand atop hers on his shoulder, shaking his head as his throat bobbed.

"Why, Da?"

She had to ask. She had asked it before, but now, he seemed calm rather than angry or demanding as he had so often been before. "Why Angus MacKinnon? Of all the men ye might have chosen for me, why him? Surely, there were other men who might've offered ye just as much and more?"

He looked at her, and his eyes were red and shining. "I was afraid of losing you, Ava—I couldn't bear the thought after losing your mother."

Ava stared at him, more confused than ever.

He looked her in the eyes. "I was afraid if you married Dermot you would"—his throat bobbed—"I was afraid you would leave, and I would never see you. At least with Angus . . ."

"I'd be at Benleith," she finished for him.

All his railing, all his control, all his stubbornness had been borne of a desire to keep her close. The revelation settled on her heart, bringing relief. But it didn't change everything. "But I told ye, Da. I told ye how he made me feel. I told ye he's no' a good man."

He nodded. "I thought you were merely eager to get away— you have always been anxious to leave Glenlochan. Angus had been decent in all our interactions. I had never seen the side of him you claimed to have seen." His face contorted with pain. "But I saw it at Glengour yesterday. I was wrong about him, Ava. I am sorry I did not listen to you. I should have trusted you." He took her hand from his shoulder, pulling it toward his lips to set a kiss upon the back of it.

Her voice shook when she spoke. "I only wished ta leave Glenlochan because of the painful memories I have here, Da. We lost Ma so soon after we came that I canna so much as walk from one room to another without rememberin' it all."

He nodded and looked at her, pleading in his watery, blue eyes. "It is the same for me. Forgive me, Ava."

She pulled him into her arms, and they embraced for the first time since the death of her mother.

"He told me ta speak with ye," Ava said softly as they held each other. "Hamish did. But I refused."

Her father pulled away and looked at her with an understanding grimace. He took her hands in his, holding them between the two of them as they faced one another. "So. This is the man you love? An innkeeper?" He grimaced, and she saw the disappointment there. "His father was a Jacobite, Ava."

She took her hand from his and reached into her pocket,

pulling out the medal. "His father may have been a Jacobite, Da, but no' Hamish." She held it out, and he took it from her hand, squinting at it.

She chuckled and reached for his spectacles, which he took from her with a smile that set her heart just a bit more at ease. She had missed her father—*this* father—for so long.

As he turned the medal over in his hand, peering at the inscription, his brows rose.

"He's a good man, Da. The verra best of men. Ye'll see that if ye give him a proper chance."

He looked up at her, holding up the medal. "And this man is willing to marry *you*?"

She nudged him and chuckled, though her smile faded after a moment. "I dinna ken if he wants ta marry me, Da. I hope so. I hope it more than I've ever hoped for anythin' in my life. I've been nothin' but trouble ta him since we met, but he hasna complained once—even when it put him in gaol."

Her father looked down at the medal again. He sighed and gave it back to her.

"Medal or no," she said, "I love him, Da." She brought her head up to meet his eyes. "And I ken ye'll love him, too. But, whatever happens, he doesna deserve ta be in gaol."

Her father's eyes searched her face, and his hand found hers, pressing it with his wrinkly, rough skin.

"Will ye help me, Da?" she asked. "Will ye help me set him free?"

30

———

Hamish awoke with a start—quickly enough to hear the last of his cellmate's snort before the man turned to his side and settled into a softer, less rumbling snore.

Hamish's very bones seemed to ache. There was certainly a difference between sleeping on the wood floor of the Glengour office and doing so on the unyielding—and dirty—stones of the Craiglinne gaol. Sleeping on the wood had been made even easier, too, by the knowledge that Ava was only a dozen feet away.

Hamish shut his eyes and sighed. That night seemed a lifetime ago.

He glanced over at the thief—Quinn, Hamish had discovered his name to be. Quinn could hardly have been more different from Ava, and Hamish stifled a groan as he rolled onto his back and stared up at the ceiling.

Lachlan had promised to help him, and while Hamish trusted his friend implicitly, he was no fool. Lachlan had only been at Dunverlockie for a matter of months. How could his influence possibly compete with that of Sir Andrew MacMorran and Angus MacKinnon?

He shut his eyes, trying for the hundredth time to reconcile himself to the knowledge that Ava and Dermot were likely halfway to Glasgow by now. The thought made him sick to his hollow stomach, though—or perhaps it was his heart. He rolled over yet again and shut his eyes, pleading for sleep to return. In time, he would accustom himself to reality, but it was difficult to do so when there was nothing to prevent him from reliving the past in the gloom of the gaol cell.

He focused on the pattering of rain outside and the increasingly frequent sound of dripping as water found its way into the cell and puddled on the stone floor below.

It was three weeks until the assizes, and part of Hamish just wished for his trial to arrive, whether that meant transportation or death. The prospect of being confined to this cell with nothing but Quinn, his thoughts, and the ghost of what might have been for companions was unbearable.

The muffled jangling of keys sounded somewhere in the distance, soon growing nearer. Hamish would have recognized the shuffling footsteps of the guard anywhere at this point, he had heard them so often in the two nights he had spent here.

The footsteps stopped, followed by clanking and muttering then the dissonance of a key in the grate. The sound was near enough to give Hamish reason to think it was his own cell the guard had stopped at, and he turned to look.

The lock clicked, and the guard pulled it from its place, opening the door with a dissonant, creaking sound.

"Ye're free ta go," said the guard.

Hamish stilled. It was dark enough that he couldn't tell whether the guard was looking at him. But Quinn was still asleep.

"Up ye go," the guard said impatiently.

Hamish scrambled to his feet. "Ye're speakin' ta me?"

The man let out a sound of annoyance. "Aye, but if ye wait

any longer, I'll shut the door again and keep ye locked up for idiocy. On ye go!"

Bemused though he was, Hamish needed no further persuading. He hurried to his feet and strode past the guard into the narrow corridor between the cells, feeling disoriented and confused. "I dinna understand. Who ordered I be freed?"

The guard set himself to putting the lock back in place, but he turned toward Hamish at his question, looking at him with annoyance. "Do ye wish ta keep askin' questions, or do ye wish ta go? Perhaps ye'd like ta sit down for tea and have a wee chat together?"

Hamish shook his head, though a dozen questions buzzed in his mind.

The guard turned away from him again. "Orders of the sheriff. That's all I ken, and 'tis all I need ta ken. Mayhap if ye learn ta mind yer own business, too, ye'll keep out of here."

The guard led him through the corridor and out of the small building that acted as a gaol for the small town. Hamish blinked as he stepped out into the streets. It was gray and rainy, but his eyes had become accustomed to the dim gaol, and the amount of light outside was blinding by contrast.

A donkey cart sat in the street, the driver standing at the animal's head.

"Ta take ye home," grumbled the guard, and he didn't wait for a response before turning back inside.

Hamish stared at the cart, trying to make sense of what had just happened, of his freedom—something he had thought never to have again. He looked for any sign of someone to thank for his release, but the only people in sight were merchants and tounspeople, hurrying through the rain from one destination to another. How had Lachlan managed it?

This cart was meant to take him back to Glengour, he gathered. He could only imagine how Glenna, Dorcas, and Mark were managing on their own. The donkey was old and stooped, and he imagined he could walk just as quickly as the over-worked animal could pull him. He would rather walk the distance to Glengour—stretch his legs and allow the slow fall of rain to wash away the grime that lingered on him from the gaol. It would give him time to accustom himself, too, to the life ahead of him.

His newfound freedom gave him a keen appreciation for the road to Glengour. He had been so anxious to reclaim Dalmore House, he had hardly taken notice of the beauty of the area surrounding Glengour, with its clusters of green forest, its braes, and the smell of the nearby sea. His eyes settled on the gorse that lined the side of the road nearest the sea as it turned toward Glengour, and he let out a sigh that ached in his heart.

He walked toward the gorse, and the column of his throat grew tighter with every step. Would these ubiquitous flowers always remind him of Ava? He breathed them in, along with the salty sea air and the loamy scent of wet dirt.

As he continued on his way and the inn came into view, his eyes searched of their own accord for any sign of Dermot's carriage. It was not there, and that was for the best. What good could it possibly do for Hamish to see Ava now? It would be more pain than he felt prepared to manage right now.

His skin and clothes were soaked, but he let a few more drops of rain fall on his face before squaring his shoulders and stepping inside. With time, not everything there would remind him of Ava, surely. All he could do until then was press through the discomfort.

There was no one in the entry as he stepped inside, but immediately, the smell of spices and burning peat filled his lungs. It made his stomach growl and his heart ache.

Glenna emerged from the kitchen, a basket on her hip, overflowing with folded laundry.

He smiled at her in all his dampness, and she set it down and embraced him.

"Ye dinna look as surprised ta see me as I thought ye'd be," he said.

She stepped back and picked up her basket. "Nay, I kend ye'd no' leave us for long." She gave him a significant look. "I hope ye're well and rested from yer bout in gaol, for I mean ta set ye straight ta work!"

He chuckled softly, a strange sound to his ears after the past few days. "Have ye appointed yerself innkeeper now, then?"

She gave a teasing nod. "Till ye can be trusted no' ta leave us."

"Fair enough," he said. "Can I have a wee slice of pie afore I begin my duties again?"

"Ye must be starvin'. Wait right there." She hurried back to the kitchen and emerged shortly with a plate and a fork.

"Eat that ta fill yer belly, and then, for the love of Bonnie Prince Charlie, go and change inta somethin' dry." She smiled teasingly at him and took the laundry up the stairs.

Hamish was already eating the pie. It warmed him like a glass of whisky, reminding him of the first time he had tried Ava's creation. He had burned his tongue—and perhaps fallen a bit more in love with Ava—in that moment.

He set down the fork. Somehow, the thought of her had chased away his hunger. If every bite of food at Glengour reminded him of Ava, he would have a difficult time of things. He was grateful for the knowledge that a great deal of work was awaiting him already. It would keep him occupied.

He hurried out of the coffee room and through the office, pushing open the door to his quarters and stilling.

Ava stood at the table, fussing over something, though she turned at the sound of his entrance and faced him. The vase of gorse sat on the table behind her, full of fresh, bright yellow blooms.

Hamish blinked harshly, certain his mind was tricking him, creating images of what he wished to see. But she was still there when he opened them.

"Ava," he said.

She smiled slightly, but it was not her usual smile. There was a timidity in it.

He looked around the room for any sign of Dermot—he badly needed the reminder that the Ava before him, familiar as she was, was not the same one from even two days ago; she was not the same Ava he had held in his arms and kissed in this room. Everything had changed since then. What was she doing here? Had she come to say goodbye? Did she think a fresh vase of gorse would somehow make up for everything Hamish had lost when she had chosen Dermot?

"What're ye doin' here?" His arms itched to hold her, and he walked toward the fireplace and took up the poker to keep himself from doing anything he would have cause to regret. "I thought ye'd be halfway ta Glasgow by now." He poked at the remains of a peat brick.

"I'm no' goin' ta Glasgow, Hamish."

His back was to her, and he shut his eyes in consternation. Did this mean she and Dermot would be staying at Glenlochan? Would he be obliged not only to lose everything he had hoped for but to be reminded of it on a regular basis? The gaol cell at Craiglinne, with all its snores and squeaks, might be preferable.

"Dermot and I are no' married, Hamish."

He was putting back the poker, but his hand stilled.

"I wished ta tell ye—ta explain it ta ye, but I couldna do so without riskin' the sheriff takin' me back ta Glenlochan. As long as I was a minor, my father had me in his power. And then ye were arrested, and . . . ."

He straightened and set the poker in its place, trying to set bounds on the hope igniting in his heart before he turned to her. But it was no use. He turned to her anyway, impatient to see her face, to see if what she was saying was true. If it meant what he hoped it meant.

But just because she wasn't married to Dermot yet didn't mean she wouldn't soon be. He changed the subject. "Was it yer father who arranged for my release?"

She was watching him carefully—as carefully as he wished to watch her but was too afraid to do. She nodded.

"How did ye manage that?" he asked.

"I did what ye told me ta do—I spoke with him." A little, rueful smile crept onto her mouth. "And I threatened ta turn meself in for smugglin' if he refused ta help ye."

"Ye did what?"

She smiled wider, apparently satisfied with his reaction, and she came closer to him. "I told him I'd join ye in gaol."

His mouth drew up at the side. "Has yer father never seen ye near a mouse? He'd never have believed ye." He didn't know if Ava still meant to marry Dermot, but the knowledge that she was at least not *yet* married filled him with a relief that made him almost giddy. He would try everything in his power to persuade her not to go through with the marriage, that it was him, not Dermot, who would make her happy.

Her nose scrunched up. "So, 'tis true. There were mice?"

He shook his head and crossed his arms, letting his eyes rake over her face and her hair, finally free of cap or kertch— sights he had never thought to see again. "Rats."

"How did ye survive?"

"Och"—he waved away the question with a hand—"rats dinna bother me now. Ye grow used ta them after the fifth or sixth time of findin' 'em chewin' on yer shoes."

She gave an involuntary shudder, and he couldn't stop himself from chucking her under the chin playfully. He didn't know how to stay away from her.

Her smile softened, and she looked up at him, eyes

searching his. "I meant it, Hamish. I'd have turned meself in ta be with ye."

His heart skipped and thudded, and his breath stuck in his lungs.

She looked down. "I dinna ken how ye feel anymore, after all that's happened—after all I've put ye through." Her gaze returned to his slowly. "Anyone would forgive ye for throwin' me out and never forgivin' me, but—"

He pulled her into his arms, pressing his lips against hers. Her surprise lasted a moment, but soon her hands were on his chest, slipping inside his damp jacket and onto his shirt as she kissed him back with all the eagerness threading through his own veins.

To have her in his arms, to kiss her and be kissed in return after all that had happened in the last week—it was ecstasy.

The passion gave way after a moment to something more slow and soft, and the tenderness Hamish felt inside felt almost as unbearable as his loneliness had felt just hours ago. Finally, their lips parted. He could feel her chest rising and falling in concert with his, and he let his cheek rest against her temple, shutting his eyes and breathing her in.

"I thought ye meant ta marry him," he said softly. "And when he said ye *had* ... " He gave an attempt at a chuckle, but it strangled in his throat at the memory. "It felt like dyin'."

Her head shook, and she stroked his wet hair with a hand. "I never truly wanted ta marry *anyone* 'til I met ye, Hamish."

He took in a deep breath, allowing the words to fill him and settle into his heart, impossible as they seemed. He pulled back and held her face in his hands so he could look into her gleaming eyes.

"I have no home ta offer ye but this one, Ava. Ye deserve more—ye were born for more."

"As were you, Hamish. But I dinna wish for more." She looked up into his eyes and put a hand on his cheek, letting her thumb graze his short beard. "Without ye, even the finest home would be naught but a prison ta me."

He shut his eyes and rested his forehead against hers.

"I only wish ye could have Dalmore," she said softly.

He shook his head against hers. "Ye're my home now, lass. Wherever ye are, I'll be. Rats and all."

"I'm nothin' but trouble, Hamish." She looked up at him with the smiling eyes he loved.

He brushed her cheek with his thumb. "I ken, lass. And I hope ye'll bring me trouble for the rest of my life."

She lifted her chin, and their lips met again.

EPILOGUE

Glengour Inn, June 1763

Hamish ran the damp rag he held in circles over the table. A soiled tartan tablecloth was heaped on the floor by his feet, a casualty of the glass of whisky Mr. Milroy had spilled a few minutes ago—a favorite pastime of his. The vase full of yellow gorse which, unlike the dram, had managed to escape being spilled by the drunkard, Hamish had placed next to the vase on the nearest table. The spots of yellow that dotted the room gave it a cheery appearance despite the low ceiling and dark wood walls.

Hamish's motions became mechanical as his gaze settled upon the woman across the room, who was sweeping the floor by the fireplace.

She looked up and, catching his eyes on her, shook her head and tried—and failed—to suppress a smile. "Do ye no' have work ta do, Mr. Campbell? 'Twill be easier if ye keep yer eyes on the table."

He reared back. "Och, can a man no' admire his own wife? What a pass things have come to!"

She tried to look severely at him, but the effect was ruined by the way her eyes laughed. It was one of Hamish's favorite things she did. There was something wonderfully rewarding about running Glengour Inn alongside Ava. The work was hard, and the days could be long, but they had made a concerted effort to work together whenever possible, and it made all the difference. Best of all, long days were followed by cozy nights together in their quarters, sitting under the plaid on the couch, sharing a bed, toasting bread and cheese over the fire.

"Perhaps a man can admire his wife *after* his duties are done," she said.

He stood straight. "Och, never, then?" He left the teasing aside. "Forgive me, love. I canna help but look for any sign of a wee bump."

She looked down at her aproned stomach and set a hand there. When her head came back up, there was contentment in her gaze. "Ye've no patience, have ye? I dinna expect ye'll be able ta see aught for another month or two. What's here now is only the result of eatin' too many pies last night." She winked at him.

He set down the rag and walked over to his wife, taking the broom into his hands. "I'll do that. Ye should focus on growin' our wee bairn."

She took the broom right back. "Ye never used ta complain about me workin' hard afore."

"Of course I didna complain," he said, keeping a hand on the handle of the broom. "I find ye most captivatin' when ye're at work, displayin' yer strength." He squeezed the muscle of her upper arm.

"Aye," she said dryly, "for what other person has the strength required ta wield a broom?" She wrested it from his grasp. "'Tis better the bairn come inta the world kennin' how ta sweep a floor than bein' accustomed ta lyin' abed since 'tis all his mother has taught him." She went back to sweeping but glanced at him out of the corner of her eye and, finding his eyes still upon her, she swept the broom at his feet playfully.

Hamish shuffled his feet to avoid the bristles, using the opportunity to come behind her, wrap his arms around her, and plant a kiss upon her cheek.

Glenna emerged from the kitchen and, seeing the end of the interaction, smiled at them knowingly. It was certainly not the first time she had caught them in a display of affection.

She held a paper in her hand, and she extended it to Hamish as she approached them. "I believe this is meant for ye."

Hamish let his wife out of his arms, taking the paper from Glenna and breaking the seal. It was from Christina Kincaid, and his eyes swept over the contents quickly. As he did so, his brows went up.

"What is it?" Glenna asked. "Bad news? Or good?"

He held it out to her.

Glenna made no move to take the paper. "Have ye forgotten, Hamish? I canna read."

"Och," he said. "I'm sorry. 'Twas thoughtless of me."

"I ken I've no' kept my promise," Ava said, voice infused with guilt. "I do mean to. Ye'll read and write soon enough, Glenna. I swear it."

Glenna shook her head. "Ye've been occupied with far more important things—gettin' married and growin' a bairn. Dinna fash yerself."

Hamish was certainly grateful to Glenna. Ava had had her fair share of bad days since the pregnancy had begun, and Glenna and Dorcas had worked harder than ever to see to whatever duties Ava couldn't manage, despite her stubborn insistence that she was well able to.

He folded up the letter. "It merely says that we can expect the return of Alistair any day now—and ta direct him ta

Dunverlockie if he happens ta come here in an attempt ta find his way."

Ava grabbed the paper and opened it. "Do ye mean it, Hamish? How happy Christina must be!" Her eyes ran over the lines rapidly. "They've certainly waited long enough. If only Elizabeth could be here ta welcome him back."

"No doubt she's keepin' ta her bed as is proper given her circumstances." Hamish nudged her with a teasing elbow.

Ava handed the letter back to him impatiently. "I dinna ken Elizabeth MacKinnon well, but given her reputation, I doubt she's one ta keep ta her bed for nine months."

Hoofbeats sounded outside, and the three of them turned to the window, hoping the view through the rippled glass might tell them who was arriving. But it was too difficult to see.

"I'll tell Dorcas ta prepare a plate," Glenna said, and she left to the kitchen.

Together, Hamish and Ava went to the front door. They were not always able to do so, but they tried to greet travelers together when possible. Hamish opened the door and found himself looking upon Lachlan Kincaid and Sir Andrew MacMorran, who were dismounting while Mark took their horses in hand.

The men had become friendly with one another, but the sight of them together was still somewhat surprising.

Sir Andrew came over and kissed Ava on the head before shaking hands with Hamish. The two of them had come to a good understanding, even if Hamish sometimes worried that his father-in-law was less-than-thrilled about his daughter running an inn.

Hamish welcomed them both inside, and the two of them accepted his offer of drinks and food.

"Will ye no' sit down with us?" Lachlan asked, glancing between Hamish and Ava.

They looked at one another, and Hamish nodded. "Aye, if ye wish, we'd be glad to."

The four of them sat down, and Glenna soon brought out a tray with drinks. "I'll have fresh pies out for ye in a few minutes. I thought ye'd prefer those ta the ones left over from yesterday."

"Thank ye, Glenna," Lachlan said. "'Tis kind of ye."

She curtsied and left the four of them.

Hamish glanced at Ava, who had the same slight frown on her brow as he imagined on his own. There was nothing strictly strange about sitting down with Lachlan and Sir Andrew, but Hamish had the sense that this was not simple happenstance.

"We wished to speak with the two of you," Sir Andrew said, straightening his coat. "We have some news."

Hamish raised his brows. "Is it Angus?" He and Ava had been bracing themselves for the repercussions of their marriage. It was unlikely to sit well with Angus that his intended bride had married an innkeeper—or that her marriage to Dermot had been a lie.

"Nay," Lachlan said, "though there is news in that quarter, as well."

Ava grasped Hamish's hand, which he squeezed reassuringly. "I'd thought ta see the effects of his anger by now," Hamish said. "It makes me feel uneasy that he's no' done anythin'."

"He has been licking his wounds, I do not doubt," Sir Andrew said. "But he has been too occupied to act, I imagine." There was a pause. "He is our new Justice of the Peace."

Hamish stared. The last thing they needed was Angus MacKinnon with more power to abuse. As Justice of the Peace, he would decide which cases were prosecuted in their area and how severe the punishments were. He was an enforcer of the law—a law he held no regard for when it didn't serve him.

"But," Lachlan said, "the real reason for our visit is a happier one." He looked to Sir Andrew and nodded.

"The Board of Commissioners has agreed to provide you a route to owning Dalmore House."

Ava's hand clenched Hamish's, but he was struck momentarily speechless.

"I apologize that it has taken so long," Sir Andrew continued, "but the Board is not known for its swiftness. We were obliged to apply to the Crown, you know. The fact of your valiance in the war was, we believe, a significant factor in obtaining approval—as was the participation of Mr. Kincaid here."

Hamish looked to Lachlan, who gave something between a smile and a grimace and grasped Hamish by the shoulder. "I gave the committee my assurance. That was all."

Sir Andrew shook his head. "He is being modest. He testified of your character, yes, but he also gave his personal guarantee that you would pay off the debts."

A lump rose in Hamish's throat, and he swallowed it down with effort. "Ye shouldna have, Kincaid."

"I've trusted ye with my life," Lachlan said. "'Twas a small thing ta do for a brother."

Hamish couldn't speak, so he merely nodded.

"These are the terms the Board agreed to." Sir Andrew handed him a folded paper. "They reduced the debts you are liable to pay to six thousand pounds."

"But why?" Ava asked.

Her father chuckled wryly. "They took on a great deal of debt with the attainted estates like Dalmore—more than they had bargained for, in fact—and they are desperate for money."

"Ye can take up residence as soon as ye're able," Lachlan said as Hamish unfolded the paper. "Ye'll make payments twice a year."

Glenna stepped out of the kitchen, and steam rose from the plates that sat atop the tray she held. Balancing the tray on her hip, she began setting the plates on the table. She looked at

Hamish, though, and paused. She was too polite to ask what the matter was, but Hamish could see the concern and curiosity in her eyes.

"Would ye care ta congratulate us, Glenna?" His voice was gravelly, but he smiled through it, wrapping an arm around Ava and pulling her closer. The thought of taking her to Dalmore was enough to bring on a fresh wave of emotion. "They've given us Dalmore."

Glenna's mouth opened, and her eyes widened. She covered her mouth with a hand, but the tray wobbled, and she was obliged to stabilize it quickly. Her mouth broke into a smile. "What news! I'm that happy for the two of ye!"

"A well-deserved prize," Lachlan said, "for a valiant man." He reached for a plate, apparently able to see to other matters now that their news had been delivered.

"When do ye go?" Glenna asked.

Hamish looked at his wife, and he saw the same wonder and joy there that he felt. "Once we have things in order here, I reckon."

"Who will take over the inn?" Glenna looked at Hamish intently. Of course that was a matter of great interest to her. It affected her so nearly, and she'd had her fair share of unpleasant experiences with the past innkeeper.

"We can discuss that soon enough," Lachlan said, cutting into the pie with his fork. "We have a few other matters to discuss regarding the terms the Board set."

Glenna blinked and nodded hurriedly. "Of course. I'll leave ye to it."

Once Hamish and Ava were acquainted with the document's contents and Lachlan and Sir Andrew had left Glengour, the two of them took refuge in their quarters.

Hamish shut the door behind them and immediately pulled his wife into his arms, nuzzling his face into her hair and kissing the side of her head. This was so much more than he could ever have dreamed of. His joy felt uncontainable.

"Did ye ken yer father was doin' this?" he whispered.

"Nay," she whispered back, "but I hoped he would." She pulled away and looked up at him with shining eyes. "Ye're innkeeper of Glengour no more, my love."

He laughed softly and looked around the room. The space had changed from three months ago. There was still gorse on the table—Ava always made sure of that—but the two of them had chosen a few other items to make the space more like home.

Hamish's medal sat open in its box on the set of drawers they'd had brought from Glenlochan. A trunk sat at the foot of the bed and upon it the folded *arisaid* Ava's mother had worn. Inside the trunk, resting on their clothing, was the small cap Ava had stitched when she had told him she was with child.

More than anything, though, the atmosphere was different. It *felt* like home. Hamish enjoyed spending time in these quarters now, for they were full of the life, insignificant as it might seem to others, that he and Ava were making together.

"I never thought ta feel regret at leavin' Glengour," he said.

She wrapped her arm through his and surveyed the room with him. "'Twill always be dear ta us, Hamish. But so will Dalmore."

"Aye," he said, looking over at her with a smile. "Though I canna think how we will manage ta fill the space there."

She smiled. "With love—and a few bairns, I hope." She went up on her toes to kiss him, and he closed his eyes, turning toward her and leaning down to press his lips to hers.

Their love was grand enough to fill the rooms of a place much larger than Dalmore, just as it did these small quarters at Glengour.

THE END

Read the next book in the series, The Gentleman and the Maid, to find out what happens next.

AUTHOR'S NOTE

As always, I have strived for historical accuracy in my portrayal of the time period. Where I have failed, it has not been for lack of effort, and I hope it does not detract from the story. In this note, I hope to explain some points that might be of interest to readers.

In 1747, not long after the Battle of Culloden, a number of estates belonging to leaders of the failed Jacobite rebellion were forfeited by their owners as part of their punishment for participation in the revolt. Most of them heavily encumbered by debt, some estates were sold at auction while thirteen were annexed to the Crown in 1752 and put under the management of the Board of Commissioners for the Forfeited Estates. A handful of estates did not come under the Board's control until 1770 and were in the meantime managed by prominent and loyal subjects of the Crown.

While this is the story of a set of fictional characters and estates, the premise is inspired by historical events, including the story of Simon Fraser, Lord Lovat. He was executed in 1745 and his estate forfeited to the Crown. However, his son served in the army and, because of his loyalty and service to the

Crown, was given back the estate (but not his father's title) in 1774. Hamish's story mirrors this one somewhat.

While marriage of unwilling parties was technically illegal in Scotland, the reality was not so pretty. Parties might be married without any involvement of a religious institution, but if they wished for the blessing of the Kirk, a minister could be bribed to ignore the circumstances of a marriage. As was the case elsewhere, pressure—or force—could be brought to bear upon unwilling parties.

After the Act of Union in 1707, many taxes in Scotland were increased—some by as much as seven-fold—and the people understandably saw the changes as unjust and an unfair burden on a country already struggling financially and having to submit to the country to the south. Salt was one of many items taxed at a high rate. It was one of the few forms of food preservation available at the time, making the raising of taxes on it a significant burden on the people. With its harsh winter climate, preservation of food sources was crucial to survival for people in the Highlands in particular.

While it is difficult for many of us living in the 21st century to imagine, smuggling was an almost universally accepted behavior in 18th-century Scotland. It would be more akin to the license we currently take with the speed limit than to its seeming modern-day parallel of willful tax evasion or, more dramatically perhaps, drug smuggling. Even if a person guilty of smuggling was taken to court, there was almost no chance at all of them being convicted, as there was so much support for the trade amongst society.

Most of the lodging options available to travelers in 18th-century Scotland were of the most basic type, including bothies—small, generally primitive huts. Bothies were essentially a shelter and nothing more. Travelers might also lodge for the night with an obliging inhabitant in a blackhouse near the road. Larger inns with more services offered were becoming more frequent with the expansion of commerce and the slow improvement of the sparse road network (almost nonexistent in the Highlands), but reports from the time most often describe them as significantly inferior to the inns people from England were accustomed to. They might well be run by a sole individual or family and had the most meager of services. As travel in the Highlands increased with the region's romanticization by the English, there was greater demand for inns of higher quality as well as a desire by many not to be outdone by their neighbors to the south.

I hope you enjoyed Hamish and Ava's story, and I thank you for reading it.

OTHER TITLES BY MARTHA KEYES

If you enjoyed this book, make sure to check out my other books:

Tales from the Highlands

The Widow and the Highlander (Book One)

The Enemy and Miss Innes (Book Two)

The Innkeeper and the Fugitive (Book Three)

The Gentleman and the Maid (Book Four)

Families of Dorset

Wyndcross: A Regency Romance (Book One)

Isabel: A Regency Romance (Book Two)

Cecilia: A Regency Romance (Book Three)

Hazelhurst: A Regency Romance (Book Four)

Phoebe: A Regency Romance (Series Novelette)

Regency Shakespeare

A Foolish Heart (Book One)

My Wild Heart (Book Two)

True of Heart (Book Three)

Other Titles

Of Lands High and Low

The Highwayman's Letter (Sons of Somerset Book 5)

A Seaside Summer (Timeless Regency Romance Book 17)

The Christmas Foundling (Belles of Christmas: Frost Fair Book Five)

Goodwill for the Gentleman (Belles of Christmas Book Two)

The Road through Rushbury (Seasons of Change Book One)

Eleanor: A Regency Romance

Join my Newsletter at www.marthakeyes.com to keep in touch and learn more about British history! I try to keep it fun and interesting.

OR follow me on BookBub to see my recommendations and get alerts about my new releases.

ACKNOWLEDGMENTS

There are always so many people to thank with any given book! First and foremost, my husband deserves those thanks. He makes everything possible and never complains about the strangeness that is life married to an author. He irons out plot holes with me, listens to me drone on about anything and everything writing related, and is the absolute best husband and father I could ask for. I love you, honey.

Thank you to my critique group partners and dear friends, Kasey, Deborah, and Jess. I count myself so fortunate to associate with you and to receive your input every week.

Thanks to my editor, Jenny, and to all those who provided needed beta feedback. You have made the story so much better.

Thank you to Nancy Mayer for her never-ending willingness to share her wealth of knowledge and to point me to valuable resources.

Thank you to my mom, who cheers me on every step of the way and drops everything to read my first drafts.

This book wouldn't be here without any of these people and so many others.

ABOUT THE AUTHOR

Martha Keyes was born, raised, and educated in Utah—a home she loves dearly but also dearly loves to escape whenever she can travel the world. She received a BA in French Studies and a Master of Public Health, both from Brigham Young University.

Word crafting has always fascinated and motivated her, but it wasn't until a few years ago that she considered writing her own stories. When she isn't writing, she is honing her photography skills, looking for travel deals, and spending time with her husband and children. She lives with her husband and twin boys in Vineyard, Utah.

Printed in Great Britain
by Amazon

41330365R00169